Published by Autumn Day Publishing

Copyright 2017
Cover by Toby Gray
Other work by L.S. Gagnon,
Witch: A New Beginning
Witch: The Spell Within
Witch: The Secret of the Leaves
Witch: The Final Chapter
Thea the Little Witch Series
Original release, 2017
ISBN 978-0-9967707-3-6
All characters in this book are fiction
and figments of the author's imagination.

Warlock: Descension into Darkness

Book One

by L. S. Gagnon
Facebook/TheWitchSeries

I dedicate this book to my sister, Yvonne Palafox Dominguez. It shattered my heart when you left us too early in life. I was taken back to that dark place, a darkness that robbed me of any will to fight. A piece of me is missing, you took it with you when the angels came calling. I know you're with our mother, keeping a watchful eye. I can feel you both, smiling down on me. Yvonne, you were a ray of light, shinning on all who knew you. Your infectious laugh still rings in my head. I try to think of it when times are bad. It makes me smile, thinking of all the times we spent together. I miss you more than you'll ever know. I hide my pain, my sorrow, and go on with life.

Today, your laughter woke me from my sleep. I could feel you near me, asking why I wasn't writing. I cried, ashamed to tell you I was weak. I didn't want to admit how broken hearted I truly was. You were my baby sister, and I couldn't, didn't want to, let you go. I thought of six words you said to me the last time we spoke. "*I love how brave you are.*" So, here I am, Yvonne, being brave for you. It's time to write, time to find myself again. I put your favorite color in the book. You'll find sprinkles of it throughout the chapters. I love you, sister.

Table of Contents

Prologue

I struggled to free myself as the Black Witch approached. She leaned forward, breathing her rancid breath straight into my mouth. The stench moved slowly through my nose and into my lungs. I felt I would vomit. I wanted to thrust a dagger straight through her heart, but I was far too weak to move. This would be the end of me. I had failed in every way possible. I thought of my mother as the Black Witch began moving piles of wood closer to my feet. She smiled, revealing a fire spell spinning in her hand. She slowly held it up, showed her yellow teeth, and threw it under me.

Chapter One: The Vortex

I felt I would fall into space as we traveled into the human world. I waited in anticipation to feel the ground under my feet. I was in a vortex of travel with my grandfather and a friend. It was the door to my realm, the world I'd only heard of my whole life. My grandfather's ring served as the key that opened the door to the human world. The moment he pulled it off his finger, we were pulled into this vortex.

Speckles of light surrounded and carried us as if we were feathers. I could feel only the wind blowing all around us. I was far too excited to pay attention to anything else.

We moved through the vortex with ease. I truly felt I would fall at any moment. Although my grandfather, William, had been in this vortex many times, this was my first time going with him. I had waited my whole life to leave Magia, the magical land I came from. The human world had only been a story told through the eyes of my parents. My mother, a wizard, and my father, a witch, were born in the human world. They lived there for most of their young life. My mother never told me why they left the human world, but I knew it broke her heart when she left all her friends behind.

She grew up with the people I knew as my uncles and aunt. Although we were not blood related, my mother always told me they were family nonetheless. She had been friends with them since childhood. My mother said she would not be alive if not for them. She often said they were closer than family. Even now, they came to visit us frequently. My grandfather gave them a ring so they could travel into our world. Their visits were the only time I saw my mother truly happy.

I thought of the worried look my mother gave me right before we left Magia. I was her only son, and for a moment, I thought she would never let me find my own way. I was speechless when she finally agreed that I should see the human world. Her decision came suddenly one day. I didn't question her, only gathered my belongings before she could change her mind. Her reasons didn't matter to me—I was finally free.

I felt suffocated for years. I was always under the watchful eyes of the royal guards and my parents. Even my grandfather, the Wizard King of

Magia, wouldn't let me spread my wings. I would be turning seventeen soon, and I wanted nothing to do with being a prince. They could keep their royal titles and thrones. I didn't want any part of that.

Magia was filled with rules and prophecies. I was taught as a boy, that certain things would happen. "There is no changing the future," my grandfather always said. And part of that future is that I be king one day. But there was one thing he didn't know; I didn't want to be king. A life of commanding others was not the life I wanted to live. It was bad enough just being a wizard; I didn't need the pressure of being a king as well.

I looked at my grandfather as we travelled through the vortex. His green eyes had not met mine once. I couldn't help but wonder why he left his kingdom to come with me. His decision to leave was as sudden as my mother's to let me go. I had a strange feeling he only wanted to protect me. But why would I need protecting? I had no enemies, that I knew of.

No one in the human world even knew who I was. I spent the last sixteen years sheltered from them, the humans. It was a decision my parents made when they left the human world. Although they lived for years in a town named Salem, they had never taken me there once. I never understood that, and my parents never explained why. All they ever said was that I belonged in Magia. Went on about how it was my home. I always knew they were only trying to get the idea of leaving out of my head.

I was born and raised amongst wizards and dragons. Magic has always been the only life I knew. I knew nothing of human possessions or the thing called *money* that was needed to live. Coming into the human world was a way to escape my obligations of being a prince.

My mother spoke of Salem frequently. She called Salem her first love. I wanted to see the strange sun that gave light there. My father once said it was the other side of our sun. He said his world was unlike our realm. There would be no magical garden or Tree of Life. "*Humans can't fly,*" he explained one day. "*No staff in the world can give them that power.*" He never knew this, but his stories only fueled my need to leave the kingdom.

The human life he spoke of seemed simple and uncomplicated. I was tired of being praised for what I had not yet done. I wanted to earn my way, not have it handed to me. Just because I had been born into royalty, didn't mean I expected things to come easy. I welcomed the challenge.

I wanted nothing else but to prove to myself and to others that I was much more than just a prince. The human world seemed like the perfect place to start. There, I would be just like the others, just another boy. I would use no magic or spells. I would put away the wand my mother gave me and blend into the masses. I had many reasons for wanting to come into the human world, but right now, I can think of just one.

"Vera will be happy to see you, Ethan," my grandfather said.

I hadn't noticed he was finally looking at me. He was smiling. Did he know I was thinking of her? It couldn't be. No one knew I loved Vera, or that she was my real reason for wanting to leave Magia.

Vera was a half-human witch that lived in the human world, a world she seemed to be quite happy in. My title or magic never impressed her. We'd been around each other since we were kids. Her mother, Delia, had been bringing her into my world ever since I could remember. As Vera grew, I began to look forward to those visits more and more. I found myself feeling empty when she wasn't around.

For Vera, coming into my world had become a nuisance. I knew she only did it to accompany her mother. I could see she had no desire to be in the magical world I lived in. The human world was the only place she spoke of. She'd been coming to Magia for so long that she no longer found my world enchanting.

She thought it strange that we lived without the modern technologies of her world. "*What do you do besides fly around all day?*" she would ask. "*What about watching movies or listening to music?*" I never knew what to answer. I had no idea what those things were.

Her visits to my world had become almost torture. I was finding it harder to hide how I felt. Her brotherly love for me didn't help matters. She thought nothing of sitting close to me and holding my hand. "*Let's sit on that rock*," she would say, pulling me toward the waterfall.

I couldn't remember half the things she said sometimes. I was always too busy trying to stop myself from pulling her into my arms. "*Ethan, don't sit so close*," she would say scooting away from me.

My usual answer would be, "*Then don't pick such a small rock.*"

Her long, dark hair smelled like a beautiful garden. Lavender was my favorite scent. I often got lost in her emerald-green eyes. She was short tempered like her mother, but I always loved that about her. She looked even more beautiful when she was angry, I thought.

"*I wonder what Steven is doing*," she would say. She certainly had a way of ruining a good moment.

That would only make me back away. He was a constant reminder that her heart was already taken. It didn't help that Steven lived in the same house where she lived. He was a just a boy when her parents took him in. Vera talked of nothing else. Steven this and Steven that. I often got very annoyed with her because of that. Here she was, in the most magical place ever, and all she wanted to do was talk about Steven.

"Ethan, did you hear me?"

I broke away from my thoughts of her. My grandfather was looking right at me.

"Does she know we're coming?" I asked in a calm voice. I didn't want to give away how excited I was to see her.

My grandfather smiled. "You'll have to change out of that wizard robe when we arrive," he said, looking down at what I was wearing. "I'm sure your father's clothes will fit you just fine."

Netiri, a friend that was traveling with us, began to laugh. "What's so funny?" I asked.

He pointed to my robe. "You're going to stand out like a sore thumb in that thing."

I looked down at my robe, taking note of the new ruby and sapphire my mother had added. I didn't like the draped robes my grandfather wore. Mine were more fitted and slimming. It was black velvet with gold threaded edges along the front. The jewels I earned were sewn along the collar. Apparently, this wasn't what humans wore. Even Vera had teased me about what she called, *my dress* when she came to visit. I never understood why she teased me so much.

In our world, robes were a sign of courage and wisdom. The more you learned, the more stones were sewn onto your robe. I was proud to display so many. I had earned every single stone with hard work. My robe was like a badge of honor to me. I felt no shame wearing it. Although my father, James, had given me some of his human

~ 8 ~

clothes, I had no desire to wear them. It was the one thing about being a wizard I didn't want to change.

"Hey," Netiri said, nudging me with his elbow. "I'm just kidding, kid. But you'll have to wear human clothes if you're planning on fitting in."

"Who are you calling kid?" I asked. "We're almost the same age."

"No," Netiri said, shaking his head. "You're *actually* sixteen. I just look sixteen because of the aging potion I drink. No one would know I am really two hundred years old."

"Perhaps I should call you Old Man," I answered.

We laughed as Netiri nudged me again.

Netiri had been in my life since my birth. He was the only true friend I had. He left the human world many years ago with my parents. I didn't know much about his back story, but I knew he and my mother were once enemies. I heard that Netiri had spent his whole life not knowing he was half-wizard. He'd always assumed he was just a warlock. It was my grandfather, William, who informed him of who he really was.

I was surprised when my Uncle Cory said warlocks and witches didn't get along back in the day. He explained how Netiri once hated my mother. I asked my mother about that one day, but she only answered, "That's a story for another day, Son."

I always thought it strange how Netiri's eyes would change color. Whenever he was in a foul mood or excited, his eyes would go from green to blue in the blink of an eye. His brother, Morgan, passed away before I was born. I wasn't sure how or why, I only knew Netiri had taken it very hard. He never even knew he had a brother until my grandfather brought him into my world. I wondered why Netiri was going back now.

As I thought of Netiri's past, the smell of food slowly began to fill the air. I knew what that meant; we were almost there. My mother always said she could smell Magia before she got there. I assumed it worked the same way coming back.

I knew we were traveling to my parents' old house. The mansion, as my mother called it, was a house my father left for Vera's parents when he and my mother left the human world. Although my father meant it as a gift, my uncle and aunt refused to take it. Even though they were living there now, it was always said that my parents would return one day. I didn't know how true that was.

I felt my heart would leap out of my chest when the speckles of light began to fade. I swallowed thickly, bracing myself for what I was about to see. The smell of food became more intense. The air under me was now a floor. We were here, *I* was finally here.

The wind died down and I began to make out four walls. I instantly knew we were in my grandfather's room. I'd heard so many stories through the years, I could almost picture the rest of the house. This room looked just as I had imagined. Two huge windows covered one wall. There was a large table with papers scattered over it. It almost seemed like my grandfather had never left. Had he been coming here this whole time?

There was a bed in one corner with a chair next to it. I quickly noticed a pair of slippers had been placed right in front of it. I glanced at my grandfather; it was obvious he was avoiding my questioning eyes. Why didn't he want to tell me he had been coming here? What was the big deal? There was no law that said he couldn't leave our world. He was the king. He could leave whenever he wanted.

I looked around the room again. Jars filled with something I couldn't make out, lined the shelves. Dried leaves hung all around the room. The smell of lavender filled the air. It was a pleasant smell that reminded me of Vera.

I spun around when I heard birds chirping just outside the room. My grandfather stood to one side, motioning me to look out the window. I moved closer, my heart racing as I stretched out my hand. I pushed aside the curtain— and drew breath.

This world was not what I was expecting. The light from the sun was strange. It had no rays beaming down like in Magia. Surprisingly, it hurt my eyes to look at the sun here. My eyes moved down to see what the humans called cars. They were parked below. My father was right, humans couldn't fly.

"*They drive cars*," I remembered him saying. He had shown me images of them when I was younger. He even told me how he had owned a few at one time. "*I gave them all to your uncles and aunt*," he explained. "*I have no need for them here in Magia.*"

My mouth was agape as I took in every detail of this world. I almost put my head through the glass when I saw some humans walking by. A tall, wrought iron gate wouldn't let me get a clear view of them. Greenery grew on the fence that surrounded the whole mansion. I tried to look past it. I wanted to see what kind of clothes the humans were wearing. What color were their robes? Did they wear the same kind of shoes?

A door opened before I could get a better look. A small, older woman came walking in. I instantly knew she was a half-human witch. I could see her eyes light up behind her glasses. I couldn't help but notice her smile grew wider as she neared my grandfather.

"Xander, you're here," she said, greeting him. Xander was my grandfather's middle name.

"Hello, Sharron," my grandfather answered. "I didn't expect to see you here today."

They spoke as if they had seen each other the day before. She didn't seem surprised he was here.

"We've all been waiting," she said, looking my way.

"Ah, yes," my grandfather said, motioning toward me. "This is Ethan, my grandson."

The curly haired woman seemed alarmed or shocked for some reason. She slowly moved closer as I stepped away from the window. I was a little surprised when she reached out and touched my face.

"Oh my," she whispered. "You are the spitting image of your father, James. If I didn't know any better, I would have confused you for him. You have his dark hair, his brown eyes, and you're just about as tall as him, too."

"You know my father?" I asked.

"Yes, dear," she said, pulling her arm back. "And I also know your mother, Thea. How is she?"

"Mother is fine," I answered. "She said to send everyone her love."

The woman named Sharron looked at my grandfather. "He's so handsome, Xander. Delia was not exaggerating his good looks."

"He's a good boy," my grandfather said, putting his arm on my shoulder. "He's grown into quite the young man."

"I feel as if I'm looking right at James," Sharron said, seeming amazed.

"I think he has Thea's eyes," my grandfather added.

Sharron raised one eyebrow. "Does he have her temper, too?"

What did she mean by that? My mother didn't have a bad temper. I never knew her to lose her composure once. She was a sweet, gentle woman.

As they laughed, I couldn't help but look toward the window. I wanted nothing else but to go outside. I wanted to see the town that had captured my mother's heart. Would I love this place as much as she did? I was really counting on that. Through the years, as she told me her stories, I felt I loved Salem as much as she did.

Sharron greeted Netiri before he headed out of the room. "I'll come back later, Ethan," he said over his shoulder. He was out the door before I could respond.

What was his hurry? I was hoping he would show me around town. He talked about Salem as much as my mother.

I glanced at Sharron, she wasn't taking her eyes off me. I think my grandfather sensed that I was uncomfortable about it.

"Where are the others?" he asked her.

"They've gone food shopping," she said, looking down at what I was wearing. "They should be home shortly."

She looked back at my grandfather. "Should I get him some clothes? I know James left all of his behind."

Why does everyone want me out of this robe?

"I am wearing clothes," I pointed out.

Sharron seemed surprised by my answer. "Sorry, dear. I only meant to say it might be best if you dressed in human clothes."

"Why?"

My grandfather cleared his throat. "I think I should show Ethan the house."

"Yes, of course," Sharron said, giving my robe another glance. "I'll be downstairs if you need me."

My grandfather shook his head when she left the room. "You don't have to change out of that robe, if you don't want…"

The sound of someone shouting made us both turn our heads, cutting our conversation short.

"What on earth?" my grandfather said, heading for the door.

We both stepped into the hallway to find a man pointing his finger in Sharron's face. He must be in his late twenties. He towered over her.

"You need to stay out of this," he was telling her. "She's not your daughter or your concern."

Sharron pointed her chin up. "She will always be my concern," she shot back. "You're a twenty-seven-year-old man, and she's just a child. You have no business chasing after her. You should be ashamed of yourself."

"I've already told you, witch. I've started taking the aging potion. I can wait until she comes of age. But until then, you will keep your nose out of our business."

"Why don't you make me," Sharron spat.

The man narrowed his eyes, moving inches from her face. I readied myself. It looked like he was getting ready to strike her.

"You don't want to cross me, witch," he hissed.

"You took the words right out of my mouth," I said, stepping forward.

The man did a double take when he looked my way. He instantly got a confused look on his face when he looked at my robe. I saw fear shine across his face when he saw my grandfather standing next to me. He clearly knew who my grandfather was.

He slowly backed away from Sharron. "I…I didn't know you were here," he said nervously.

"And now you do," my grandfather answered.

"He was just leaving," Sharron said, crossing her arms.

The man eyed me, a subtle streak of evil in his droopy, brown eyes. He was dark skinned with messy black hair. He wore the same kind of clothes my uncles, Fish and Cory, wore. *Jeans*, as they called them, seemed to be the thing to wear in this world. There was such an angry look about him. I got the sense that he was angry at the world.

He seemed to be very at ease here. Did he live here? Then it hit me, this man was Steven. The same man Vera was in love with. I had no idea he was that much older than her. Vera had never mentioned that to me.

It was obvious he already figured out who I was. The angry look on his face made that clear. I knew this man hated my mother, although I didn't know why. It was obvious he hated me too.

He gave my grandfather another glance before turning for the stairs.

"Wait," I called out. He froze and looked my way. "Apologize to her," I demanded.

It wasn't because Vera loved him that I wanted him to apologize to Sharron. He had been very rude to her just now. In my world, we had manners. If I even raised my voice an increment, I was made to apologize.

Sharron became visibly nervous.

"It's not necessary," she quickly said.

I ignored her, taking another step forward.

"I said…apologize to her."

Steven made a fist, his face shaking from anger. I thought I saw him reach for something near his belt, then stopped and glanced at my grandfather again. He slowly pulled his hand away from his waist. "I'm sorry," he spat and quickly headed down the stairs.

Sharron looked at me, shaking her head in disapproval. "You didn't have to do that, dear."

"But he was rude to you, madam," I answered.

"Madam?" she laughed. "Please, just call me Sharron." She looked at my grandfather. "He's got his mother's temper alright."

I heard a door slam shut. I knew it was Steven leaving the house. I thought of Vera, why did she love such an angry man?

"Come, I'll show you around the house," my grandfather said, leading me toward the stairs.

Chapter Two: The Mansion

As we descended the stairs, I recalled all the stories my mother told me about this house. Everything looked just as I imagined it. There was a foyer that was large enough to be its own room. A large sitting area was just to the left of it. A beautiful fireplace welcomed you as you entered the main floor. Priceless works of art hung on almost every wall. I was no expert on homes, but I could tell this was a very nice one.

As I looked around, I saw sections I could only guess were pathways leading to other rooms. My mother once said this house even had a ballroom. In fact, she told me my Uncle Fish and Aunt Delia were married there.

My grandfather led us through a door near the foyer. "The kitchen is through here," he said, with a big smile.

I could see this room was his favorite. I looked around the enormous kitchen. Pots and pans hung over a huge counter. It looked nothing like the kitchens in Magia. We usually just made a fire to prepare our meals. A simple wooden table served as our place to share our evening dinner.

The table in this room looked like a dozen people could share it. It was elegant and had fancy chairs. I was surprised when my grandfather said there was another room called a *formal dining room* that they used from time to time. The room we were in now was apparently where they had breakfast. Why did they need two rooms for that? How odd, I thought.

My parents didn't seem like the types to own possessions like these. I was surprised this used to be their home. Back in Magia, my father built my mother a modest home. It was small but served its purpose. Our lives were spent living outside, exploring what Magia had to offer. Money or possessions had no value in my world. Magic gave us everything we ever needed. Although my grandfather lived in a castle, he rarely stayed there. Most of the time, he would stay with us. He said he had become accustomed to living in a small space. This mansion was anything but small.

I had been to the castle to see my grandfather many times. Its glass looking walls towered over the land of Magia. Precious jewels were embedded in every space available. It was very rare to see my grandfather sitting on his throne. He always said the castle was too big and empty for him. Now, I understood why. The castle wasn't cluttered with furniture like this place. He obviously had become accustomed to the clutter.

A glass door at the end of the kitchen caught my attention. I could see a beautiful garden was just on the other side. "My mother's garden," I whispered.

I moved towards the door, my heart racing.

"Go on," my grandfather said, "step outside."

I felt the strange sun the moment I walked out. Here, the sun made me feel too warm for the robe I was wearing. It was so bright, almost hurting my eyes. It was nothing like the subtle sun in Magia. I could fly around all day and not feel the heat from our sun. Here, it felt like a blanket was being wrapped around me. I wasn't sure if I liked it. I touched the back of my hand, noting how the sun was warming my skin.

I made my way across the massive yard, and to my mother's garden. It was not what I was expecting. Although it was beautiful, the flowers didn't sparkle like the ones in Magia. Where I came from, flowers gave out speckles of light that drifted into the air. They carried healing powers to everything that lived in Magia. I remember playing with them as a child, laughing when the speckles stuck to my fingers.

I scanned the garden, noticing another house at the far end of the yard. It wasn't as big as the main house, but it was just as beautiful.

"That's the guest house," my grandfather said from behind me. "I think Steven is living there now."

I looked down at the strange grass that grew here, noticing dirt patches where the grass didn't grow. In Magia, the grass looked like a lush, green carpet covering every mountain in the land.

I closed my eyes, allowing the sounds of the city, just outside the gate, to flow through my ears. They were sounds I hadn't heard before. I smiled when I heard a car horn for the first time. It was just as my father described it. I opened my eyes when I heard it again.

"Delia is home," Sharron called from the kitchen door.

We walked back into the kitchen to find my Aunt Delia holding several bags. I always thought Vera was the spitting image of her mother. My Aunt Delia also had long, dark hair. There was always an angry look about her. It didn't help that she was rather moody sometimes.

She quickly put the bags on the counter and ran to my side. "You're early," she said, wrapping her arms around me. "I wasn't expecting you until tonight."

"Are they really here?" I heard my Uncle Fish say.

He came storming into the kitchen with far more bags than my aunt was holding. He couldn't put them down fast enough. I couldn't help but notice he had a few bruises on his face. Had he been in a fight?

"Come here, kid," my uncle said, pulling me away from my aunt.

"Hello, Uncle," I said, embracing him.

"I've already told you, just call me Fish," he said, pulling away.

I was happy to see him. I loved my uncle. He always made me laugh. He didn't look any older than me, something I knew to be not true. He and my Aunt Delia took an aging potion to stay young. At least that's what my mother told me.

Vera had her father's green eyes. She didn't inherit his dirty blond hair; rather, her mother's dark hair. My mother always said that my uncle had the face of a fifteen-year-old boy. He was always in a good mood, always very funny. My father loved being around him, laughing the whole time they were together.

"Joshua and Meaghan will be sorry they missed you," my Aunt Delia said. "They left on vacation two days ago."

She pulled me into her arms again. I could feel her love flowing through me. These people had been in my life for many years. My mother loved them more than life itself. They were her best friends and she considered them family. She spoke of them often, always making it a point that I knew how much she loved them.

"How is your mother?" my aunt asked.

"She sends her love," I answered.

"So, what do you think?" my Uncle Fish asked. "Like it here?"

I smiled. "I haven't seen much yet."

I noticed my Aunt Delia's eyes moving down to my robe. "Did you bring clothes?" she asked.

"James left a ton of clothes," my uncle said to her. "I'm sure he'll fit into them. September has been very warm this year," he said to me. "I bet you're melting in that thing."

"Who's September?" I asked, confused.

They laughed, although I didn't know why.

"We should give him a moment so he can change out of his robe," my aunt suggested.

"If you don't mind," I said, "I'd rather keep what I'm wearing."

My aunt looked at my grandfather. "Is that wise? He'll stick out like a sore thumb."

My grandfather smiled. "He'll change out of it when he's ready."

Again, I took notice how no one seemed surprised to see my grandfather. My aunt and uncle hadn't even said hello to him yet. It was as if they had spoken moments ago.

I caught my grandfather and uncle exchanging glances. I think my grandfather noticed the bruises on his face.

"Is everything okay?" my grandfather asked him.

My uncle nodded. "We'll talk later."

"Are you hungry?" my aunt asked.

I smiled politely. "If you don't mind, I would rather see the town first."

Everyone looked at my robe again. Why did they keep doing that?

"May I ask something?" I said, trying to get them to stop staring at my robe.

"Shoot," my uncle answered.

"Why is everyone's thumb sore?"

The room erupted into laughter.

"Why don't I show you to your room?" my grandfather said, composing himself. "You can put your things away before we see the town."

"Come on, kid," my uncle said, showing me the way. "You can stay in your parent's old room."

My grandfather followed as we ascended the stairs. "We removed all the flowers," my uncle was saying.

"Flowers?" I asked confused.

My uncle nodded. "I didn't think you'd like the way your father left it. He put a spell on some flowers to make them live forever. He did it for your mother, she loved flowers. He had them everywhere."

"I love flowers," I informed him.

My uncle stopped half way up the stairs. "Kid, no," he said, shaking his head. "Guys don't say things like that. No flowers, okay?"

Confused, I nodded and we continued our way up. I looked at my grandfather, wondering why it was a bad thing that I love flowers. He only smiled.

We walked down the same hallway we had been in earlier. We stopped at my grandfather's room, so I could collect my things.

"Your room is at the end of the hall," my uncle said, leading the way. "Vera's room is right next to yours. So, no sneaking around," he joked.

My head shot up when he said that.

"Is she home?" I quickly asked.

"She's at the bakery with Cory and Helena," my uncle answered. "Delia thought perhaps making her get a part time job would keep her out of trouble."

I came to a stop. "She's in trouble?"

He laughed. "No, but she will be if she doesn't keep that job. She has too much free time on her hands. Keeping her busy will do her some good."

My uncle looked at my grandfather. "I don't know what's got into her lately. I don't think I like the influence Steven is having on her."

My grandfather nodded knowingly.

We continued walking. I had to stop myself from asking more questions about Vera. What kind of trouble was she getting into?

"How many rooms does this house have?" I asked looking around.

"Eight bedrooms," my uncle answered. "Ten, if you count the ones upstairs, but we never use them."

He stopped at a set of double doors, pulling a set of keys from his pocket. "Plenty of room for you in here," he said as he unlocked the doors.

When he swung them open, I saw a beautiful sitting room. Two large chairs sat in front of a huge fireplace. Hundreds of books lined the walls.

"Where is the bed?" I asked.

My uncle walked over to another set of doors which were made of glass. "We made a few changes," he said, as he swung them open.

A huge bed sat near another set of doors that seemed to lead outside.

"That's the terrace," my uncle explained.

I quickly noticed the room was cluttered with furniture. Why would anyone need anything else besides a bed?

My uncle walked over to yet another set of doors and opened them. "This is the closet. There are plenty of clothes for you to change into. I bet you and your father wear the same size."

I walked over and looked in. I'd never seen so many human clothes before. I noticed there wasn't a robe in sight. Strange shoes lined the bottom of the closet. I remembered my father calling some of them sneakers.

"We'll give you a minute to change out of that thing," my uncle said, looking at my robe.

I looked at my grandfather again. He smiled and put one finger over his lips, motioning me to stay quiet. As soon as my uncle was gone, my grandfather closed the door.

"Grandfather, I don't want to change out of

my robe."

He crossed his arms behind his back. "So, don't. No one is forcing you."

I looked around the room again, wondering how many more doors there were.

"Do you not like your room?" he asked.

I looked at the bed, several people could easily sleep in it. I wanted to say no, but the thought of being right next to Vera was making it very hard to turn this room down.

"It's fine, Grandfather."

He stepped closer to me. "There are more important things I need to speak with you about." He put his hand on my shoulder. "I'm going to ask you to do things that may not make any sense, but I want you to obey my wishes and do them anyway. Do you understand?"

"Yes, Grandfather," I said, putting my things down.

"For starters, I don't want you calling me grandfather in this world. Refer to me as simply, William. I also don't want you referring to Delia and Fish as your aunt and uncle, even in your thoughts. Simply, Delia and Fish. Do you understand?"

"But, why?"

"For reasons I cannot tell you, I don't want strangers knowing who you are…yet. And when you see Cory, you will do the same. Understood?"

"Yes grandfa…I mean, William."

"And most importantly, do not use your

magic in the presence of humans. No matter the situation, refrain from using it. Is that clear?"

"Crystal clear."

My grandfather smiled. "I wish your mother would have followed my instructions as easily."

He motioned toward the door. "Come, it's time we see the town."

"May I ask you something?" I said, as we made our way into the sitting room.

"Of course."

I faced him. "Why did my parents finally agree to let me come here?"

He looked thoughtful for a moment. "Because it was time," he finally answered.

"You're not going to tell me, are you?"

He only smiled.

"Will you tell me soon?"

"Very soon," he answered. "I give you my word. There will be no secrets between us."

I looked around the room again. I couldn't imagine my mother living here. She seemed to love the small home we lived in now.

"Why do you like it here so much?" I asked.

My grandfather sighed, looking around the room. "I was a prisoner to this house once. I suppose I'm attached to the memories I left behind. I became fond of this place, though not because it's a mansion. I would feel the same if it were a shack."

"A prisoner?" I asked confused.

"It's a long story, Ethan. I'll tell you about it

another day."

We made our way downstairs and back into the kitchen. "I'm taking Ethan into town," my grandfather said. "We won't be gone long."

Sharron was putting away the food my aunt had purchased. She made a funny face when she realized I was still wearing my robe.

"Did the clothes not fit, dear?" she asked.

"Want to try some of mine on?" my uncle offered.

I didn't answer and only looked out the window. Steven was coming out of the guest house, and he was not alone. Three other men were with him. They had the same kind of angry look Steven possessed. They all looked to be the same age. They began making their way toward the house. One had blond hair and was rather short. The other two were tall with dark hair.

My Aunt Delia spotted them. "Oh, I hate when he brings warlocks here, especially the new ones in town. They've been acting very odd, causing all sorts of trouble. Everything was so quiet until they got here."

Again, my grandfather and uncle exchanged glances.

"I'll take care of it," my uncle assured her.

Steven stomped his way in, but froze when he saw me. We stared at each other for several long moments. His hatred toward me was obvious. I had to admit, I was starting to feel the same towards him.

"I won't be home for dinner," Steven said, storming past me.

The three men looked me up and down before following him across the kitchen and out the door.

"I need to speak with you, Steven," my uncle said, following behind them.

My grandfather looked at Delia. "When?" he asked.

"Few weeks ago," she answered.

He nodded. "We'll be on our way now. I'll be back to help you prepare dinner." He turned to me.

"Come Ethan, I'll show you the town."

Chapter Three: Salem

We stepped outside to find my uncle arguing with Steven. The men that were with him were not far away. They waited near the gate as Steven's conversation with my uncle began to get heated.

"I'm not having this conversation with you again," my uncle was saying. "I don't want you bringing the likes of them into my house."

Steven glared at him. "This isn't your house, remember? You're as much a guest as I am."

My Uncle Fish stepped up to him. "And, as of this moment, your reservation has been cancelled."

Steven laughed. "What? You're kicking me out now?"

"Would you rather I just kick your ass?" my uncle shot back.

I saw Steven reach for something around his

belt, but my uncle was faster. He flicked his arms, revealing two hook-like weapons from his sleeves.

"Go ahead," he said, getting in Steven's face. "Let's see how tough you are. Pull that thing out, I dare you."

Steven's eyes darted down to the hooks. He made a fist, slowly moving it away from his belt. I stepped forward when the other men moved closer. They also seemed to be reaching for something.

"Fish," I said awkwardly. "Is everything okay?"

"I don't know," he answered. "Is it?" he said, glaring at Steven.

"Why don't you go back inside, pretty boy?" one of the men said to me. "You might get your pretty dress all dirty."

Steven's eyes grew wide when he saw my grandfather. He looked back at my uncle. "I'll be back for my things later," he hissed.

"I'll have your things waiting by the door," my uncle said getting closer to him. "And if you come near my daughter again, I'll skin you alive."

Steven gave my grandfather one last glance before turning on his heels. My uncle stood there until Steven and his friends disappeared down the street. He flicked his arms again, causing the hooks disappeared into his sleeves.

I'd never seen my uncle so angry. My mother was right; despite being a half-human witch, he was very brave. I wondered about the strange weapons he had up his sleeves. I knew my uncle couldn't wave his hand like me. My mother told me that half-human witches need spells to use their magic. Is that why he carried a weapon?

I watched Steven and his friends walk away. I thought the bad blood between warlocks and witches was a thing of the past. My uncle didn't seem to like them very much. I couldn't help but wonder why. Were all warlocks bad? Did they all have bad tempers like Steven and his friends? That couldn't be. I knew my parents had plenty of friends that were warlocks.

"You did the right thing, Fish," my grandfather said, eyeing the men.

Fish turned and faced us. "I never wanted this for him, William. He gave me no choice. His new friends are nothing but trouble. I have to look out for my daughter."

"No need to explain," my grandfather answered. "His new friends seem to have changed him."

Fish looked down the street. "Tell me who your friends are, and I'll tell you who you are."

My grandfather followed Fish's gaze down the street. "Indeed."

I was suddenly aware that I was outside. My heart began racing all over again. I looked beyond the gate, eager to explore this world.

"Hey, are you really going into town wearing that thing?" my uncle asked.

"Yes," I said, gazing all around me.

The mansion was much bigger than I

thought. I saw the name *Wade* on another building next to the house. "That's the garage," my grandfather explained.

He motioned towards the gate. We walked across the massive driveway, making our way out the gate, and onto the street. My uncle quickly filed in behind us, staring at my robe the whole time.

"It even moves like a dress," he said, under his breath.

Trees lined the street the mansion sat on. I walked in amazement at what my eyes were taking in. There were no wizards flying above us, no dragons for me to mount. It was a world paved in stone. The ground was covered in it. Why did humans need to walk on stone?

There were subtle yellows and reds on some of the trees. I remembered my mother telling me about the changing of the leaves. It was her favorite time of year. She called it autumn. I knew that soon, the trees would transform and become radiant with colors. At least, that's what my mother said. That didn't happen in Magia, so I was looking forward to it.

"What do you think?" my uncle asked, as we made our way down the street.

I forced a smile. "It's lovely."

He stopped. "Kid, no," he said, shaking his head at me. "Guys don't say that. No lovely, okay?"

Confused, I nodded and we continued

walking. Again, I glanced at my grandfather, wondering why it was a bad thing that I say lovely. And again, he only smiled.

My eyes almost came out of their sockets when I saw two humans walking our way. I got a little confused when they gave me a strange look. They stared at my robe as they past us.

"Is it October already?" one of them said to the other.

What did they mean by that?

A large vehicle full of humans caught my attention. "Oh look, it's a warlock," one of them said. They began holding up small boxes. I couldn't help but wonder; why did they think I was a warlock?

My uncle began laughing. "See, you should have changed out of that robe."

Confused, I looked at him.

"That was a tour bus," he explained. "They were taking pictures of you because they think you're in costume."

I looked at the thing called a *bus* again. The humans were still holding up their boxes as the *bus* drove away.

"Ethan, they're just taking pictures of you," my uncle assured me.

Why would they take pictures of me?

"Come on," my uncle said, putting his arm on my shoulder. "Essex Street is just a few blocks from here. The bakery is just off it. We'll stop by and see Cory."

I was taken aback when we reached the street named Essex. I quickly stopped. There were hundreds of humans walking around. Some were even dressed as witches. I saw one human dressed as, what I could only say was, a monster. He had what appeared to be fake blood running down his face. That was odd. Why did this human feel the need to put fake blood on his face like that?

My uncle laughed as we continued walking. The street was lined with shops. Stands with what my uncle called t-shirts were everywhere. Most of them had the word *Salem* imprinted on them. There were witch hats, brooms, and trinkets of all sorts.

I looked at the human that was dressed as a monster. The fake blood on his face looked very real. Was he trying to scare people? I stopped again as he got closer to us.

"Hey," the bloodied man said. "That's a cool costume," he said, pointing at my robe.

Bewildered, I watched as he smiled and walked past us.

"Ethan," my grandfather said. He waited until I tore my eyes away from the human.

"How did you know that man was human?" he asked.

"What do you mean, grandfa…I mean, William?"

He looked at the humans around us. "Them, how do you know they're human?" he asked again.

I wasn't sure how to answer his question.

~ 37 ~

"I'm not sure," I answered. "Something inside of me just knows."

"And, can you spot the real witches?" he asked.

I looked around the busy street. I saw a witch standing behind her stand. She seemed to be selling trinkets. "She's a witch," I said, pointing. "And her, she's also a witch," I said, pointing to a woman walking into a building. "But him," I said, pointing to a man sitting at a table. "He's not half-human or a witch. He's a warlock."

My grandfather shook his head and mumbled, "Thea. I should have known."

"Did you really expect her to stay out of this?" my uncle said to him.

My grandfather ignored him. "And the men Steven was with today, did you know they were warlocks?" he asked me.

"Yes."

"I see."

"Even I know Thea wouldn't send him without tools, William," my uncle said.

"What are you both talking about?" I asked.

My grandfather only smiled. "Come, Cory is waiting."

We continued walking through the crowded streets. I felt all eyes were on me. One man stopped and asked where I had purchased my robe. When I said Magia, the man asked where that store was. "I have to get me one of those," he said, admiring my robe.

My grandfather was quick to say I shouldn't tell people about my world or say the word, Magia. "Try to pass off as human," he suggested.

"Good luck with that," my uncle laughed.

"Ethan," my grandfather said, nudging me. "I told you, not even in your thoughts. Think, Fish. Simply, Fish."

"Yes, William," I answered.

I was starting to realize that humans had no idea wizards and witches were real. I found it amazing they had no idea we walked among them. It would appear witches went to great lengths to keep it that way.

The smell of bread hit me the moment we walked into the bakery my Uncle Cory owned. I smiled as I pictured my mother working here. She'd shown me images of this place my whole life. She loved this bakery. When Norm, the original owner, retired, my uncle purchased it. My mother said she had lived some of her happiest moments working in this small, little place. She explained that this was where she had reunited with my father.

The bakery was small with two huge glass counters, both filled with pastries. A few small tables were scattered around. Boxes and bread lined the walls. Two wall-sized windows gave perfect views of the tourist walking by.

"Cory, he's here," I heard his wife say.

My uncle's wife, Helena, was a striking woman. She was tall, thin, and very beautiful. She had golden locks that shimmered in the sun. I could never understand how my mother had once hated her. She seemed to be a very pleasant person.

I was shocked to learn that she and my mother had once been enemies. My mother had said Helena was once a very bad person. Of course, my mother loved her now.

Helena walked from around a counter and gave me a hug. "He'll be so happy to see you."

"Where is he?" I heard my Uncle Cory call out.

He came out from the back of the bakery, a smile spread across his face. I was a little shocked that he too, had bruises on his face. I wasn't surprised to see him and my grandfather exchanging glances.

I had never ignored the special relationship my mother shared with Cory. She talked of him often, calling him a beautiful Polish man.

"Even that nose can't take away from his beauty," she once said.

His visits into my world were something my mother looked forward to. She always referred to him as her brother. Truth was, even I couldn't ignore how handsome he was.

"Come here, kid," Cory said, pulling me into his arms.

"Hello, Uncle."

"Please, just call me Cory. How is your mother?" he asked, pulling away from me.

"She sends her love."

"And your father? How is he?"

"Father is well."

Again, I noticed my grandfather's presence surprised no one.

"How do you like Salem?" he asked, looking down at my robe.

Before I could answer, Vera came walking out of the back room, holding a tray of pastries.

Our eyes met. I slowly smiled. She looked different somehow.

"Hello, Vera," I said softly.

"I see you're still wearing a dress," she said, placing the tray on the counter.

I could smell her lavender scent from here. She looked more beautiful than the last time I'd seen her, and that was just a few days ago. Her dark hair fell across her face like an angel. Her green eyes spoke to me and called me to her.

"Don't be rude," Fish hissed at her.

She rolled her eyes. "Hello, Ethan," she said, strolling to the back room again.

"I'm walking you home," Fish called to her.

She was back within seconds. "Why? I know where I live."

"Oh good," he answered. "Then maybe you can show me."

She rolled her eyes again. "I really wish you wouldn't do that. People always think you're my boyfriend or something. I hate having to explain why my father looks like he's seventeen. I really wish you and mother would stop taking that aging potion."

"Then, maybe Ethan can walk you home?" Fish suggested.

Vera slowly looked at my robe. "No, I'll walk home with you," she said, heading to the back again.

I stepped forward. "I was hoping you could show me around, Vera."

She gave my robe a sour look. "Are you serious? In that thing? All you need are heels and maybe some lipstick."

She flipped her hair and strode off to the back. I heard her mumble, "What a loser," as she disappeared.

This wasn't the reaction I expected from her. I thought she would at least be a little happy to see me. I hoped she'd want to show me around, like I had done with her on her visits to my world. Here, she seemed a little rude, spoiled even. I wasn't sure I liked this side of her. I always found her temper charming, but the rude part of her, well, it wasn't very pretty.

She was only gone a few moments when she returned, holding up one of those boxes like the humans had on the bus.

"You threw him out?" she shouted at Fish.

He smiled. "What? Did the baby call and tell you?"

"Where is he supposed to go?" she asked.

"Tell him to sleep in the woods. Maybe he'll

learn some manners there."

"I hate you!" Vera shouted.

Fish stepped up to her. "Did I ever tell you about my belt collection? I have several of them. I have leather ones, suede, even alligator skin. Want to see them?"

Vera burst into tears, stomping her way past him and out of the bakery.

Fish sighed. "Time to go be a dad," he said, chasing after her.

"He threw Steven out?" Cory asked my grandfather.

"Yes, and I think it was time," he answered.

Cory looked thoughtful for a moment.

"I was really hoping that kid would straighten his life out. Those warlocks he's been hanging out with are bad news. Maybe I'll go look for him and try to talk some sense into him."

"I believe the time for talking is over, Cory. There is only one way he's going to change his life."

They both glanced at me. Why did they keep doing that? It was starting to get a little annoying.

I had been quiet this whole time. This world had me a bit unsettled. I thought of the one place my mother said she had always found peace.

"Grandfa...I mean, William. Do you mind if I go explore the town on my own?"

"I'll show you around, kid," Cory said. "Just give me a few minutes. You might get yourself lost."

I smiled politely.

"If you don't mind, I'd rather go on my own. I'd like to see the places my mother told me about. I think I can find my way back."

Cory and my grandfather looked at each other.

"Don't be long," William said. "I'll be back at the mansion, waiting."

"Thank you, grandfa…William."

I walked out, disappearing into the crowd. I ignored all the strange glances and odd comments about my robe and finally made my way into the woods. Once clear of human eyes, I pulled out the wand my mother had given me. When I waved my hand, the wand quickly turned into a long, wooden staff. It was old and rustic looking. It had once belonged to my mother. It still had indentations from where her fingers once had been.

I slowly put it between my legs. The wind suddenly picked up beneath me, made me hover, then took me away.

It felt good to feel the wind in my face again. Flying always gave me the feeling of freedom I so desperately wanted.

My original plan had been to never use the wand. It was my intention to live without my magic. But this world had me on edge. I wasn't finding the feeling of freedom I thought I would. Surprisingly, I was missing Magia and my parents.

Vera's reaction to me didn't help matters. I expected to find the sweet girl I had fallen in love with. Her eyes showed no sign of happiness when she saw me just now. In fact, she could care less that I was here. Something was different about her, I could feel it. She had never been this rude.

I flew through the trees, using them as cover, and found my way to my mother's lake. So many times, she had shown me images of this place. I knew exactly how to get here. I would have been able to find it with my eyes closed.

The lake was just as she had shown me. I landed and tossed the staff to the ground. Trees surrounded the murky lake. It was nothing like the crystal-clear lake in Magia. There were no flowers or draping ivy. I found no waterfall or dancing fairies. I began to question my mother's reasons for loving this place so much.

I stood at the edge, trying to understand her love for this world. It wasn't the world I had expected. Everything seemed so dull and lifeless, I thought. Even the leaves that blew in the wind seemed lifeless. What had my mother fallen in love with? Were her eyes blind to the dullness of this world? Magia was full of life and color. You could hear the leaves whistling in the wind a mile away. Here, the forest was silent and dull.

I looked down at the ground, happy to see it wasn't covered in stone. I removed my shoes, sighing as I felt the grass under my feet. It was only making me think of Magia more and more. Had I made a mistake by coming here? I didn't feel very welcomed in this world. Things were off to a bad start.

"Well, look who's here," I heard from behind me. "It's pretty boy, and he's still wearing his pretty dress."

I looked over my shoulder. It was the three warlocks that had been with Steven.

I turned and faced them.

"What's the matter, pretty boy?" one of them asked. "Did you get lost?"

"Look at his stupid shoes," the blond one said, pointing to where my shoes lay. "Are they bedazzled?"

They laughed.

"His dress is bedazzled too. These half-human witches sure do dress odd."

I couldn't understand it. Why did these men think I was a witch? Better yet, why did they hate me?

"These stones are badges of honor," I informed them.

"Did the girl scouts give them to you?" a dark haired one asked.

They laughed again.

"No, my mother did," I answered.

They laughed even harder.

"Did you hear that?" the blond one said. "His mommy gave them to him."

I couldn't understand why they were laughing at me. "Don't laugh at my mother," I demanded.

"Why? Are you gonna cry, pretty boy? Or,

are you gonna run and tell your mommy?"

I didn't like the way the word *mommy* flowed from their mouths. I had a feeling they meant it as an insult.

I stepped forward. "If you call her *mommy* one more time, you will find out why I earned these badges."

They stopped laughing. The blond warlock slowly put his hand near his mouth. When he spat into his palm, a spell came out, spinning and making a strange sound. It would seem these warlocks couldn't just wave their hands like me. The other two quickly followed suit, spitting spells into both of their hands.

"Are you preparing to fight me?" I asked.

The blond one slowly smiled. "No, we're preparing to tear you apart, pretty boy."

I had no idea why they wanted to fight, but if it was a fight they wanted, I was prepared to give it to them.

I stood there, looking deep into their eyes. I could feel hate coursing through their veins. It wasn't just hate for me, they hated everything. I grew more curious about these warlocks by the minute. Did they not have the capability to love? Why had my mother been at war with them? It was a question I would pose to my grandfather when I got back.

"Thinking about running, pretty boy?" the blond one asked.

Just as I was about to command my staff

into my waiting hand, I heard a woman's cries from within the forest. Suddenly, another man emerged from the trees, dragging a human girl behind him. Looking terrified, she was kicking and screaming for him to release her.

The man dragged her over the ground as if she were garbage, pulling and tearing at her hair.

"I said, shut the hell up!" the man said, kicking her in the face.

The girl screamed louder.

I broke into a run. Spells began flying over my head as I ran to help the girl. I had no idea what was going on, but I couldn't stand by and do nothing.

"Get him!" I heard behind me.

Chapter Four: Nancy Girl

I waved my hand at the man dragging the girl, sending him flying into the water. I waved my hand again, making a wall of leaves around the girl as I faced the other three.

I could hear their spells spinning as they approached me. One of them spat a spell near my feet. I was surprised when snakes began coming out of the ground, hissing and trying to bite me.

I heard a sword being pulled from its sheath. Before I could wave my hand, a warlock's head fell to the ground, leaving the body standing. When the headless body dropped, Netiri was standing right behind him.

The other two men spun around, seeming surprised at who it was.

"Traitor!" blond-hair yelled at Netiri.

Netiri smiled as his eyes began changing

color. "Xander sends his regards," he said, right before cutting off their heads.

The spells the warlocks had been holding fell to the ground, leaving burn marks on the grass. As the snakes faded away, I spun around and removed the wall of leaves protecting the girl. I heard what I thought was moving sand as I knelt to check on her. Before I could touch her, Netiri pulled my hand away.

"Let me deal with this," he said, gently pushing me away.

"They were hurting her," I explained. "I had to help."

Netiri pulled back the girl's hair. It was then I noticed they had also beaten her. Despite the dirt and tangled hair, I could see she was quite beautiful.

"Is she well?" I asked.

"She's going to be fine," Netiri answered.

"Why did they do this, do you suppose?"

"They were going to have their way with her, I have no doubt."

That shocked me. What kind of place was this?

"We should get her home," I suggested.

Netiri quickly shook his head. "You stay here. I'll take care of her. We can't be seen together again. There's a lot you don't understand."

Netiri had just killed three men, yet he acted like it was so normal. I got the sense that he did this often.

"Netiri, why did they call you traitor?"

I hadn't missed that.

Netiri locked eyes with me. They started changing color again. First green, then blue, now brown.

"You'll find out soon enough, I promise."

He turned and chanted a spell at the girl. When he lifted her up with ease, I knew what kind of spell he had chanted.

"Stay here," Netiri ordered, "at least for a few minutes. I don't want anyone seeing us together, okay?"

I nodded, and he disappeared into the trees, carrying the girl. I didn't know what to do. I had no idea what was going on. This place was full of cruelty and evil. It wasn't a happy place at all. Why did my mother love it so much?

I looked out towards the lake. I waited for that solace my mother had spoken of so often. I wanted the lake to calm me, like it had calmed her so many times.

I thought it best that I listen to Netiri. I sat at the lake's edge and began to think, perhaps I should leave this world. I knew it would certainly make my mother happy. I thought of Vera, questioning if I had given up on her too quickly. Perhaps being alone with her would have a different outcome.

I sighed and decided it was too soon to leave. I would give Salem another chance. There were too many unanswered questions. My gut told me something awful was going on. Why did Cory and Fish look like they'd been in a fight? And, why couldn't I call them my uncles, even in my thoughts?

"You're going to ruin that beautiful robe," a woman's voice said.

I rose to my feet. "Afternoon," I said, facing her.

The moment our eyes met, she drew a long breath. "Oh my," she whispered.

"Is something wrong, Madam?"

She wouldn't look away from me. She had strange white hair and dimples on her cheeks. If I had to guess, I would say she was about fifty years old. I could also sense she was a witch.

"Is your father James Ethan Wade?" she asked.

I quickly remembered what my grandfather had warned me about. He didn't want people knowing who I was. I wasn't sure why, but I would respect his wishes. "No," I lied.

"No?" she said, with a strange look on her face. "But you look just like him."

She began to look me over. Her eyes darted to my robe, then at the stones on it. When she spotted my staff on the ground next to my shoes, she raised an eyebrow.

"I'd know that staff anywhere," she said, with suspicious eyes. "If you don't want people to know who you are, you shouldn't carry that thing around. People aren't stupid, you know."

I tried to talk my way out of it, but this woman was having no part of it.

"I know your mother, Thea," she informed me. "I also know James, your father."

I could see it was pointless lying to her. I wasn't prepared to answer about the staff. My mother had obviously used it a lot.

"I apologize for lying to you, Madam."

"Please, call me Melanie."

I instantly knew who she was. My mother had told me all about her. "You're the Smiling Witch," I said brightly.

"The Smiling Witch?" she asked, confused.

"Yes, my mother says you smile a lot. In fact, she says you smile all the time. You own a shop, correct?"

"Yes," she said, looking away. "But I don't have much to smile about anymore."

"I'm sorry, but my mother said you had auburn hair?" I said, looking at her very white hair.

"What else did she tell you?"

"About you? That's pretty much it."

"I see," she said, looking away again.

"Is there something I can help you with?" I asked.

She looked back into my eyes. "You shouldn't be out here dressed like that. It will be a dead giveaway of who you are." She looked at the staff. "And don't carry that around. People will recognize it—bad people. Don't be stubborn like your mother."

She turned on her heels before I could respond. I kept my eyes on her until she disappeared into the trees. There was a certain sadness about her. She had a broken heart, I was certain of it.

I looked down at the staff, wondering just how many people knew it belonged to my mother. Anyway, why was it a bad thing if people knew who I was? Why would my grandfather not explain that to me?

One thing I did know, I had to keep it a secret until I got some answers. I would also have to find a way to carry the staff so it wouldn't be seen. I couldn't take the chance of it slipping from my robe.

I decided to head back into town. Netiri had to be a good distance away by now.

I gathered my shoes and staff, and waved my hand. When I shrank the staff back down, I placed it in my robe. Flying didn't seem like a good idea right now. Besides, maybe a good walk would clear my head.

By the time I reached town, about a dozen people had stopped to ask where I had purchased my robe. I finally settled for telling them I made it myself. That seemed to impress them even more.

I walked the streets, admiring some of the homes along the way. I realized not all the homes in Salem were mansions. There were many humble looking ones as well. I think the tall ones were my favorite. They had a certain charm to them.

I stopped when I reached a park. My heart began to race when I realized it was my mother's park. Well, it didn't belong to her, she just called it that. I searched for the white gazebo she spoke so much about. I smiled when I spotted it in the middle of the park. The place was lined with trees and benches.

Witch Museum, I read on a building across the street. They had a museum for witches? I laughed a little at that one. I would make it a point to visit that building soon.

"Look at this guy?" I heard someone say. "He's a Nancy girl."

Five men burst into laughter as I turned to face them. "He's wearing a dress," a long-haired man said, pointing at my robe.

"Look at those ridiculous shoes," another said, pointing at my feet.

I sighed. "Not again."

"I think he even smells like a girl," the long-haired one added.

"Do all you warlocks have bad manners?" I asked, looking at the group. "Or are you all just not capable of having them?"

There was silence. The men looked at each other. They eyed me, unsure of who I was.

"How the hell did you know we were warlocks?" long-haired asked.

I smiled. "Because, you're just as stupid as the ones I met earlier."

Before I knew it, there were spells flying right at me. I heard them spit out one after another. One spell hit me on the leg, instantly breaking several bones. As I dropped to my knees, another spell hit my arm. It felt as if my arm was being ripped apart. In an instant, my temper rose to the surface. It was time to defend myself.

I waved my hand at my leg, repairing my bones instantly. When another spell hit my shoulder, I waved my hand toward the men. They screamed in agony as my magic lifted them and tore their bones apart.

"How do you like it?" I asked, rising to my feet.

I felt pain shooting right through me. My shoulder was being torn apart. I quickly waved my hand, breaking the spell's effect. I ran my palm over my injured arm. The pain was gone moments later.

A woman's screams made me spin around. There was a crowd forming, and they were all human. This wasn't good. How could I possibly fix this?

I looked at the warlocks still floating in the air. Their bodies were distorted from where my magic kept breaking their bones. One of them had already passed out from the pain.

"Ethan, put them down!" I heard a voice call.

It was Sharron, running out from the house across the street. My heart leaped to my throat when my grandfather was next to exit the house. He waved his hand, silencing the screaming humans. They simply hung their heads and went to sleep.

I felt shame wash over me. I knew I had disobeyed him. I allowed my temper to get the best of me. I never knew I had a temper like that. There had never been a reason for me to get so upset in the past. I wasn't sure if I liked that side of me.

The sound of breaking bones made me realize the warlocks were still suffering. I quickly waved my hand, sending their bodies crashing to the ground.

Chapter Five: Friends?

I checked on the warlocks as my grandfather crossed the street. Sharron was on his heels.

"I warned you this would happen," she kept telling him.

I ignored her and waved my hand at the warlocks, commanding my magic to heal them. I was stunned when they didn't respond. I waved it again, nothing.

"Your magic isn't working because they're already dead," I heard my grandfather say from behind me.

"Dead?" I whispered.

"Yes, that means not breathing," he snapped.

I slowly faced him, head bowed.

"I'm sorry, Grandfather."

"William, I said to call me William."

"You can't do things like that," Sharron

hissed at me. "Where do you think you are?"

"Sharron, please," my grandfather shot at her. "I can handle this—alone."

Sharron gave me such a dirty look, then turned on her heels. She mumbled all the way back to where the humans were. "Always cleaning up the messes," I heard her say.

"They won't remember a thing," my grandfather said when he noticed I was looking that way.

I sighed. "I'm very sorry, Grandfather."

He made a fist. "I said to call me William!" he shouted.

Stunned, I took a step back. He had never yelled at me like that.

"How many times must I remind you?" he said, in such an ugly voice. "This isn't Magia. You can't go around using your magic like that. Do you realize what you could have done? I warned you about using your magic around the humans. Most importantly, you're using up precious energy."

"What do you mean?"

"It means, you're going to get people killed."

I didn't know what to say. If he would just explain things to me, I would understand the magnitude of what was at stake.

"I was left no choice but to defend myself," I tried to explain.

"No choice? Was something wrong with your feet that you couldn't just walk away?"

I hung my head again. "Please don't do that," he spat. "I never liked it when your mother did it, and I don't like it now."

It made me a bit angry when he brought up my mother.

I locked eyes with him. "They were trying to kill me, *William*."

I said his name with bitterness in my tone. I had taken just about all I could today. Why couldn't he see that I had no choice?

The sound of moving sand broke up our conversation. I spun around, shocked to see the warlocks were turning to dust.

"Why did you do that?" I asked William.

He shook his head. "There's so much you don't know, Ethan."

I remembered hearing that same sound back at the lake. Those men must have turned to dust as well.

"There were others?" William quickly asked.

I closed my eyes, remembering he could read my thoughts.

"Ethan, did you kill them?" he asked. "Did they figure out who you were?"

I didn't answer.

"Did you kill them?" he shouted.

"It wasn't me. Netiri killed them."

He sighed, seeming relieved.

Sharron was back, giving me the evil eye.

"It took them longer to turn to dust this

time," she said.

Again, William sighed. "Yes. I noticed that as well. Someone is helping them."

"Gran...I mean, William, why can't you tell me what's go..."

"Go home!" he shouted. "You've done enough damage for one day."

Feeling brokenhearted, I slowly walked away. The walk back to the mansion took longer than I wanted. I didn't want to give myself time to think. I wanted to go home, back to my parents and back to Magia. I planned on packing my things the moment I got back to the mansion. It had been a mistake coming here. Even my grandfather was acting different in this place. Back in Magia, he was nothing but loving toward me. He'd never raised his voice once.

This world was filled with hate. It changed people, even me. I had killed not just one man, but several. In just one day, I had taken lives. What was this human world turning me into?

As I neared the mansion, I noticed Steven was standing outside the gates. "Great, just what I need right now," I said to myself.

My plan was to walk right by him no matter what he said to me. But when he said, "Just the person I wanted to see," I had to stop.

His tone wasn't aggressive. In fact, it was friendly.

"You want to see me?" I asked, surprised.

I couldn't get past his sad eyes. They were

naturally droopy. "Yeah," he said, with a big smile. "I know we got off to a bad start, but I wanted to apologize for earlier. I know my friends can be a pain sometimes."

His friends.

Netiri had just killed them.

"Listen," he said, moving closer. "I get a little crazy when it comes to Vera. I feel no one understands my feelings for her. Sharron can be quite mean sometimes. I guess she got the best of me today."

"Yeah, I can understand that," I answered.

"She already yell at you?" he laughed.

I nodded. "Just a little."

"Don't worry, there's more."

I managed to smile.

"So, friends?" he said, extending his hand.

I was starting to think that maybe everyone had Steven all wrong. He wasn't such a bad guy after all. He seemed friendly enough right now.

"Friends," I said, shaking his hand.

"So, do you think you can get Fish to let me move back into the house? I really don't have anywhere to go. He may listen to you."

I hesitated. "Um, I can try."

Was that the only reason he was making peace with me? Was it because he wanted to be near Vera? I wasn't sure if I liked that.

"Thanks, man. That's all I ask, that you try."

I wasn't sure what to make of him as he walked away. I decided to go ahead and speak to

Fish about him. Maybe having him closer was a good thing. I could keep an eye on him to make sure he didn't hurt Vera. I guess that meant I was staying for a bit. Besides, I didn't like the kind of friends he had. Was Steven the same way?

When I walked into the mansion, I heard someone call my name.

"I'm in the kitchen. Come talk to me."

It was my Aunt Delia, I mean, Delia. I wasn't in a talking kind of mood, but I didn't want to be disrespectful.

I walked into the kitchen to find her serving up some food. "Are you hungry?" she asked.

"Not really," I said, looking at the strange food she had put on the plate. It had a stick coming out of it. Why did she make food with sticks?

"Oh, come have some corn dogs," she said, placing the food on the table.

"Dogs?" I said making a face.

She laughed. "I just realized you don't have dogs in Magia. But these aren't real dogs. They just call them that. Sit down and try them."

I looked down at the strange food. I really was rather hungry. I took a seat and reached for my fork.

"No, just pick them up," Delia instructed. "Here, try them with some mustard," she said, placing a yellow bottle on the table.

She took a seat next to me. "Go on, try them. Your mother loved them."

I slowly picked one up. She had served me

three of them. I took a bite. "Good, right?" she said with such a big smile.

I didn't have the heart to tell her the food was horrible. "It's lovely," I answered.

Just then, Fish walked in.

"Kid, no. Don't say that word. Guys don't say lovely. Stop doing that."

"Will you leave him alone," Delia said.

"Where's Vera?" I asked, taking another horrible bite.

"Upstairs," Fish answered, opening a strange metal looking box.

When he pulled out a can made of tin, I couldn't help but stare at him. I watched as he drank from it, then placed it on the table. He noticed my stare.

"You want a soda?" he asked.

"What is soda?" I asked.

Fish didn't seem to know what to say.

"This is going to be a problem," he mumbled.

"Any corn dogs left?" Vera asked, as she walked into the kitchen.

"You can have mine," I said, offering up my plate to her.

She rolled her eyes. "Why do you still have on that dress?"

"Don't be rude," Fish hissed at her.

"I'm still mad at you," she shot back.

"You'll get over it," Fish teased.

"Where is he supposed to go, Father? We're

the only family he's got."

Fish took another drink of his soda. "I told you, he can stay in the woods."

This was my chance to speak up. "It's not my place to give opinions, but can't you give him another chance?"

"You see," Vera quickly said. "Even Ethan thinks that was cruel."

The sound of my name coming from her lips made my heart race. "He's not such a bad guy," I added. "He even apologized to me."

Fish was thoughtful for a moment. I continued. "Perhaps you shouldn't give up on him so easily. He seems to feel bad about what happened."

"Yeah, I bet he does," Fish said with sarcasm.

"Father, please," Vera said, grabbing his arm. "I promise he won't be any more trouble. He really doesn't have anywhere to go."

Fish looked at Delia. "What do you think?"

After several long moments, she finally said, "Just one more chance, but that's it."

Vera leaped into her arms. "Thank you, Mother."

I couldn't look away from her. She truly looked like her mother. Her emerald-green eyes were sparking. Her white, milky skin was calling to me.

Vera ran and gave Fish a kiss on the cheek. When she did the same to me, my heart almost exploded. She was gone in seconds.

"Hello, Grandfather," I heard her say.

I closed my eyes, knowing I was in terrible trouble.

Chapter Six: Memories

The moment William walked in, Fish took one look at him and shook his head.

"I'd know that look anywhere," he said, looking right at me. "What did you do?"

"Already?" Delia added.

Sharron was next to walk in. "He's just like his mother. I knew this would happen."

I instantly felt my temper rising to the surface. "If I'm so bad," I said, rising to my feet, "why did you welcome me here?"

I pushed the plate away and made my way out. I hurried up the stairs to pack my things. I'd had enough. It was time for me to go.

I stormed into my room, slamming the door behind me. I felt angered by the fact that everyone was expecting me to fail. It was like they were counting on it. If that were the case, why was I here?

It didn't surprise me that William followed me up the stairs. I gave my back to him as he walked in.

"You're so much like your mother," he said.

"I'm getting real tired of hearing that," I said, shaking my head.

"Look at me, Ethan."

"Why? So you can tell me how I've disappointed you?"

"Would you mind asking your son to face me, James?"

I quickly spun around. Was my father truly here?

"Father?" I said, searching every inch of the room.

"It's pointless to hide," William said. "I can smell you."

When the closet doors slowly began to open, I knew it had to be him.

He was wearing the blue robe my mother made him. It had twice as many jewels as mine. I was happy to see him wearing his crown. Although William had turned over the throne to him, my father never wanted to rule. He always said William was the true king. When William and I left Magia, my father had no choice but to take the throne.

"Father," I said, embracing him.

"Hello, my son."

"I thought we agreed you would stay away,

James?" William snapped. "The boy has only been gone one day."

My father pulled away from me and faced him. "I'm sorry, William. I had to know Ethan was safe."

"So, you think I would let harm come to him?"

"I'm sorry, but I was worried."

"After only one day?"

"Was it only one day?" my father said, looking away.

"And, what's your excuse, Thea?" William asked.

"She's here?" my father asked surprised.

A huge smile spread across my face when my mother emerged from the sitting room. She was wearing a beautiful red velvet dress. Her long, brown hair pinned up with emeralds.

"Going for a walk, huh?" my father said.

"A quick fly around Magia?" my mother shot back.

They both laughed.

My mother quickly ran to my side. She threw her arms around me and pulled me to her.

"Mother," I whispered.

"Ethan," she said, squeezing me tight.

"I'm coming home, Mother. I don't like it here," I said, pulling away from her.

"What happened?" she quickly asked.

"Your *son* killed some warlocks today," William informed them.

"What?" my father said, stepping forward. "I thought our war with the warlocks was over?"

"You thought wrong," my mother said, touching my face. "Did they hurt you?" she asked.

She didn't seem surprised.

"Nothing I couldn't handle," I answered.

Fish burst out in laughter the moment he saw my parents. "I knew you'd be here sooner than later. He's only been gone one day, for Pete's sake."

My father laughed and shook his hand. "Still the same Fish, I see."

"Were you expecting someone else?"

"Where is Delia?" my mother asked.

"In the kitchen," Fish answered.

"The kitchen? Since when does Delia cook?" my mother laughed.

"Are we quite done now?" William asked. "We have other problems to deal with."

My mother's smile quickly faded.

"What is it, Father?"

"It's your son; we need to share our memories of this world with him. He's having a hard time adjusting. There is too much to explain. It's time he knew."

"Already?" my mother asked seeming shocked.

"He's only been here one day," my father added. "We can't fill his head with horror."

"We must," William insisted.

My mother considered William's eyes.

"Will it change anything?" she asked.

What did she mean by that?

"I don't think so," he answered.

"I can't take that chance, Father."

He sighed, seeming frustrated. "They know he's here, Thea."

She gasped. "Father, no. It's too soon."

"How?" my father asked.

William looked at me. "Netiri told me they ran into some warlocks at the lake. I would assume one of them figured it out."

"Netiri killed them," I pointed out.

"He didn't know you had sent one flying into the water. He got away."

I closed my eyes. I had forgotten all about that one.

My mother spun around, a horrified look on her face. Before I could move, she placed her hands over my head and closed her eyes.

I felt the room spin as memories from her past flowed through my head. I saw a man named Simon standing over my mother, torturing her. My mother screamed as Simon pierced long needles through the bottoms of her feet.

There were memories of her and my father in not-so-happy times. I saw my mother fighting warlocks with a sword. She was brave, much more than I imagined.

Memories of my uncles flowed through me. There was a costume ball, Simon was there. I saw a dead body on the floor, Sammy, my mother called him. Memory after memory was filled with horror. I cringed when I saw my mother's skin being torn from her bones. She had been hit with a bat that disappeared under her skin. My father's agony was hard to watch as he tried to heal her.

I saw the horrific things a wizard named Wendell had done to her. I felt her pain when she thought I was dead. She had suffered so much so that I may live. There wasn't one battle she backed down from. She even went toe to toe with my grandfather.

I saw the bakery my uncle now owns. My mother had been truly happy there. The image of my mother's lake was next. I saw her there often. I could feel her love for it; I understood it now. I could see the beauty she found in it, the solace too. I allowed every memory to sink into the depths of my brain. The horror of what she'd been through truly shocked me.

When she was done, my grandfather instructed my father to go next. I kept my eyes closed as he placed his hands over my head. I instantly felt his pain. He had been separated from my mother for hundreds of years. She had sent him away to protect him. I could feel his love for her. She was his life, his air, his everything.

I saw my father being tortured in a dungeon. His heart was shattered when the one named Javier was stabbed in the heart. The warlocks did horrible things to my father. I could see them spitting spells at him. My father cried in agony until my mother rescued him.

I made a fist every time I saw the man named Simon. There wasn't one good memory of him to share. Then I saw a woman, the Black Witch. She had killed her children. She was helping him.

"No," I said, as they tried to cut me out of my mother's womb. My mother fought hard. I couldn't get over how truly brave she was. The Black Witch wanted what had been promised to her.

I sank into darkness as the memories continued. It felt like hours had passed. When I finally opened my eyes, it was dark. I was on the bed, surrounded by loved ones. Cory was there, so were Fish and Delia. It didn't take me long to realize they had all taken a turn sharing their memories with me.

I felt closer to them than ever before. The love my mother had for them was never ending. She adored them, lived for them, loved them. I knew from this moment on, I would love them just as she did.

"How do you feel, Son?" my mother asked.

She was sitting next to the bed, eyes filled with tears. I realized I loved her more than I thought myself capable. She had suffered so much for me.

"I love you, Mother."

She smiled. "Of course, you do."

I felt different. Something inside of me had changed. There was a bitterness towards the warlocks because of what they had done to my parents. I also knew not all warlocks were the same. My parents had good friends that happened to be warlocks. My mother had fond memories of a warlock named Ciro. He had taken his place next to my mother, fought the battles no one else would. My mother always said he had risked so much to keep her safe. She called him a man of honor, a man of great respect.

I knew what cell phones were now, although I would never be able to use one. My wizard energy was too powerful. I was almost certain I could drive a car, work a computer, even make a corn dog. They had shared all their knowledge of this world, answered every question I had. I understood everything. I could feel every moment of their lives flowing through me. I understood the bond between my mother and Cory. He had once loved her, lived to protect her. She would have married him if she'd never met my father. Every moment they had lived was now stored in my head.

"Was that too much for you?" my mother asked.

I tried to sit up.

"We're not done yet," William said, gently pushing me back down.

When he placed his hands over my head, I sank back into darkness.

Chapter Seven: The Wooden Ring

I had the oddest dream that night. I was standing in the middle of a fort with an enormous flat-screen TV hanging on one of the walls. There were corridors branching off the courtyard where I stood. Nearby, I spotted a platform with four nooses mounted on it. I could hear words being whispered in my ear. I couldn't quite make them out. I could have sworn it was William's voice.

I had many dreams that night, each filled with puzzles I couldn't piece together. The last thing I remembered was seeing several witch hats thrown about the fort. Then a voice, a horrible, raspy voice, whispered in my ear, "How do you like it?"

When I awoke, my mother was still sitting by my side. I could tell she'd been crying all night.

She reached for my hand, holding it to her face.

"Good morning," she whispered.

My eyes darted to the window. It really was morning. I felt I had been asleep for days.

William was there, holding a cup of tea. He looked very tired and drained. The dark circles under his eyes gave away how much he had shown me.

"We're with you, Son," my father said from the other side of the bed.

"You have to leave now, James," William said, in a tender voice. "The longer you stay, the more things will change."

My father nodded and leaned down, placing what looked like a small knife on my chest.

"I made a few changes to it. Use it well, my son."

My mother began crying. She held my hand to her cheek. "Please, Father. Let me stay. I can help him."

"The only way to help him is to leave," he answered.

My father walked around the bed, gathering her in his arms. "Come, my love. William will take good care of him. We can't risk his life."

My mother mouthed I love you before my father slipped on his ring. Within seconds, they were gone.

I slowly sat up, but paused when I felt something in the palm of my hand. It was the same hand my mother had been holding. I glanced at

William, quickly slipping whatever it was under the blanket. Somehow, I knew she didn't want him to know she had given me something.

"Do you remember everything?" William asked.

When I looked up at him, images of what he'd shown me began flowing through my head. He eyed me intensely, not looking away until I remembered every detail of his life. I leaned back, his puzzles unraveling in my head.

"Do we understand each other?" he asked.

It took me several long moments to understand what he was asking me to do. I felt unsure.

"You're not mistaken," he said. "Every detail is correct."

"I don't understand, William."

"Yes, you do," he said, placing the tea on the table next to me. "I was very clear."

"I'm not sure I can do it," I said, realizing how much he was asking of me.

"I disagree."

He turned to leave, pausing at the door.

"Ethan," he said, with his back to me. "I have the same faith in you as I had in your mother. There is more of her in you than you realize."

He walked out without another word. The moment he was gone, I pulled away the blanket. There, shimmering on the sheets, was a ring. I picked it up, gazing at how rare it looked.

The bottom half was made of wood, the top

was glass. It was light as a feather. What was inside it, what made it rare, was the waterfall from Magia. The forest was there, too. Even some clouds were floating around. I saw small speckles of light, just like the ones in Magia, floating in the air. I smiled, realizing my mother had left me something to remind me of home. I would make it a point to carry it always.

I jumped out of bed, unsure what the day would bring. I needed time to absorb what William had shown me. There was a lot to think about. I smiled, feeling the need to visit my mother's lake. I had all but forgotten how ugly I once thought it was. I was looking forward to seeing Salem through her eyes today.

And with that thought, I knew what I was doing today.

I opened the closet, knowing I wasn't ready to wear human clothes. My robe gave me a feeling of security I wasn't willing to give up yet.

I grabbed a clean robe, this one black and orange, and put it on. I placed the wooden ring into the pocket of the robe, making sure William never saw it. I looked at my shoes, considering whether to put them on. The precious jewels on them seemed to attract too much attention. I spotted a pair of black sneakers and decided they would work. The moment I slipped them on, I knew I wouldn't have a problem wearing them.

There was a knock on the door.

"Come in," I called.

Delia walked in, holding a platter of food.

"Thought you might be hungry," she said, placing the tray on a table.

I eyed the food, hoping it wasn't corn dogs. I was relieved when all I saw were scrambled eggs.

"Well, that's a start," Delia said, placing her hands on her hips.

I followed her eyes, she was looking at the sneakers I was wearing.

"You have to tie the laces," she said, pointing.

I looked down. "Why?"

"Well, because you'll trip and fall."

"Why would I do that?" I asked.

Confused, she shook her head. "Because, you'll step on the laces."

"I'll make it a point not to step on them," I assured her.

She shook her head again. "You are so much like your mother. It's kind of scary."

After she left, I sat and ate the salty eggs she had prepared for me. I had to admit, Delia was a horrible cook. I would make it a point to help with the cooking sometimes. Perhaps I would prepare some meals from my world; rose petal soup, perhaps.

As I made my way down the stairs, dirty plate in hand, Vera came out of the kitchen. Her lavender scent hit me softly across the face. My heart instantly began racing.

She wore jeans, which happen to hug every

inch of her body. I could see every beautiful curve, every breath-taking part of her. Her red blouse was tucked in, revealing her tiny waist. She wore her hair up today, showing her long, beautiful neck.

"What are you staring at?" she snapped.

I quickly realized I was ogling her.

She took one look at my robe, rolled her eyes, and headed for the front door.

"When are you gonna get out of that dress?" she said, over her shoulder. "It's wicked ugly."

"It's not a dress," I reminded her.

"Whatever," she said, shrugging her shoulders. "You want to walk into town with me?"

I was a little shocked. I wasn't expecting her to say that.

"Um, sure. Just let me put this plate in the kitchen."

"Just leave it there," she said, pointing to a table near the door. "We'll get it later."

I partially threw the dirty plate on the table and followed her out the door. Vera flipped her hair, brushing it softly across my face. I froze, taking in her wonderful scent. Was she trying to drive me mad?

"Hey, thanks for defending Steven," she said, as we made our way out the gate. "He moved back in last night."

"Where is he now?" I asked.

"He got a job. Works long hours now."

"A job?"

"Yeah, you know, that thing that pays you money?"

As we made our way down the street, I couldn't help but feel an enormous love for Salem. I wanted to walk slow, just so I could take it all in. My mother's memories of this place had changed me. Salem was full of charm and mystery. I knew the trees would finish changing soon, making it my favorite time of year.

"People are staring at us," Vera said, looking at my robe. "I really wish you would change out of that thing."

"Let them stare," I answered. "I really don't care. Where are we walking to, anyway?"

"The bakery. I'm supposed to take you there so you can start work."

"Work? No one told me this."

"I'm telling you, silly. Besides, you were sleeping when Uncle Cory came over and said he had a job for you."

That was odd. Why hadn't William told me about it?

As we made our way to the bakery, I noticed blue and red lines painted on the pavement.

"Why are there lines here?" I asked.

Vera looked down. "That's for the tourists. You know, so they can find their way around."

"They need lines to guide them?" I asked confused.

"Well, yeah, to help them find all the cool stuff here. It also helps them find their way back."

I didn't want to tell her, but I wanted to follow the lines to see where they would take me.

When we walked by a small alley, I felt my heart come alive. "Delia's alley," I whispered.

I could see my mother here, helping Delia work her stand. She would stop by after work to visit her favorite witch. It hadn't changed much at all.

I laughed at some humans taking pictures with a wooden witch. It was a piece of plywood with a witch painted on it. The face had been cut out, making it possible for the tourist to place their own in it. I found it rather funny.

As we neared the bakery, I noticed a young girl sitting on a bench just outside of it. She held a book on her lap, her eyes glued to the pages.

"What is *she* doing here?" Vera snapped. "I hate when she hogs up the only bench we have for customers. She takes up the whole thing."

I looked at Vera, not liking the awful words coming out of her mouth.

"She's not hurting anyone," I pointed out. "She's just reading."

Vera snorted. "Yeah, well, she's going to break that bench. She needs to stop buying our donuts and get a life."

Although Vera was being nice to me, she was still horribly mean to everyone else. That was rather disappointing.

The girl never looked up as Vera made her way into the bakery. I reached for the door, pausing to look at the girl. Something was familiar about her. I tried to get a look at her face, but she was glued to her book.

"Good, you're here," Cory said, from inside the bakery. "Come on in, kid."

I peeled my eyes away from the girl and walked in.

Chapter Eight: Caramel Apple

I took in the smell of bread and pastries from the door. You couldn't help but inhale the aroma of sugar in the air. There were hundreds of empty boxes lining the walls.

"Those are orders we have to fill," Cory said, when he noticed I was looking that way.

He looked at my robe. "Do you plan on working in that thing?"

I looked down. "I didn't realize I was working," I explained. "Vera told me on the way here."

"Well, why don't you go home and change. Put on your father's old jeans and a t-shirt."

I tried my best to smile and not be rude. I really hoped that by now, they would understand that I didn't want to take off my robe. Why wouldn't they just get over it already?

"If you don't mind," I said, for the third time today, "I'd rather leave it on."

"Ok, but you may get hot in that thing."

"Robe, it's called a robe," I said, as Cory walked to the back of the bakery.

As I followed him to the back of the bakery, my mother's memories came alive. I could sense her everywhere. She was by the mixers and near the ovens pulling out cakes. She was in every corner of this bakery. My head was filled with memories of this place. Suddenly, I realized what else my mother had stored in my head…her recipes.

"Hey, you want me to get started on some cakes?" I asked Cory. "What do you want? Coconut or chocolate?"

Cory froze near the ovens. "She gave you the recipe for her coconut cake?" he asked, hopeful.

I nodded. "I think she gave me all her recipes."

A huge smile spread across Cory's face. He untied his apron and reached for something on a shelf. "You think you can write them down?" he said, pulling down some index cards.

"She never gave them to you?" I asked.

He laughed. "I never thought to ask."

I reached for an apron. "Then, we'd better get started."

For the rest of the morning, I showed Cory how to make my mother's eclairs, her coconut cake, and even her red velvet brownies. I had to admit, I really enjoyed baking. It was rather soothing to me.

Cory had Vera and his wife, Helena, boxing up all the orders that were ready to go. When the coconut started selling out, Cory sent the women for more supplies. "Buy two cases of snowflake coconut," he instructed them. "Not shredded. It has to be snowflake."

Cory looked beyond happy. "I should have sent for you years ago," he said, taking pies out of the oven.

When we were done, Cory instructed me to start boxing up more orders. "Use the boxes I folded earlier," he said, pointing toward the front.

I nodded and reached for the stack of slips.

"Tape each slip to its box," he ordered.

"Got it," I said, heading to the front.

As I began to spread the orders on the counter, something outside caught my eye. It was the girl, she was still out there, still reading. I moved closer to the window, trying to remember where I'd seen her.

She had long, brown, wavy hair and a larger build than most girls. I couldn't see her face, only the profile of her small nose. I smiled when she reached into a bag, looked in all directions, and took a huge bite of a chocolate donut. She wiped her mouth, looking in every direction again.

I chuckled when she folded the rest of the donut in half, looked around, and shoved it into her mouth. She chewed with one hand over her mouth, always making sure no one was watching her.

I was about to go offer her another donut when she looked over her shoulder, spotting me in the window. I drew breath. It was her; the same girl that warlock had been dragging through the woods. The same girl Netiri had taken away. What was she doing here?

The girl looked halfway over her shoulder again, checking to see if I was still there. When I didn't look away, she bit her lip and nervously looked down. I was glad to see that Netiri had cast a good healing spell on her. There were no signs of yesterday's events on her face or anywhere else.

I tapped on the window, hoping she would look up again. When she did, I waved hello. She had honey-brown eyes with a rather shaggy look about her. I was sure she was embarrassed I had seen her eating the donut.

I was about to step outside and talk to her when, "We're back," Helena said, as she walked into the bakery. "There's more bags in the car. Can you go help Vera?"

I nodded and made my way out, pausing at the door. "Afternoon," I said, politely.

The girl kept her head bowed, looking only at my shoes. "Afternoon," she answered awkwardly.

"Why are you still here?" I heard Vera ask.

I spun around, hoping she wasn't talking to the girl. To my dismay, she was.

"We didn't put this bench out here for you, fat ass. You need to find somewhere else to read."

I couldn't believe how rude Vera was being. It was more than rude, it was downright mean.

"Vera," Helena said from the door. "We don't talk to our customers like that."

"Well, she's been out here all morning," Vera shot back.

"What's that got to do with it?" I asked. "Do we charge to sit on this bench?"

The girl rose to her feet, glanced at Vera, and began walking away.

Helena sighed. "Why would you do that, Vera? She wasn't hurting anyone."

Vera mumbled under her breath and walked inside. Before Helena could go move her car, I managed to ask her about the girl.

"Who is she?"

Helena looked in the girl's direction.

"Her name is Viola. Cory says her mother was killed by warlocks many years ago, back when we didn't get along. She comes here almost every day. Sits on this bench and reads."

"Why do you suppose she comes here?" I asked.

Helena looked thoughtful. "You know, I'm not really sure. She seems to be at ease around us. Well, the bakery, I mean. Don't know why, but she seems to really like it."

"Does she come every day?"

"Mostly, yes. Although, she wasn't here

yesterday. I didn't see her all day."

As Helena left to park the car, I couldn't help but wonder about Viola. I wasn't sure why, but I wanted to know more about her.

I spent the rest of the day boxing up all the orders. There were a few more in the back I still needed to grab. I headed back there, pausing near the doorway when I heard my name.

"I catch him staring at me all the time," Vera was saying. "It's annoying sometimes. It's obvious he's in love with me. I've always known that. I hate that my parents are always trying to push us together."

"So, you know he loves you?" Cory asked.

I pressed my back to the wall as I listened.

"I've always known," she answered. "I don't feel the same about him. He's such a dork. Look at the clothes he wears. And that hair, it looks like a cow licked it to one side. He looks wicked stupid."

I could almost picture her rolling her eyes.

"Clothes don't make the man, Vera," Cory said. "He's a good person."

"Yeah, well, so is Steven. I wish everyone would stop trying to push that dork and me together. It's not going to happen…ever."

"That's too bad," Cory answered. "It would have made your parents very happy."

"They'll get over it."

I looked down, realizing what a fool I'd been. She was never going to love me. I had this unrealistic dream in my head, a dream I was trying to make come true. My whole purpose for being here was to win her over. That seemed so laughable now.

I threw my apron on the counter and walked out. I wasn't sure where I was going. I just knew I needed to clear my head.

I walked the streets of Salem, ignoring the comments about my robe, and made my way to the park. I took a seat on a bench, feeling like the world's biggest fool.

"You idiot," I said to myself.

Vera had shattered my heart to pieces. Her words kept going through my head. *"He's such a dork. Look at the clothes he wears. And that hair, it looks like a cow licked it to one side. He looks wicked stupid."*

I touched my hair, pulling it to one side, just as I always did. What was wrong with wearing my hair like this? I closed my eyes, realizing Vera wasn't the sweet girl I had always dreamed of. In fact, she was spoiled, mean, and rather snooty. I didn't like who she was in this world. What had I ever seen in her? She was right, I really was a dork.

"Would you like a caramel apple?" a voice asked.

The question pulled me from my thoughts. I hadn't even noticed the apple cart going by. An old woman was pushing the cart. Her raggedy clothes gave me the impression that she really needed the money.

"Sure," I said, reaching into my pocket.

She held up her hand. "That won't be necessary, young man. I'm done for the day. I'm giving away the rest of them."

That was a good thing. I remembered I didn't have any money.

"Thank you, Madam," I said, taking her last apple.

She waved goodbye. "Enjoy the apple."

The apple smelled delightful. It was covered in caramel and crushed peanuts. I'd never had a caramel apple before. This was going to be wonderful.

I took a bite, savoring the rich taste of the caramel in my mouth. The next bite was even better than the first. I could taste the apple now. Its tartness really complemented the caramel.

When I took another bite, the caramel began oozing down my fingers. It tingled as it made its way down my wrist. I switched hands, unsure as to why the caramel was melting. When it continued up my arm, I tried to throw the apple to the ground.

I jumped to my feet when the apple wouldn't budge, sticking to my hand as I tried to shake it off. Within seconds, the caramel made its way up my shoulders, leaving me unable to wave my hand. I fell to the ground when the caramel reached my legs. It was covering my whole body.

I looked across the street, hoping to see Sharron. Luck was not on my side.

The caramel began making its way up my neck. Soon, it would cover my face.

"William!" I shouted.

I tried to breathe as the caramel incased my body. There was a tingling feeling traveling throughout my body. This was a strong spell, a deadly one. I thought of commanding the spells effect to release me, but there was no stopping it.

I took a deep breath as the caramel traveled up my cheeks, and over my entire face. I tried with all my might to pull the cursed caramel off me. Suddenly, the caramel began to harden. It felt like a rock was crushing me to death.

For a moment, I thought William had arrived. I lay breathless as the caramel slowly began to peel itself away. Then I felt it, pain like I'd never felt before. As the caramel peeled itself away, it was taking my skin with it. I gasped as my skin was pulled away from my bones, skinning me alive.

"How do *you* like it?" a voice whispered into my ear.

I tried to see who it was, but my agony wouldn't let me think straight. I choked on my sobs as my skin was being torn away. My body shook violently, leaving me close to begging for death. The pain was unbearable, endless.

"William," I said, one last time.

"He's over here," I thought I heard.

"Hurry, put it all over him," a distant voice answered.

There was panic in the voices. I couldn't make out who it was. I wasn't sure if it was a woman or a man. The voices seemed so far away. They were sinking into the darkness with me.

"Hurry, he's dying," another voice said.

"I think it's inside of him, too," was the last thing I heard.

Chapter Nine: Poison

When I opened my eyes, I found myself in a bed, covered in something wet. William was standing over me, a concerned look on his face. A searing, agonizing pain quickly shot through me, reminding me I had been skinned alive.

"P…pain," I mumbled.

William quickly leaned over me. "I've already cast a spell, Ethan. It's the best I can do until your skin begins growing back."

How was that possible? He was a wizard, with unlimited powers. How could he leave me in such pain?

"I would make it go away if I could," he whispered.

His clothes were covered in blood, my blood. I tried reaching for him. I wanted to beg him to help me. When I grabbed onto his shirt, I saw that my nails had been ripped away from my skinless fingers. Every nerve on my arm was exposed. There wasn't an inch of skin left.

Pools of blood oozed from every part of me. The agony I felt was indescribable. I felt like a coward, unable to cast a death spell upon myself. I wanted to die, release myself from all this pain.

"I know, Son," William whispered. "The pain will end soon enough."

My salty tears burned the surface of my face as I cried out in agony.

"Please, kill me," I begged.

"I'll get more sheets," a woman's voice said.

William nodded but kept his eyes on me. There was pain in his eyes, knowing he couldn't help me.

A cold, shaky hand stroked my head. It was Delia. Tears streamed down her face as she managed to crack a smile. "You're going to be just fine," she tried to assure me.

She jumped to her feet when I began choking on something. It felt like a rock was stuck in my throat. "Here comes another one," Delia said, reaching into my mouth.

For a moment, I thought I was vomiting. When Delia pulled out a hard piece of caramel from my mouth, I realized what she was doing.

"You think that's the last of it?" she asked, placing the hard caramel on the table next to me.

Before William could answer, Sharron walked in, holding some large leaves in her hands.

They looked odd. I could have sworn they were made of plastic.

"I used stronger spells this time," she said, placing the leaves on the bed. "We'll have to change them every hour until they take."

William nodded and stood aside as Sharron began placing the leaves all over my body. It was then I realized I was completely naked.

I closed my eyes, welcoming the relief the leaves were giving me.

"It's not skin," Sharron explained, placing some of them on my face. "They'll fall off as your real skin begins to grow back."

I began to choke again, feeling the hard caramel in my throat. Delia quickly reached into my mouth, pulling out the cursed caramel.

"Can't you go faster with those leaves," William said, through his teeth. "He's in agony."

"I'm going as fast as I can," Sharron said, wrapping some on my neck.

For every leaf she placed on me, the pain lessened.

"Thank goodness," William sighed.

I began to choke again. Delia had her fingers in my mouth at once. "Why did you have to send him here, William?" Delia growled. "We've been through enough already. I thought this was over. How could you do this to us?"

"He would have ended up here anyway, young Delia. I couldn't kill him in Magia. It has to be here, in the human world."

She threw the cursed caramel on the table, giving William such a look.

"Why here? Why Salem? Why couldn't you send him far away, then kill him?"

William sighed. "I've told you, he would have ended up here, no matter where I sent him."

"Thea will never forgive you if something happens to him," she said, pointing to me.

When I began choking again, William asked Delia to leave the room.

"I've got it," Sharron said, reaching into my mouth. "There shouldn't be much left," she said, forcing my mouth open.

Sharron's touch sent pain shooting across my head. She wasn't a very gentle woman. She reached into my mouth, grabbed another piece, and forcefully threw the cursed caramel on the table. When she tried forcing her fingers down my throat, William quickly stopped her.

"You can't force it," he said, pushing her aside. "It has to come out on its own. Making him gag will not work."

"Fine, I'll finish placing the leaves on him," she said, grabbing more of them. "I don't think these will be enough. I'll have to search for more."

I thanked William with my eyes. He smiled and gave me a subtle nod.

"Who poisoned him, you suppose?" Cory asked. "Do you really think it was Wendell?"

I'd heard that name before. I knew he was a wizard William had cast out of Magia years ago.

He had betrayed all the wizards and even caused a lot of suffering in this world. From my mother's memories, I knew Simon had risen to power because of Wendell. Strange thing was, why hadn't William shared those memories? I knew who Simon was. Why wouldn't he share Wendell's story? And, why hadn't William killed him? Delia was right. Why send him here?

William avoided my eyes, knowing I had questions.

"I found more sheets," a curly haired woman said.

I recognized her from my mother's memories. Her name was Kym. She was a witch that once turned warlocks into cats. My mother had a lot of respect for her, mostly because she stood up to my mother.

"We'll change them when I'm finished," Sharron said to her.

When Sharron finished placing the leaves on my body, a strange sensation began traveling throughout my arms. It was as if something was crawling all over me. My legs were next, then my torso.

It took me several moments to realize it was Sharron's magic leaves. They were moving, becoming part of my body. I could feel the ones on my face getting tighter, giving me the sensation of skin.

"Good, they're finally taking," Sharron said.

I closed my eyes, feeling my agony drift

away. I could feel the leaves wrapping themselves around my fingers. I drew breath as the leaves tightened around my neck last. I felt warm, as if I had been wrapped in a blanket.

"Is that better?" William asked.

I opened my eyes. He had his hand on my face, but I couldn't feel his touch. I knew it was there, but I couldn't feel the warmth of his fingers.

I opened and closed my eyes, hoping he would understand.

"I understand," he said.

It was times like these I was grateful he could read my mind.

"So, it's going to be poison, is it?" Kym hissed. "Well, I've got a few tricks up my sleeve, too."

"Not the cats again," Sharron laughed.

"You'll see soon enough, witch," Kym said, pointing her chin out.

"Stay out of it," William said, over his shoulder. "It's not time yet. You'll only complicate things."

Kym grunted once, and turned on her heels. "I'll be downstairs," she said, slamming the door behind her.

With the pain manageable, I closed my eyes. I wanted to remain sleeping until this nightmare was over. Why had I taken that apple from the old woman? *The old woman!*

My eyes shot open. "William," I whispered.

"He can talk?" Sharron said, spinning

around.

"Silence," William said, holding up his hand.

He leaned down. "Yes, Ethan?"

"There was an old woman," I mumbled. "She had an apple cart. She gave me a poison apple."

"Apple cart?" Sharron asked confused. "There are no apple carts in Salem."

"Silence," William yelled.

He kept his eyes on her until Sharron nodded and stepped back. He leaned closer to me.

"Did she say anything to you?"

"She said she was done for the day," I explained. "That's why she gave me a free apple. But…"

I began to choke again. I could feel the next piece coming up, and this one was very large.

"I've got it," William said, pulling it from my mouth.

I swallowed down the bitterness the caramel left behind. "There was someone else there," I continued.

"Someone else?" William said, leaning closer. "Who?"

"I don't know, but they asked how I liked it?"

His eyes narrowed, studying my face. He made a fist, his face turning red with anger.

"I see," he whispered.

"What is it, Xander?" Sharron asked.

William looked at her from the corner of his eye. "They wanted to know how he liked being skinned alive."

Sharron quickly put her hand over her mouth. "Oh my," she gasped.

They both looked at Cory, who had been sitting near the bed.

He seemed surprised about something. "You think they confused him for Fish?" he asked.

William thought it over. "That's very possible. It would explain why they attacked Ethan so soon."

William looked down at me. Before I could say another word, he waved his hand.

"Sleep," he chanted.

The heat awoke me from my slumber. I was drenched in sweat. The pillow was soaked, my hair, damp. Why was it so hot? I licked my lips, feeling the need for water to quench my thirst. Was there a fire under me? I wanted to tear off my robe, run naked into ice cold water.

Was there lava trapped in my head? Was someone holding a torch to it? It was so hot. I could have sworn I was burning alive. I let out a long, agonizing sigh, hoping some of the heat would escape through my mouth.

I slowly looked around the room, hoping William would be there. Why was he allowing me to burn?

"Water," I said, in a dry, raspy voice.

There was no one there. I was alone, dying

of thirst. Fighting through the pain, I managed to get myself out of bed. There was an odd sound in the room, and it was coming from me. Every time I moved, my body made a strange sound. Almost like the wrinkling of paper.

I didn't try to make sense of it and headed for the door. The only thing I could think of was drinking gallons of water. I was so parched. I was practically going mad over it.

"Water," I said, as I walked out of the room.

Where was everyone? And most importantly, where was the water?

I took a few steps down the hall, pausing when I heard running water. I licked my lips again, feeling the torture of the heat killing me slowly.

I managed to find where the sound was coming from. I imagined a beautiful, cold waterfall hitting me in the face as I drank every drop. I opened the door. "Water," I gasped.

"Who is it? Get out!"

It was Vera. What was she doing in my waterfall? "Please, water," I begged, pulling on a curtain hanging in front of her.

She let out a loud, screeching scream the moment the curtain was pulled back.

Three things happened at once. First, Vera tore the curtain from the hooks on which it hung and wrapped it around herself. Second, someone burst into the room, hitting me over the head with something. And third, I fell, reaching for the water I so badly needed.

"What is that thing?" was the last thing I heard.

Chapter Ten: Scary Leaf Man

I could hear voices as the heat became more intense. I was quickly reminded how thirsty I was. I was back in my bed, still dying of thirst.

"How was I supposed to know it was Ethan?" Fish was saying. "Vera screamed, so I jumped into action."

"I was naked," Vera proclaimed. "He didn't even knock."

"You're not naked anymore," Fish reminded her.

"Yes, but I was."

"If you had locked the door," Fish pointed out. "He wouldn't have gotten in there."

"Sorry Father, but I didn't know a scary leaf man was going to intrude on my shower."

"Is he okay?" Delia asked.

They all looked at me.

"Please, water," I begged.

"He looks so creepy," Vera said, making a face.

Why wasn't someone giving me water? Unable to wait any longer, I waved my hand, hoping my magic would reach some blessed water. I was not disappointed. Seconds later, a cold pitcher of water came floating into the room.

"What the heck?" Vera said, taking a few steps back.

I reached for the pitcher, ignoring the pain it was causing me and pulled it to my mouth. The more I drank, the more I could sit up. I cursed myself for not thinking of using my magic earlier.

"Another," I commanded.

"Fish, go get him some water," Delia yelled.

Before Fish could make his way out, another pitcher came floating into the room.

"How many pitchers do we have?" Fish said, standing aside.

I reached for it, quickly pouring the water all over my body. "More," I said, throwing the pitcher on the floor.

"Okay," Fish answered, "Let me go see if we have anymore pitchers."

I waved my hand at the empty pitchers, commanding them to fill themselves. I knew my magic would be much quicker than Fish.

"Um, okay," Fish said, as the pitchers flew out of the room. "I guess we don't need anymore."

"What's wrong with him?" Vera said,

stepping next to her mother.

"Vera, why don't you go to your room?" Delia suggested.

"What? And miss all this?" Vera asked looking back at me. "I want to see what he does next."

"This isn't funny," Fish snapped at her. "Can't you see he's been hurt?"

She rolled her eyes. "With what? A tree?"

They stopped talking when the two pitchers came floating back in. I sat at the edge of the bed, commanding the pitchers into my hands. I held them up, pouring as much as I could into my mouth. I knew I was making strange noises, but I didn't care. I was finding it hard to catch my breath. The more water I managed to swallow, the more I wanted.

"Is he going to *actually* pour some water into his mouth?" Vera asked. "He's getting it all over the bed."

"I've got an idea," Fish said, reaching for my arm. "Delia, grab his other arm."

They helped me up and out of the room. We were back in the room with the waterfall. Fish leaned down and twisted a knob. Water began coming out of the wall.

"Come on, kid," he said, helping me under the water. "Maybe a cold shower will help."

I closed my eyes, sighing as the cold water hit my head. I could feel the heat calming.

"I like showers," I said, putting my face up

to the cold water.

Fish laughed. "Next time, wait your turn, okay?"

As the water cooled me, I began to look around the small room. I searched my memories, and realized this was a bathroom. Now I understood why Vera was so upset. She had been bathing herself. She didn't know that I hardly noticed her naked body.

Some leaves on the floor caught my attention. They were scattered everywhere. That was odd. Why were there leaves in a bathroom?

I put my head down, allowing the cold water to hit my neck. I was surprised to see more leaves in the tub I was standing in.

"The drain is clogging up," Fish said, reaching for a handful of leaves.

"I'd better call Sharron," Delia said, pulling out a phone. "We're going to need more leaves."

Feeling cooler, my mind began to piece together the awful events that took place. I remembered the old woman, eating a caramel apple, then being skinned alive.

Vera's scream made both Fish and I jump back. "What's wrong with him?" she said, pointing at me.

I looked down, remembering Sharron's magic leaves. They were being washed off with the water. You could see my red, skinless body.

"Get her out of here!" Fish yelled to Delia.

Fish quickly turned off the water. "Well,

that didn't go as planned," he said, helping me out.

When Fish leaned over to grab a towel, he exposed the mirror that was hanging behind him.

I froze. "No," I gasped.

I didn't recognize the monster in the mirror. I looked positively horrifying. There were only a few leaves hanging from my fleshy face. Blood clots were everywhere. The water had soaked the leaves and made me look worse. It was no wonder Vera screamed. I think I would have done the same.

"Is it hurting?" Fish asked, placing a large towel over my fleshy shoulders.

Surprisingly, there was no pain. I was very thankful for that. "I'm fine," I answered.

Fish helped me back into my room. With every step I took, I could hear my flesh making a horrible squishy sound.

"I'll change the sheets," he said, helping me into a chair.

"Can I have some clothes, please?" I pleaded.

Fish looked me over. "Um, I think we'd better wait for Sharron. She'll need to wrap you in leaves again."

"Can I at least have a blanket or something?" I said, grinding my teeth.

I felt like a freak for all to see. I was all set with being everyone's amusement for the day. I didn't miss how heartless Vera had been just now. It was like a show to her, with me as the clown. I don't know what I ever saw in her. She was not the sweet girl I had hoped for.

As Fish threw a clean sheet over me, William opened the door. "Oh, William," Fish said, sounding relieved.

"What happened?" William asked, closing the door.

Fish was quick to explain.

"He walked in on Vera, she was taking a showe…"

William held his hand up. "If you don't mind, I'd rather Ethan explain."

William looked at me. "Ethan?"

I pointed to the bed. "The heat woke me. The bed was soaked with sweat. I was dying of thirst, almost going mad over it. I heard water, walked in, and she was there."

"He drank about four gallons of water," Fish chimed in.

"I was afraid of that," William said, seeming to know this would happen.

"What are you talking about?" I asked.

"It's the leaves. They made you warm, a bit too warm. Leaves don't breathe, so your body heat got trapped."

"He can't walk around like that," Fish pointed out. "He'll scare the whole town of Salem."

William glared at him. "I have no intentions on leaving him like this, Fish."

There was a knock at the door. "Come in,

Sharron," William called.

Sharron walked in, holding a large bag in her hand. "I hope you're right about these leaves," she said, placing the bag on the floor.

"Please, not the leaves again," I said, pleading with William.

Sharron dumped the leaves all over the bed. She held up her hands and began a chant. "Grow his skin and make it heal, guard him like a shield of steel."

The leaves began to vibrate. William stepped forward and waved his hand over them. With one last jolt, the leaves stopped moving.

"I put a spell on them, so they won't make you warm," he explained.

Sharron clapped her hands. "Okay, everyone out. I have to wrap him again."

Chapter Eleven: James' Double

I lay perfectly still as Sharron wrapped my legs and arms with the leaves. I tried not to think of my nakedness. This woman, whom I hardly knew, had seen every part of me. Embarrassed was not enough to describe how I felt.

"You're even built like James," she said, as she wrapped my chest. "Not all men keep themselves so fit, ya know."

I closed my eyes, horrified that she had even noticed.

"James was also *full* of muscles," she continued. "A lot of women took notice when he entered a room."

I wanted to beg for her to stop.

"Look at you," she said, spreading her arms, "you're James' double."

"Are you almost finished?" I asked, hoping

the answer would be yes.

"A few more spots," she answered, looking at my groin area.

Embarrassed and horrified, I closed my eyes, turning my head sideways. I tried to make my mind wonder and drift away. I didn't want to feel any part of her touch.

I quickly opened my eyes, realizing what could happen when she touched that area. What if…

"There, all done," Sharron said, reaching for a sheet.

I swallowed hard, thinking the worse thing possible. When Sharron noticed I was trying to look at my groin, she laughed.

"Don't worry, dear. I didn't wake it."

I squeezed my eyes shut. Her words were like poison to my ears. Why wouldn't she stop talking already?

"Besides," she continued. "It's a natural thing. You're a man, and…"

"Please," I begged. "Just close the door behind you."

I let out a sigh of relief the moment she left the room. I wanted to crawl into a hole when I heard her and Delia giggling out in the hallway. I knew they were talking about me.

I looked away when someone walked in. I was hoping it wasn't Sharron or Delia.

"It's just me, kid."

When I looked towards the door, Cory had

his mouth wide open.

"Whoa, I guess you won't be leaving this house for a while."

"How bad is it?" I asked.

He looked me over, debating on his answer.

"Let's just say, you look like a leaf gave birth to you."

Fish was next to walk in. "We all better?" he asked, closing the door behind him. "No more showers, right?"

He looked at Cory. "You tell him yet?"

Cory shook his head. "I was about to."

"What's going on?" I asked.

Fish pulled up a chair, pointing to another one in the corner. "Grab that one," he said to Cory.

I slowly sat up, trying to ignore the pain. Cory quickly grabbed another pillow and placed it behind me.

"There, that's better," he said, helping me sit back.

"Man, you look like a leaf mummy," Fish said, shaking his head. "They really did a number on you."

"They?" I questioned. "There was only one person."

"Oh, trust me," Fish answered. "There's a *they*."

Cory cleared his throat. "Listen, I know I told you that I would give you a job at the bakery. I feel really bad about it, but I don't think that's a good idea."

This surprised me. Were they scared?

"Tell him why," Fish said, motioning with his head.

Cory nodded. "You see, my wife, Helena, has gone through a difficult and traumatic event. It would seem they're targeting you, and I can't put Helena in danger like that again. She's been through enough, and the trauma would send her over the edge."

"And my daughter works there, too," Fish said, pointing to himself. "If these guys are going to be looking for you, I don't want Vera anywhere near them."

"Fighting them is not an issue for us," Cory continued. "I'll stand next to you, just like I stood next to your mother. But the thought of Helena going through what she did with Simon, well, would be very wrong. It took me years to help her out of her traumatic state. I can't put her through that again."

"Perhaps I should just leave?" I offered. "If my being here is going to put you all in danger, why wouldn't I just leave and take the danger with me?"

"You sound just like Thea," Fish laughed.

"You can't leave," Cory answered. "And I don't want you far away, either. That's why I found a solution, one where I can still keep an eye on you and not have you at the bakery."

"How are you going to do that?" I asked.

Cory smiled. "I'll explain that when you get

all better. For now, try not to be seen. Stay in the house and read a book or something."

I offered to leave again. The thought of causing problems didn't sit well with me. I knew I had an important role in this. I had seen it in William's thoughts. Was risking so much worth it?

"Yes, it's worth it," I heard from the door.

It was William, and he didn't look happy.

"If you leave," he said, entering the room. "Things will change. Not only will our loved ones be killed, they will be tortured. Salem will become a playground for those warlocks who have gone to the dark side. There is more at stake then you'll ever know."

William looked at Fish. "As for *why* I sent Wendell here. This is where it all began. It is where he was meant to die. The only way to truly end this is to kill him here."

Fish got to his feet. "Then kill him. Why risk our lives trying to find him? Why risk his?" he said, motioning to me. "Put a knife through his heart and put an end to it."

William looked away. "It doesn't work that way, Fish. If it were only that easy."

"Then why?" Cory asked. "Can't you at least tell us why?"

William looked past Cory and out the window. "Days before Ethan and I arrived, the Black Witch had already taken something away from you, something you didn't even notice. If I kill Wendell now, you'll never get it back."

"What is it?" Fish quickly asked.

William slowly looked at him. "You know better than to ask me that question."

Fish's face turned white as a ghost. "But I've done everything to stop it."

"I warned you, Fish. You can't change the future. You can only guide it to the right path."

Fish began shaking. For a moment, I thought he was going to strike William.

"I hate your visions," he yelled and stormed out of the room.

William sighed as Fish stomped his way down the hallway. The room was silent.

"William," Cory said, stepping up to him. "Please, tell me everything is going to be okay."

More silence.

"I give you my word. I will not allow any of you to perish," William finally answered.

"What did Wendell take?" Cory asked.

William locked eyes with him. "I cannot tell you. I do, however, promise I will get it back."

William looked at me. "And Ethan is the key we need. Without him, we will all perish."

My heart grew heavy as William spoke his words. How could their lives be gambled on my choices? I didn't know what to do, what to say. I didn't even know what was going on. How could they put their lives in my hands?

"But for now," William said, removing the second pillow from my back. "Ethan must rest."

I rested my head on the pillow, searching for

answers in William's eyes.

"You'll find them when it's time," he said.

For the next few weeks, I did nothing but sit in my mother's garden. I tried to unscramble William's words and explanations. Nothing made sense to me.

By now, the leaves I had been wrapped in looked more like scabs. They were falling off, a few at a time, leaving behind new skin. Wearing my robe covered the few leaves I had left. Sharron grew my hair back with a spell. She said my nails would grow back on their own, which they did. I was ready to leave the house again, ready to face the future that was awaiting me.

"Thea loved this garden, too," I heard from behind me.

I looked over my shoulder. It was Delia.

"Miss her?" she asked, taking a seat next to me.

I smiled. "I always miss her."

Delia reached for my hand, placing something in my palm.

"Found this in the robe you had on the day you were hurt. Thought you might want it back."

I looked down. It was the ring my mother had left me.

"Oh yes, my mother gave it to me so I would be reminded of home."

Delia laughed. "Oh, Ethan. You don't know your mother very well, do you?"

"What do you mean?"

She rolled her eyes. "If I know Thea, that ring does a lot more than remind you of home."

I looked down at the wooden ring again. I couldn't imagine what else it could possibly do.

"Do you know what it's for?" I asked, hoping she knew the answer.

She shrugged her shoulders. "With Thea, the possibilities are endless."

"Mom, are you giving me a ride or what?" Vera yelled from the house.

"I'm coming," Delia answered. She rose to her feet. "See you later, sweetie."

The sound of Vera's voice no longer made my heart race. In fact, I'd hardly seen her the entire time I'd been stuck in this house. Not once did she ask how I was doing. Her time was spent with Steven, in and out of the guest house. They were closer than ever.

Fish had set rules for Steven, but it didn't seem like Steven was abiding by them. He still came and went as he pleased; still brought warlocks home at all hours of the night. Fish seemed to turn a blind eye to Vera's conduct around Steven. I had decided to stay out of it. Vera was not my problem. If Fish and Delia had no problem with her relationship with Steven, why should I care?

I looked down at the ring again, wondering what Delia meant about my mother. Just as I was about to put the ring on, I smelled something burning.

I jumped to my feet, searching the massive yard for the fire. I quickly noticed smoke coming from the back of the guest house. I put the ring into my pocket, and made my way there.

As I neared the house, Steven came running out the front door. He seemed eager to stop me.

"Wait there," he yelled to me. "I'll come to you."

I stopped, looking up at the smoke bellowing in the air. "Yeah," Steven said, in a nervous tone. "We were grilling some steaks back there. I guess we burned them."

"No fire?" I asked.

"Um, no, there's no fire. We got it under control. Like I said, just burned a few steaks," he said, scratching his head.

I looked up at the smoke again.

"They were pretty big steaks," Steven explained.

"Very well," I answered. "I'll go back to the house."

"Yeah, thanks. Go back to your garden. Cut a few flowers, you know, cuz they're pretty and you like them."

He laughed and made his way back in.

"Ethan, my mom wants you," Vera yelled.

I couldn't look away from Steven. There was something odd about him. I hadn't known him very long, but I could tell he was somehow different.

I turned away, looking over my shoulder as

he entered the guest house again. I could hear him laughing from where I was.

I made my way through the kitchen and into the foyer. Delia was coming down the stairs, car keys in hand.

"Yes, Delia?" I asked.

"Yes, what?" she answered.

"Vera said you wanted to see me."

"I did?"

"Yes, she just told me."

"Vera," Delia yelled.

Vera came out of the kitchen. I hadn't seen her when I walked through it just now.

"When did I say I wanted to speak with Ethan," Delia asked her.

Normally, I would have noticed how beautiful Vera looked in her tight dress. Her lavender scent would have turned me into putty in her hands. There was nothing, and I was grateful for it.

"No matter," I said, walking past them both. "It's not important."

"Ethan, you want a ride into town today?" Delia asked. "I'm taking Vera to buy a new dress for the party next week."

"Why did you tell him?" Vera said, giving Delia a look.

"Aren't you going to invite him?" Delia asked.

"I don't go to parties," I answered, walking out the front door.

Chapter Twelve: Viola

I left the house feeling angry. Vera was disappointing me at every turn. Her mood swings had become intolerable, making me want to forget all about her. I tried not to think of the times she visited me in Magia. She was never this rude, never mean or arrogant. I had always been able to find beauty and tenderness in her personality. At the time, her temper had been endearing to me. Now it was only aggravating. I realized I had never truly known her.

As usual, I ignored the comments about my robe and made my way to the bakery. It was time to jump back into life. I needed to speak with Cory and learn all about his plans. He was right to protect Helena. I had seen the horrible things Simon had done to her. My mother's memories were very vivid.

I stopped as I neared the bakery. The girl named Viola was sitting outside, book in hand. Her long, brown hair was covering her face. I could only see her nose from where I stood.

I continued walking, taking note of her shoes. She had taken them off. I could see red marks from where the shoes were a tight fit. From what I could see of her dress, it was two sizes too big for her, making her look larger than she really was.

I paused at the bakery's door, looking down at the girl. Her head moved slightly, eyeing my shoes. She was startled when I spoke to her.

"Hello," I said softly.

She looked around, making sure I was talking to her.

"It's a beautiful day, isn't it?"

She slowly looked up at me. "Are you talking to me?" she asked nervously.

I gazed into her honey-brown eyes. I took in the details of her face. She wasn't typical in any way. Vera wore layers of make-up. This girl wore none. She had thick eyebrows that arched perfectly over her brown eyes. Her nose was thin and pointy, with a subtle curve at the end. I thought she was quite beautiful.

"Is there someone else sitting out here?" I asked playfully.

She looked around again. "My name is Ethan," I said, offering my hand. "And you are?"

She looked at my hand, pulling back a bit.

I smiled.

"Eventually, my arm is going to get tired," I said, moving it closer to her.

She lowered her book, reaching for my hand. "Viola," she said, shaking it.

"That's a beautiful name," I answered. "I don't think I've ever heard it."

I could see her eyes traveling the length of my robe, ending at my shoes.

She pressed her book against her chest. "Did you want me to move?" she asked. "I can go read somewhere else."

Why would she think that?

"No, of course not. I just wanted to say hello."

"Oh, hello," she said, looking at my shoes again.

I turned, reaching for the door.

"You changed your shoes," she said, over her shoulder.

"I beg your pardon?"

She looked down. "Your shoes, you changed them. I can tell those aren't the right ones. They don't go with your robe."

I looked down at my sneakers. "You know what Viola, I agree with you."

I swung open the door, giving her one last glance.

"Hey, look who's all better," Cory said, coming out from around the counter. "You're all back to normal."

I held out my arm. There were a few leaves still on it. "Almost," I answered.

"At least you're not all fleshy looking," he laughed.

"Yeah," I said, looking out the window.

Viola was still there. Don't know why, but that made me happy.

"You sure you're okay to work?"

I wanted to tell him that I didn't even know I was working, that no one had bothered to tell me.

"I'm fine," I said instead.

"Let's go next door," he said, putting his arm on my shoulder. "I want you to meet Sean."

Viola eyed me as we headed to a shop next to the bakery. "Sean and his wife bought the deli a few years ago," Cory was saying. "They make the best grinders in town. Helena and I bake all the bread they use."

I only heard half of what he was saying. All I kept thinking was, *what is a grinder?*

A bell dinged as Cory opened the shop's door. The odor of cured meats hit me at once. There were two large glass display cases filled with sliced meats. On the counter were vegetables, sliced tomatoes, onions, olives, and more. The layout was just like the bakery with a large room in the back. I could see wooden tables and dried meats from where I stood. A sign hung above one of the display cases: Order here.

"Big Sean," Cory called. "You here?"

A very tall, curly-haired man came walking

out from the back. He must have been over six feet tall. He had a large build, with very broad shoulders. I couldn't help but notice how many tattoos were on his arm. I looked closer; they were tattoos of strange looking knives.

"Hey, Cory," the man said, shaking his hand. "How's it going, man?"

All eyes were soon on me. I didn't miss the look on the man's face as he checked out my robe.

"Who we got here?" he asked, looking down at my robe.

Proudly, Cory introduced us.

"This is Ethan, the kid I told you about."

"Hey, sorry about what happened to you," Sean said, offering me his hand. "It's nice to meet you."

I shook it, feeling week compared to his mighty strength. He had quite the handshake.

"My friends call me Sean," the man said, looking down at my robe again.

"Ethan," I answered, glancing at his tattoos.

I'd never seen knives like the ones tattooed on his arms. Each knife had two blades, one larger than the other. They were connected by small pieces of metal.

Sean noticed I was admiring them.

"Oh, you like them?" he said, holding out his arm. "They're called razor swords, and they come in *very* handy."

Confused, I looked at his arm again. What did he mean by, *they come in really handy*?

"Those are swords?" I asked confused.

Sean looked at his tattoos, seeming proud of them. "That's all the sword I need, kid."

I knew Cory and Fish had tattoos. They were both covered in them. I never understood why people would cover their bodies in drawings.

"By the way," Sean said, pointing to my sneakers. "Your shoelaces are untied."

"I like them that way," I answered.

There must have been about twenty people stopping to inform me about my laces. It was getting as annoying as hearing about my robe.

"You're going to be working for Sean," Cory began. "He'll show you how to make his famous grinders. He makes the best."

"Yes, and Suzie Lou will show him how to run the register," Sean added.

"Who is Suzie Lou?" I asked.

"That would be me," a woman said, coming out of the back. "And we have lots of orders to fill today," she said, opening a display case.

The woman had straight, long brown hair. I was surprised to see her wearing glasses. I never understood why witches never used a spell to correct their vision. Did they like wearing glasses?

"Did you bring work clothes?" Sean asked, looking at my robe again.

Cory cleared his throat. "Would you mind if Ethan wore his robe for a bit?"

Sean glanced at my robe. "Costume?" he asked Cory.

Cory tried to hold it in, but his laughter came suddenly and loud.

"Sorry," Cory said, trying to compose himself. "But I tried to warn you."

"He'll have to wear a hairnet," Suzie Lou said, as she filled the display case with sliced meats.

I ignored them and asked Sean to show me around. "I'd like to get started," I said, still wondering what a grinder was.

Cory excused himself and walked out. Sean pointed to the back of the deli, then followed behind me. "This is our prep area," Sean said, as we entered the room.

It was a very large room with three wooden tables taking up most of the space. Knives hung over one of the tables, cutting boards and pans sat to the left of them.

"The meat slicers are there," Sean said, pointing to a small stainless-steel table. "The door next to that is the walk-in. I store some of the meats in there. Meats to one side, produce on the other. You'll have to clean it at the end of each day."

I nodded. "Where are the mixers?" I asked.

"We cut, we don't mix. The mixing happens next door," Sean said, patting me on the back.

I almost hit the floor when he did that. Did he *not* realize how strong he was?

He gave me an apron, instructing me to put a strange net on my hair. "You're working with food," he explained. "So, make sure you wear it."

I nodded and placed the odd net over my head.

"Are you sure you're up to working so soon?" he asked.

It was obvious Sean knew about what happened. This surprised me. I was positive Sean was a warlock. Not a half-human witch like Cory, but a full-blooded warlock. Why did Cory trust him so much? I didn't remember him from any of their memories.

Unsure of him, I tried to be polite.

"I'm fine. Just anxious to get started."

"Well, that's a good attitude," he said, patting me hard on the back again.

He was strong—a little too strong. He could probably crush my neck with one hand—one massive hand. His arms were quite impressive and intimidating. I had no plans on messing with him, magic or not.

"You're going to be slicing salami," Sean instructed. "I have a big order to fill. There's a party tomorrow, and I'm catering it."

"We need pepperoni, too," Suzie Lou said, placing a bag of bread on one of the tables. "Make sure he knows how to use the slicer first."

She disappeared into the walk-in, mumbling something under her breath. I got the impression she didn't want me here. At least she wasn't staring at my robe.

"Go wash your hands," Sean said. "I'll show

you how to use the slicer. Then I'll get you started on the tomatoes."

For the next few hours, I sliced meats and cut vegetables. The sound of the bell dinging as people walked in was constant. "Give me an Italian, with extra hots," I would hear from the back. The deli was very popular.

Suzie Lou hardly spoke to me. I was convinced she didn't like me, although I couldn't understand why.

I would glance at Sean from time to time, admiring his tattoos. He was working on the table across from me, cutting a large piece of meat. It was odd how his tattoos would move, appearing to slice when he did. I couldn't get past how much bread Sean ate. Never any meat, just large pieces of bread. He ate it almost every hour, on the hour.

Suzie Lou stepped into the room, looking at the clock on the wall.

"He's late, again," she snapped at Sean.

"Give him a break, Sizzles. He'll be here soon enough."

I wasn't sure who they were talking about, but Sean started looking at the clock after that. By mid-day, I was feeling the need for food. My stomach was growling.

"Whoa, I heard that from here," Sean said, reaching for some bread. "I'll make you a grinder, so you can take your lunch."

I removed my apron as Sean placed assorted meats between the bread. He added vegetables, poured a liquid over them, then cut it in half. He threw it on a parchment paper and held it out.

"Here ya go," he said with a big smile. "I put plenty of oil and vinegar on it."

I grabbed the strange food with both hands, unsure if I would like it. Was this going to be like the corn dogs?

"Ever had a grinder before?" Sean asked.

I looked at the grinder.

"No, I don't believe I have."

"Well, have at it, kid. Go sit out front, enjoy your food."

"Thank you," I said, heading for the front.

I sat at one of the tables, placing the grinder in front of me. I could smell the vinegar, it didn't smell half bad. I picked up one of the halves, opened my mouth, and took a bite.

Flavors I'd never experienced, danced about in my mouth. The foreign spices, well, foreign to me, made my mouth come alive. I took another bite, savoring the delightful taste. I licked my fingers, not wanting to waste a single portion.

"Here," Suzie Lou said, slamming a drink on the table. "Enjoy the sandwich."

I didn't even look at her. I took another wonderful bite and closed my eyes. I moaned in delight as I chewed my food slowly. I could taste the olives, peppers, onions, tomatoes, and all the wonderful meats. This was truly magical. Why hadn't my parents told me about *grinders* before?

I looked at the drink, feeling the need to

wash down my food. The dark liquid didn't look very inviting. No matter, it would have to do.

I held the glass to my lips, allowing the liquid to slide down my throat. My eyes shot open, realizing how delicious the drink was. It took me only seconds to down the rest.

"Want another soda?" Suzie Lou snapped at me.

I didn't even care about her tone. "Yes, please," I quickly answered.

As I ate the delightful grinder, I got the sense that someone was watching me. I paused, looking around the deli. When I looked toward the window, I saw a man looking in. Our eyes met, a wicked smile spread across his face as he slowly walked away.

What was that all about? Maybe he wanted a grinder? I didn't give it a second thought and dug in. I was already on the second half of the sandwich. When the last bite was gone, I asked Suzie Lou if I could have another.

She pointed her chin out and headed to the back.

"He already ate it?" I heard Sean say.

Chapter Thirteen: Like Them?

With my second grinder in hand, I decided to finish my lunch outside. Besides, I couldn't take Suzie Lou's glares any longer. She had almost tossed the grinder at me when she brought it out.

When I stepped outside, I was surprised to see Viola was still there—still reading. I looked at my grinder, deciding I would share it with her.

I wasn't sure why she giggled when I sat next to her. "Want half of my grinder?" I asked, holding it out.

She looked at me, giggled again, and said no. "I assure you, they are very good," I said, offering it up.

She eyed it, unsure of what to do.

"You like leaving my hand out, don't you?" I said jokingly.

I offered it again, this time she took it. I

leaned back and took another wonderful bite.

"These are amazing," I said, with a mouthful of food. "Have you ever had one?"

She kept giggling. "I eat there all the time," she answered, taking a small bite.

"This is my new favorite food," I said, stuffing more of the grinder into my mouth.

"Haven't you ever had one?" Viola asked.

My mouth was too full to answer. I just shook my head and took another massive bite.

Viola laughed. "You really like those, don't you?"

"They're delightful," I managed to say.

Trying to hold in her laughter, she asked, "What did you say?"

I swallowed down some of the grinder.

"I said, they're delightful."

She chuckled.

"What?" I asked, wiping vinegar from my mouth.

"Well, guys don't usually say delightful. Then again, they don't dress like you either."

"Wow, guys around here don't say a lot of words, do they? It's a wonder they even manage to speak."

"Ethan, where are you?" I heard Sean call.

He was standing outside the deli, an apron still hanging from his neck. He marched his way towards us when he spotted me.

"Hey, you have a license?" he asked.

"A what?

"A license to drive?"

"I don't think so."

He sighed, seeming frustrated.

"Is everything okay?" I asked.

He looked up and down the street. "No, it's Wayne, my delivery driver. He's late, and I need to start the deliveries."

He looked up and down the street again. "Come inside when you're done with lunch. We'll figure out something."

He turned to leave. "Oh, by the way," he said, pausing, "you can take off the hairnet when you're not working. You look kind of silly. It only needs to cover your hair, not half your head."

Viola giggled again. I quickly reached up, pulling it off my head. No wonder she was giggling.

"Why didn't you tell me?" I asked.

She laughed again. I liked hearing her laugh. It brightened up her face.

"Considering the robe," she said, looking at it. "I assumed it was part of your outfit."

I looked down at myself. "Fair enough," I said, taking the last bite of my grinder.

"Are you like… them?" Viola asked softly.

Confused, I looked at her. "What are you talking about?"

She instantly became nervous.

"Um, never mind," she said, rising to her feet. "I have to go."

I sat there, watching her march down the

street. What an odd question to ask. I didn't give it much thought and made my way back to the deli. Sean was bagging up some grinders when I walked in.

"I guess *I'll* have to make the deliveries," Suzie Lou hissed.

"Leave them there," Sean said, grabbing a bag from her. "Ethan and I will take care of it. I'll stop by Wayne's, find out why he didn't report for work today."

I could see the idea of getting rid of me for a bit made her happy. "Take your time," she answered, smiling as she looked my way.

I thought of asking Sean why his wife didn't like me, but thought better of it when I realized I could be wrong.

I helped Sean load up the van. When I took a seat inside, the wonderful odor of grinders filled my head. Sean pulled the seat all the way back before getting in. Even then, his legs needed more room.

I held on tight when Sean pulled away from the curve. This felt odd. It wasn't the same as flying, more like riding Attor with my eyes closed. This van was no dragon, but I got the same sensation, well, almost.

I took a deep breath, wishing I could eat another grinder. "It smells delightful in here," I said.

"Did you just say delightful?" Sean asked.

I nodded.

"No," he said, shaking his head. "Don't say that. Instead, say it smells good, but not delightful. Guys don't say that."

"What's wrong with delightful?" I asked perplexed.

Sean hung one arm over the steering wheel.

"You're a guy, not a girl."

What did that have to do with it? What was up with these men? Why did certain words seem to almost offend them?

"How about flowers?" I asked. "Do you like flowers?"

Sean made a face. "I'm starting to wonder why you wear that thing," he said, looking at my robe.

"Tell me something?" I asked, hoping he would be honest.

"Shoot."

"What's wrong with what I'm wearing?"

He raised an eyebrow. "You really want to know?"

"Why else would I ask?"

Seeming on the verge of laughter, he glanced at my robe again. "Well, if you were married and someone asked who wore the pants in the family…" He paused, "well, that would be a hard question for you to answer." Then he erupted into laughter.

What was so funny?

I stopped asking questions when Sean asked how many different color robes I had.

"You have some with flowers on it? You seem to like flowers."

More laughter.

It would appear I had to learn how to ignore comments like these. I was determined not to let it bother me. Like it or not, I was not going to stop wearing my robe.

Sean stopped laughing when I asked why his wife didn't like me. Several long moments passed before he said, "We'll stop by Wayne's house. It's not like him to miss work like that."

I didn't miss the fact that he ignored my question. That meant I was right about his wife. She hated me, I just wasn't sure why.

We drove to a small house just outside of town. There was a lot of clutter scattered about the yard. An old, rusted truck sat in the front yard.

"I bet he's still sleeping," Sean said, turning off the van.

Sleeping? It was mid-day.

We stepped over tools and opened beer cans as we neared the door. "What the heck was this guy doing?" Sean muttered.

He froze when he noticed the front door was cracked opened. A sudden uneasiness washed over him. He took short, quiet steps and pushed open the door. "Wayne?" he called. "You okay, man?"

The house was in disarray. Things had been turned over and thrown about. There had been a struggle, that much was clear. I tapped Sean on the shoulder, pointing out some blood on the kitchen floor.

"Go wait in the van," Sean said, looking down at it.

I readied myself, ignoring his wishes. I could sense warlocks, and they were near.

Sean made his way through the kitchen, stopping when he looked out a window that was over a sink.

"What the…" he gasped.

In the back yard, near a shed, were four warlocks. They were struggling to get another man on the ground. The man was fighting for his life, kicking and swinging his arms.

"Wayne!" Sean shouted.

He kicked open the back door, sending it flying about ten feet. The four men spun around, drawing their weapons. They held strange looking swords with needle like objects coming from the blade. The swords made a strange humming sound as they held them up.

I followed Sean out, wishing I had a weapon of my own. I pulled out the only thing I could think of, my mother's wand. It instantly turned into the staff as I held it up.

Sean came to a sudden stop. He noticed what I had seen right away. One of the men looked identical to the one named Wayne. Same dark hair, both in their late forties. They were carbon copies of each other. The only way of telling them apart were the clothes they wore. The Wayne that was being attacked wore chef's clothes, while the other was in jeans.

Sean spread his arms, smiled at the warlocks, and spat a spell into his arms. I was surprised when his tattoos began to move. Sean slowly took his left hand and pulled the razor sword from his right arm. When he did the same with his left hand, the tattoos that were once on his arms, disappeared.

In an instant, the warlocks came at us. Sean spun his swords and sent one flying right at the warlocks. I heard the swift sound of a blade cutting as a head dropped to the ground. Sean whistled, causing his sword to come flying back into his hand. He spun it again, looking at the other two warlocks.

"I was hoping for three heads," Sean said, with a wicked smile.

The warlocks began spitting spells at us. One hit Sean on the shoulder, dropping him to the ground. A bearded warlock held up his hand to his partner, eyeing me the whole time.

"I have a special spell for him," he said, spitting one into his palm.

From the ground, Sean whispered, "Run."

Why would I run? Did Sean think me a coward?

"Throw it," the other warlock yelled to the man.

I ran at them, holding the staff with both hands. When the warlock threw the spell, I tapped the ground with my staff, and vaulted over it. I swung the staff, slapping both warlocks across the face with it. I stood still, patiently waiting for my magic to take effect.

I held the staff next to me, smiling at the warlocks. They seemed confused at first, wondering why I wasn't attacking them. When their cheeks began to crack, they dropped their swords, grabbing at their faces. I knew my magic would cause them pain—horrible, awful pain.

They began to scream in agony as the cracks spread throughout their bodies. The more the cracks moved, the thicker they got, cutting them almost in half.

There was silence. I could only hear Sean moaning on the ground behind me. I moved towards the warlocks' bodies, realizing they hadn't turned to dust like the others. Pieces of them were still moving. I waved my hand, deciding to be merciful and end their misery.

When I faced Sean, he had a look of shock on his face. "Are you well?" I asked.

He huffed. "I'm delightful," he answered.

I helped him up, eyeing the wound on his shoulder. I waved my hand, breaking the spell that was causing him pain. I could tell it had been a powerful spell. Sean should have been screaming from its effect.

We quickly checked on Wayne, who was still twisting on the ground. "I think he's been poisoned," I said.

I spied a cauldron near the shed, a fire still

burning under it. A thick, yellow substance bubbled inside of it. "A potion," I muttered.

Wayne's body went limp. He drew breath, and began to vomit. Sean sat him up, patting him on the back.

"Get it all out, buddy."

"We have problems," Wayne managed to say.

"Of what nature?" I asked.

When Wayne began to vomit again, Sean asked me to help get him inside the house.

Chapter Fourteen: A Spy?

Sean was pushing clutter aside as he tried to look for a glass to fill with water. Everything was broken and moved around as if they were looking for something.

"What the hell happened?" Sean asked from the kitchen.

I looked down at Wayne, who was lying on the sofa. He kept coughing and shaking his head.

"The water will help," I assured him.

"If I can find a glass," Sean answered from the kitchen.

With my eyes on Wayne, I waved my hand. Within seconds, the house began to repair itself. Broken glass floated off the floor and put itself back together. The curtains lifted themselves off the floor and onto the rods. Legs flew back onto chairs and back under the table. Every picture, every item, was back in its place.

Sean came walking slowly from the kitchen, glass in hand. "They want *me*, to protect *you*?" he said.

I looked at him. "Why would I need protecting?"

Sean looked at the glass, then at me.

"I have no idea, kid."

With the glass finally filled with water, Wayne grabbed it with both hands and quickly drank.

"What happened here?" Sean asked him.

Wayne held up the glass. "Please, more water."

As Sean left to get the water, I observed burn marks on Wayne's neck. The burns had a strange look to them, like they were coming from inside his throat.

"Here's the water," Sean said, sitting next to him.

Grabbing at his throat, Wayne began coughing up blood. Sean jumped to his feet, pulling a phone from his pocket. "Hey, I'm at Wayne's," he said into the phone. "I think he's been poisoned. Get Donna to the deli. I'm on my way."

I wanted to help, but breaking the effect of poison wasn't something I was familiar with. It was the one thing my mother said our magic was weak against. In fact, it was how Morgan, Netiri's brother, had died. I saw that in one of her memories when Fish was poisoned.

"Help me get him in the van," Sean said, reaching for Wayne's arm.

Sean ran every light on the way back to the deli. Suzie Lou was waiting outside when we arrived. "I knew this would happen," she cried.

"Go inside, hun," Sean said, throwing Wayne over his shoulder.

Cory was already there with a tall, blond woman by his side. Sean took Wayne to the back of the deli.

"Tear off his clothes," the woman instructed.

She knelt, pulling a bottle from her purse.

"Open his mouth," she said, pulling off the cork.

I stood back as the woman emptied the contents into Wayne's mouth. Cory grabbed my arm, pulling me into the other room.

"You have the staff on you?" he asked.

I pulled the wand from my robe. "Yes."

"Unshrink that thing," he ordered.

"What?"

"This happened before," Cory explained. "You have to fly him around so the poison leaves his pores."

"If it will help."

"Oh, trust me, it helps," Cory said, running into the back again.

I already had my staff between my legs when they dragged Wayne out. Sean ran to the door, checking for human eyes.

"I think it's clear," he said, over his shoulder.

Cory quickly threw Wayne over the staff.

"Try not to be seen," he said. "Stick to the clouds. Don't come back until you see he's feeling better."

"Okay," I said, preparing myself.

Sean had his hand up, warning me to wait. He looked in every direction, opened the door, and waved for me to go.

The wind picked up under me, made me hover, and I was off.

I flew as quick as I could into the clouds. When Wayne began breathing in the fresh air, the vomiting returned. I noticed a strange, oozy substance coming from his skin. The moment it hit the air, it disintegrated and drifted away.

"I understand," I said to myself.

It was clear what I needed to do. I flew faster, trying to stay clear of human eyes. It was a clear day with not many clouds to choose from.

"Are we flying?" I heard Wayne ask.

I had to grab his arm when he realized how high we were. "We really *are* flying," he said, in a panic.

"I'm not going to drop you," I said, grabbing a fist full of hair.

He struggled to free himself, vomit covering his lips. He finally stopped fighting when the vomiting was too much. I tried to ignore the sounds he was making. It was making me nauseous to hear him.

I flew until there was no oozing from his skin. He wiped his mouth, looking up at me.

"What the hell are you?" he said, trying to pull himself away.

It was time to head back. It was clear he was feeling better.

I hovered in a cloud when we neared the deli. I looked down on Salem, hoping no one would see me. It was still daylight and lots of tourist still walked about. Things got worse when I spotted Viola in her usual place. Now what was I going to do?

"Do you have one of those phones?" I asked Wayne.

Trembling, he reached into his sock, and pulled it out. "Can you please call Cory?" I asked. "Tell him we're right above the deli."

"I must be dreaming," Wayne said, pushing on the numbers.

There was a pause. "Sean, I know this is going to sound crazy, but we're above the deli, hiding in a cloud."

Another pause.

"Yes, I feel better now...I think," Wayne said, glancing up at me.

I looked down, waiting for the signal. Suzie Lou came out of the deli, handing something to Viola. She looked at whatever Suzie Lou was holding, nodded, and took it from her. I was relieved when Viola began making her way down the street.

Cory opened the door, looked up, and waved me in.

"Hold on," I said to Wayne.

I flew down from the sky like a flash of lightening, coming to a dead stop the minute we were inside the deli. Wayne fell off the staff the minute I lifted my protection. The others ran to him, asking if he was okay.

All Wayne could do was look my way.

"He can fly," he kept saying.

I shrunk down the staff and put it into my pocket, noting the horrible look Suzie Lou was giving me. The woman named Donna was looking Wayne over.

"He seems fine now," she assured us. "I don't think he drank much."

The tall, blond woman faced me, a look of amazement in her eyes. "You're right, Cory," she said. "He really does look like James."

Cory ignored her.

"What happened?" he asked Wayne.

Wayne shook his head. "They broke in, tore the house apart, made me drink something, and dragged me outside."

"Did they say anything to you?" Sean asked.

"No, but I heard them talking when one of the warlocks drank from a cauldron and turned into me."

"What were they saying?" Cory asked.

Wayne looked thoughtful for a moment. "They were giving instructions to the one that drank the potion. They wanted him to come here, work, and pass off as me."

"A spy?" Sean asked, looking at Cory.

Every eye in the room was now on me. I was a little shocked when Suzie Lou stepped forward, raised her hand, and slapped me across the face.

"Susan," Sean said, pulling her back.

"I knew this would happen," she said, pushing Sean away. "He shouldn't be here. We waited so long to return to Salem, and now it's happening again."

"This isn't his fault," Cory said, stepping forward. "He's here to help, remember that."

"Help?" Suzie Lou spit back at him. "How the hell is putting us in danger going to help?"

"I can answer that," William said from the door.

I still hadn't grown used to seeing William in human clothes. The fact that he was wearing a hat threw me off a bit.

He entered slowly, eyeing Suzie Lou. "You, Madam," he said, stepping up to her, "are blaming the wrong person. It wasn't Ethan who wanted you to come back to Salem. It was your husband's choice."

Suzie Lou bowed her head.

"And when he wanted to come help fight Simon," William continued, "that was also his choice. Not one person was forced to stay in Salem back then. You were one of the many who fled."

"I did it for her," Sean explained.

"You've held that over my head for years," Suzie Lou cried.

Sean gently grabbed her shoulders. "Suzy, this is our home. How can you expect me not to defend it? I left Salem the first time because I wanted to protect you. I realize now, the only way to keep you safe, is to fight."

He pulled her close and wrapped his arms around her. "I said no to Simon because I wasn't like them. You have no idea how much I regret not warning the others about his lies."

"Simon approached you?" Cory asked, seeming uneasy.

Sean nodded. "He approached all the warlocks, near and far. He wanted us to come fight—fight the witch with the unmatched powers. He offered riches and glory, said the human world would be ours. He wanted to make slaves of them, the humans, make them pay for what they'd done to him."

"Why did you say no?" Cory asked.

Sean pulled Suzie Lou away, gazing into her eyes. "Because when Simon learned I had married a half-human witch, he tried to kill her."

Suzie Lou's eyes spilled over with tears.

"Is that why we really left?" she asked.

Sean smiled. "I wasn't going to risk your life. You mean too much to me."

"But why now?" she cried.

"The reasons are the same," Sean answered. "If I don't stay and fight, they'll find you."

"But Simon is dead," she reminded him.

"The Black Witch is not," William shot back.

He looked around the room. "Before Simon was killed," he began, "he left certain things in place, assuring that his wishes were carried out. Killing Simon didn't end things, only delayed them. Unfortunately, Simon sought out the Black Witch, made her promises he never intended to keep. The Black Witch doesn't care if Simon is dead. She wants what was promised to her."

I noticed Cory looking at me from the corner of his eye. "What other promises did he make?" he asked.

William sighed. "I wasn't quite sure at first. That's why I've been coming here for the past few months. I'm searching for answers, trying to figure out what the Black Witch's plans could be."

"Have you figured it out yet?" Sean asked.

William nodded. "Yes, and I'm afraid her plan has already begun. She's taking things right from under your noses, replacing it with something of her own."

He looked at Wayne. "I'm sure your double was ordered to keep a watchful eye, report every word that was spoken here."

"What has she already taken?" Cory asked.

"That, I cannot tell you," William answered.

"However, I will tell you this, there is only one person capable of finally ending your nightmare, and he's standing in this very room."

I didn't know what to say as all heads turned to me.

Chapter Fifteen: On the Hunt

I knew they had questions, all of which I couldn't answer. I already knew my part in this, William had shown me. I also knew I couldn't say a word about it, fearing it would change things.

"One thing I must warn you about," William continued, "your lives cannot change. If the Black Witch suspects we know her plan, she will change it. I will no longer have control over the outcome. That is why you must live your day to day routines. Work, play, act as if nothing is wrong."

"You're asking us to just sit here, like sitting ducks?" Suzie Lou asked.

"We're not just sitting here," Cory answered. "We've been hunting down warlocks, taking them out, and leveling the field. William says the Black Witch has no idea how many men she has, so it's easy to get rid of them."

Sean spoke next. "Being a warlock myself, I can tell you that we've always relied on our spells. There's never been a need for us to physically fight someone. That's why we're bad fighters, well, not me, I've been training with Cory."

"They *were* bad fighters," William said. "Have you not noticed the weapons they carry? They've been training, I'm certain of it."

"So far," Cory interrupted, "we've only come across the weak ones, the unskilled ones. We've had to protect ourselves from their spells, not their weapons."

Now I understood Cory's appearance. He and Fish had obviously been fighting warlocks.

"What's going to happen?" Suzie Lou asked. "How can we possibly know which warlocks are friend or foe? We can't go around killing all of them."

"She's marked them," William answered. "It's not hard to spot the scars on their necks."

Suzie Lou gasped. "Blood promises?"

William nodded. "And I believe they are taking a potion to disguise the darkness in their eyes, but there is no disguising the scars."

William began pacing the room. "Soon, they will do nothing but think evil thoughts. It will consume them. A blood promise is unbreakable, causing the person who made the promise with the Black Witch to do her will."

"Can't we find a way to break it?" Sean

asked.

"That's not possible," William answered. "I know of only one person who has broken a promise like that."

Again, all eyes were on me.

"Why are you looking at me?" I said, stepping forward. "I've never made such a promise."

"It was your mother," Suzie Lou spat. "Everyone knew about it. She was a fool."

"Suzie, stop it," Sean said, pulling on her arm.

"It's true," she said, yanking her arm away from him. "We didn't even live here then, but we heard what she had done."

"Enough!" William shouted. "You are alive because of her. I will not stand here and allow you to disgrace her in front of her son."

I was speechless, shocked from what I had just learned. Had my mother really made a blood promise? If so, to whom? My mother neglected to share that memory with me. In fact, I was starting to realize she didn't share a lot of things. What possible reason could she have for making such a promise? How desperate could she have been?

I knew little about a blood promise, but I knew it was an awful thing. It began with a request, followed by a promise to pay the darkness. Blood was given to seal the promise, ensuring it would be kept. If the promise was broken, the person who made the promise would die a horrible death before being pulled into the darkness. If the promise was kept, the blood which had been given would just disappear. I'd even heard stories about someone keeping the promise, but they were never the same again. They became evil, consumed with power and dark thoughts. There was no easy way to escape a promise like that. You paid a heavy price for the help you asked for.

"You heard him," Cory snapped at her. "There's no reason to bring up the past. Life goes on, and we must go on with it. All we can do is be patient, and wait for the Black Witch to make her move. Find the Black Witch, find our answers."

"There's something I need to know," Sean said. "Why would you ask *me* to protect *him*? It's obvious Ethan can take care of himself."

William smiled. "I didn't ask *you* to protect Ethan. I asked *Ethan* to protect *you*."

William looked around the room. "Protect all of you."

It was true. When William placed his hands over my head, he asked me to do things I didn't understand, one of them being to protect the ones my mother loved so much. That's why I didn't question Cory when he asked me to work for Sean. Cory thought he was keeping a watchful eye on me, but it was I keeping a watchful eye on him. I knew William's requests would get harder and harder, but I was determined to follow his instructions, no matter the cost. I knew my purpose. I knew my job.

"I believe you have deliveries to make?" William said to Sean. "Shouldn't you be done with them by now?"

The room quickly cleared. Cory returned to the bakery as I prepared myself to help Sean make the deliveries. Sean made Wayne take the day off.

"Why don't you stay in the basement for now?" Sean suggested to him. "It will be safer."

Wayne quickly agreed.

I heard the bell on the door ding. It was Viola.

"I have the change Susan asked for," she said, holding out some money.

I smiled, admiring the beautiful dress she wore today. It was three sizes too big, but she looked lovely nonetheless.

"Change?" I asked.

"Um, yes. She asked me to get her one-dollar bills from the bank."

"Suzie Lou," I called. "Viola is here to see you."

Suzie Lou came storming out. "You don't get to call me that," she hissed. "It's Susan to you."

She bumped shoulders with me as she headed to Viola. Apparently, she was still blaming me for all the troubles we were having.

Viola took her place on the bench outside after giving *Susan* the money. Sean and I left soon after.

Sean didn't say much as we delivered

grinders to some of the shops in Salem. I knew he felt uneasy. He cleared his throat as he draped his arm over the steering wheel.

"Um, I'm sorry Susan struck you," he said awkwardly. "She's not normally that rude."

I looked out the window. "I understand."

"She'll warm up to you, I promise."

I wasn't sure if I wanted her to. Maybe things were better this way. I didn't want to spend my time trying to win her over.

"That's not necessary," I answered.

With the last order delivered, we headed back to the deli. Vera was standing outside the bakery talking to Viola. The moment Sean parked the van, I jumped out.

"Why do you always have to sit here?" Vera was asking her. "Salem has tons of benches. Why can't you sit on any of those?"

"Because I like this one," Viola shot back.

"Well, I don't want you here," Vera said, trying to grab her arm.

"Viola," I called from in front of the van. I was about to fix this little problem. "There's a lovely bench in front of our shop. Why don't you sit ever here?"

"She was just leaving," Vera said, trying to pull Viola to her feet.

"Actually," Viola said, pulling her arm away. "That bench looks more comfortable than this one."

I chuckled as Viola made her way to the

bench. I liked that she had some spunk in her. For some reason, I thought she never defended herself. She was always so quiet—so shy.

As Viola made her way to me, I looked at Vera. She was beautiful as ever. She wore her hair up with a beautiful butterfly pin in her hair. How I had loved her, fantasized about our lives together. She was the reason I was here, the reason I was doing all of this. At least, it was back then.

"She doesn't like me very much," Viola said from the bench. "She never has."

I took a seat next to her. Viola looked at my robe. "I'm glad you haven't stopped wearing that."

"What? My robe? You really like it?"

She nodded. "You should go back to wearing your other shoes. Those sneakers don't go with the robe."

I laughed.

"Ethan, may I speak with you?" Vera asked, in a sweet tone, a little too sweet. "I want to show you something."

"What is it?" I asked.

A flirty smile spread across her face as she approached us. Her lavender scent filled my head the closer she got.

"I want to show you around Salem, silly. I'm sure Sean will let you out early."

I didn't know what to make of her as she moved closer to me.

"Oh, come on," she said, running her fingers along my arm. "I've been looking forward to this."

"You have?"

"Of course. I've just been having a few bad days," she explained. "I planned on showing you around Salem all along."

"I have to go," Viola said, grabbing her book.

"There," Vera said, seeming proud of herself. "No excuses."

Just then, Sean came out of the deli.

"Ethan, you can get out of here for today. I need to speak with Susan. I'll see you in the morning."

He went back inside before I could answer.

"Come on," Vera said, pulling me up from the bench. "Let's go for a walk."

"What about my robe? I'm still wearing it. Doesn't that bother you?"

She still had a smile spread across her face.

"It's fine. Besides, it's almost October, you'll blend right in."

I decided to go with her. Why had she changed her tune so suddenly?

"I'm sorry I've been acting like a brat," Vera said, as we walked down the street. "It has nothing to do with you."

"Are you sure about that?" I asked.

I stopped and faced her. "I heard what you said to Cory, about how I'm a dork."

She bit her lip. "You heard that?"

"Isn't that enough?"

We began walking again. "Listen, Ethan. I

didn't mean those things. It's just that, well, my parents have been hounding me about you my whole life. I feel they've been training me to make you happy. What you heard was me trying to teach them a lesson."

"That's odd," I answered. "You were talking to Cory when you called me a dork."

She stopped. "Don't you get it? He's just like them. Ethan this, and Ethan that. By the time I would visit you, I was aggravated. I thought you were the one telling them to do that. I never knew they were acting on their own."

I thought back to all the times she came to Magia. She was right; there was always an angry tone to her voice. I always thought she was just a little moody, but now it all made sense.

"Ethan," Vera said, taking hold of my hand. "I realize now that you had no idea what they were doing. You weren't trying to make me love you, they were."

She moved closer, brushing my cheek with the back of her hand. "I would have loved you all on my own."

Her sweet lavender scent hit my face, sending my heart racing. I tried not to read into her words, but it was too late. I wanted her, now more than ever.

"I only acted that way to anger my parents," she continued. "I never meant to hurt you. I care about you. Nothing could ever make me hate you."

"What about Steven?" I asked.

"Another way of pissing them off," she explained. "When I overhead them almost planning our wedding, I used him to get back at them. I knew that would drive them crazy. I guess it kind of backfired on me a little."

She moved a little closer. "I know it didn't seem like it, but I always looked forward to my visits with you. I didn't dare tell my mother about it, she would have bought me a wedding dress right away. I wanted our love to grow organically, not forced into our hearts. I know deep in my heart I may already love you. I just don't want people telling me I have to love you."

I gazed into her green eyes, allowing her words to give me hope. I looked at her lips, pulled her to me, and pressed my lips to hers.

She wrapped her arms around my neck as my tongue touched hers. I trembled as I pulled her closer, kissing her more intensely. I had waited years for this moment, dreamt of tasting her lips. There wasn't a part of her I hadn't fantasized about, hadn't thought about touching. She was in every thought, every desire I had.

"Ethan," she whispered into my mouth.

I closed my eyes, squeezing her tighter and tighter. The sound of my name coming from her lips was sweet. I wanted more. I wanted her.

She ran her fingers though my hair.

"Are you still angry with me?" she asked, between kisses.

"Does this answer your question?" I asked,

crushing my lips to hers.

The heat from her body traveled through me, sending me to a place I'd never been. My heart was pounding, burning with desire. I was overcome with happiness. No amount of danger could take this way from me. She was all that mattered, all I wanted. I would do anything for her. Drop to my knees, if she wished it so.

When I squeezed her even tighter, she pulled away from me. "We'd better slow down," she said, looking around.

I wanted to pull her back into my arms. I didn't like the distance between us.

"Come on," she said, giving me a peck on the cheek. "Let's go to the lake. There's no one there this time of day. We can talk there."

Unwilling to wait, I pulled out my staff. We were in the air in seconds.

Chapter Sixteen: Loose Girl

Vera squeezed me tight as I flew over Salem. I couldn't get to the lake fast enough. I wanted her in my arms, her lips touching mine. The happiness I felt was overwhelming. To learn that she never hated me, never thought those horrible things, filled my heart with joy. I knew I had been lying to myself when I said I would forget her. There was no forgetting my first love.

When we reached the lake, I threw the staff to one side and took her in my arms again. I pulled the butterfly pin from her hair, allowing it to drape down her shoulders.

"You're so beautiful," I whispered.

I had to force myself from ripping away her clothes. I was starting to lose control of myself. All I could think of was her naked body. I pictured myself beside her, our bodies becoming one.

I felt out of breath as I tightened my arms around her waist. One of my hands was already traveling to places I could be slapped for. I couldn't stop the flood of emotions I was feeling for the first time. My body was on fire.

"Ethan, you're going too fast," she said, trying to pull away from me.

I tried to kiss her.

"No," she said, pushing me away.

She gave her back to me. "I told you, my plan backfired. I really do have feelings for Steven," she confessed. "I guess I spent so much time with him, that I developed real feelings. I can't just start seeing you. It wouldn't be fair to him."

I spun her around. "What does your heart tell you? Right now, at this moment, what does your heart feel?"

She touched my face. "I feel I could love you. I want to love you."

"Do you love him?"

I wasn't sure if I wanted to hear the answer. When she said, "I think so," I let go of her shoulders.

"Why did you let me kiss you then?" I asked.

She sighed. "I'm not sure. I think I wanted to know for sure that I didn't have feelings for you. When I saw you talking to Viola, it made me a little jealous. It confused me."

"And, what did you discover?"

She moved closer, something I wished she would stop doing.

"I discovered I missed my friend," she answered.

I felt like a fool. I had given myself hope yet again. She wasn't to blame. I was the one that had taken liberties when I kissed her. I had even dared to almost undress her.

I took a deep breath, trying to stop my heart from racing. I didn't want her to notice how aroused I had been.

"Can I sit with my friend, like old times?" Vera asked.

"Is there a rock around here?"

We both laughed.

We sat, facing the lake, talking about Salem. I was surprised to hear that Vera didn't like it much here. "There's always so many people," she explained. "Tourism fizzles out in November, that's my favorite month around here. That and January."

"Why January?" I asked.

She smiled. "The snow, the quietness, the empty streets. It's when Salem really comes alive."

"Can I ask you something?" I said.

"What?"

"Why don't you like that girl, the one that sits on the bench? Why are you so rude to her?"

"You'd be rude too, if you knew what I knew."

"What do you mean?"

"She's a loose girl, Ethan. Half the men in Salem have taken their turn at her. She gets around, trust me."

This surprised me. I never got that from her. She seemed very nice to me.

"I think she's very shy," I said. "She seems nice, well mannered."

Vera burst out in laughter. "She's a fat skank. Why would you even waste your time on her? You're just new meat to her. She doesn't care about you. You know she used to have her eyes on Cory, right?"

"She did?"

"Yeah, she was all in love with him. Helena needs to watch her back. She tries to play all innocent and shy, but I've seen her out in the woods, with three guys taking their turn at her."

I found this very hard to believe. We couldn't be talking about the same girl. Then it hit me, the day the warlocks were dragging her through the woods. Had she been out there willingly with them? It just didn't make any sense.

"I think my father took a shot at her, too," Vera shockingly announced.

"Fish?"

She nodded. "I could almost swear to it."

"Does Delia know?"

She huffed. "No, but I have a good mind to tell her. I think it happened more than once, too."

Shocked by the news, I stared out into the

lake, trying to understand. I had been so wrong about Viola. How did I miss it? Better yet, why did I care?

"So, are you going to the party?" Vera asked.

I had drifted away.

"I'm sorry, what?"

"The party? Salem has a party to launch the season. They start with a parade, ending the day with a big party. October is next week; all the events get going. You think it's busy now, wait till you see October."

I really didn't care much about this party. I just couldn't get the news about Viola out of my head. How could I have been so wrong about her?

"We better get back now," Vera said, rising to her feet. "Grandfather is cooking dinner. That means I don't have to pretend to like the food."

I laughed, understanding her comment.

I reached for the staff, shrunk it, and put it in my pocket.

"What, no flying?" Vera asked.

"Not really in the mood," I said, walking past her.

I wasn't sure why the news about Viola had upset me so much. I was finding it very hard to believe that she could be like that. She seemed so innocent, so pure. I always considered myself a good judge of character. How could I have been so wrong about her?

I thought of Fish. How could he do that to

Delia? There was anger growing inside me. He wasn't the man I thought him to be. What a hypocrite he was. I wondered what my mother would say if she knew he did such things. I'm sure she wouldn't hold him in such high regard.

William was in the kitchen when we walked into the mansion. I could smell his cooking before I even walked in. If I was lucky, there would be no corn dogs in sight.

"How was your first day of work?" Fish asked, as I walked through the kitchen door.

"Fine," I said, taking a seat at the table.

"Just fine? Did you like it? Try any grinders while you were there?"

"It was fine," I repeated coldly.

William raised an eyebrow, eyeing me intensely.

"Was Vera with you?" Fish asked. "Cory said he saw the two of you together."

"Upstairs," I said, flatly.

William kept his eyes on Fish until he left the room. "Is something wrong?" he asked, looking back at me.

"Couldn't be better," I lied.

William stirred something in a pot.

"It would appear you are not in the mood for friendly conversation," he said, adding salt to the food.

"I suppose not."

"Did you and Fish have a falling out?"

I looked at the floor, debating if I should say

something. Then I remembered, William could read my mind. I couldn't hide anything from him.

"It's Fish," I explained. "I thought he was a man of honor."

"He still is," William said, opening a cabinet.

He pulled out two cups, placing them on the counter. "Tell me," he said, pouring some tea. "What makes you think he's not a man of honor?"

"He cheated on Delia," I announced.

William smiled. "That, my boy, is a fib. In fact, it's impossible."

"Impossible?" I asked confused. "Anything is possible."

"Anything, but that."

"William, how can you say that? He betrayed his wife. I assure you."

"You can assure no such thing, Ethan."

William picked up the two cups and joined me at the table. He placed one of the cups in front of me. "You can't assure what I know to be fact," he said, taking a sip of tea.

"I have no reason to lie," I said, a little offended.

"Yes, *you* may not have a reason."

"What do you mean by that?"

William shook his head. "You're so much like your mother, Ethan. Always jumping to conclusions."

He seemed so certain of himself.

"*I am* certain of myself," he said, taking

another sip.

When he saw the perplexed look on my face, he put the cup down.

"Ethan, there's no reason why you would know this, being that you're not a witch and all. But there's something you don't know about them, something that will prove I am right."

"What is it?"

"It's called, *Witch Bonding*. When a woman gives herself to a male witch, she belongs to him forever. Her thoughts belong to him, her body becomes his prisoner, a willing prisoner, of course. For the males, when they lay with a witch, their bodies can no longer perform for another woman. So, you see, it's impossible for Fish to cheat on Delia, physically impossible. Do you understand?"

"Are you certain of this?" I asked surprised.

"You doubt me?"

I looked away. "Why would Vera lie to me like that? What purpose would that serve?"

"It would appear she wants to hide you safely in the shadows, only to bring you into the light when it's convenient for her."

I gave his words some thought.

"Did she ever approach you, Ethan? Before you started talking to the girl, I mean?"

"No," I said, realizing he was right.

William reached for his cup again. "I know this girl, Viola. She's a sweet, decent girl, and pure, if that's what you were wondering."

I don't know why, but William's words

made me happy. Viola wasn't a harlot, in fact, she was a decent woman.

"Please call me when dinner is ready," I said, leaving out the back door to the kitchen.

I soon found myself in my mother's garden, sitting on her favorite bench. I wanted to clear my head, figure out why Vera had lied to me. Maybe she didn't know about this, *Witch Bonding*? Was it possible she really believed her father had cheated? Then I remembered what she told me out by the lake.

"*She tries to play all innocent and shy, but I've seen her out in the woods, with three guys taking their turn at her.*"

"Why?" I said, trying to understand her lies.

"Vera," Delia called from the house. "Are you out there? It's time for dinner."

Moments later, the door to the guest house swung open. I saw Vera in the doorway, her arms wrapped around Steven's neck. I watched as they shared a passionate kiss. Vera gave Steven a few more pecks before running toward the house.

I made my way toward the front of the house. I didn't want Vera knowing I had seen her.

"Good evening," I said, entering the kitchen.

William was placing platters of food on the table. I tried not to look at Vera.

"How was your day?" Delia asked.

I pulled out a chair and sat next to Fish.

"Sorry I was rude earlier," I said, nudging him. "I was just tired."

"It's okay," he said, looking at my robe. "You were probably just having a heat stroke."

I laughed. My father was right, he really was funny.

"So, how was the deli?" he asked.

"They make the best grinders," Delia added.

"I had two of them," I said, reaching for some food.

"Large, or small?" Fish asked.

"I believe they were large."

"Attaboy," Fish said, patting my back.

I looked down at the food I had just served myself. I couldn't quite make out what it was.

"What is this?" I asked.

"It's called, American chop suey," Fish answered.

I looked down at the strange food. It was covered in a red sauce, with ground beef all over it. I wasn't sure what the mushy things were.

"Suzie get you all started?" Delia asked.

Not wanting to tell her the truth, I lied and said she had been very helpful.

William placed a basket of bread on the table, and took a seat. "Vera," he said, serving himself some food. "Didn't your parents tell you to stay out of the guest house?"

Fish's head shot up. "You were in the guest house?"

Vera froze, with the fork half way to her mouth. "I just went to ask if he was hungry," she said, putting it down.

"Since when does he eat here?" Delia asked.

Vera gave William such a dirty look.

"If I catch you back there again," Fish warned, "I'll throw him out for good."

Vera pushed her food away. "Why can't you stay out of my life?"

"You know," Fish said, wiping his mouth. "I think that collection of belts needs some using."

"I hate you!" Vera said, storming out of the kitchen.

William reached for some bread. "You know, Fish. Threats are meaningless when you throw them around so much."

"Are you saying I should beat her?"

"I didn't say that," William answered.

"What are we going to do with her?" Delia asked. "I blame Steven for the way she's been acting."

"She'll grow out of it," Fish said, returning to his food.

Not another word was said about Vera. We ate quietly, only speaking to compliment William on the food. This American chop suey was actually very good, but I didn't like it as much as the grinders.

After dinner, Fish and William disappeared into a nearby room. I overheard them talking about Vera as I made my way up the stairs. I didn't want to intrude, so I headed to my room.

I stopped half way up the stairs when I heard someone tapping on the front door. "Steven, you in there?" I heard someone ask.

They tapped on the door again.

"Coming," I said, descending the stairs.

I swung open the door, surprised to see three warlocks standing in front of me. All three had blond hair, with dark, penetrating eyes. They were holding large pieces of metal in their hands. Why were they carrying large pieces of metal around?

"May I help you?" I asked.

They seemed surprised to see me.

"Um, I think we got the wrong house," one of them said. "We're looking for Steven."

"He lives in the back," I said, pointing to a path on the side of the house.

"Who is it?" Fish asked.

William was right behind him.

"They're looking for Steven," I said, standing to one side.

Fish took one look at the warlocks and made a fist. "Steven isn't allowed to have visitors," Fish spat. "Not at this hour."

The warlocks exchanged glances.

"We'll come another day," one said, stepping away from the door.

They disappeared into the night.

Fish spun around. "Did you see their eyes?" he asked William.

William nodded.

"That's it," Fish said, heading into the kitchen. "I'm throwing him out."

Chapter Seventeen: Forge

I followed Fish and William to the guest house. The lights were out, but that didn't stop Fish. He kicked the door open and called for Steven. "Get out here!" he shouted.

When William flicked on the lights, we all froze. "What the hell...?" Fish said, looking around.

There were tools of all sorts, scattered throughout the house. I recognized some of these tools. We had similar ones in Magia.

There was an anvil used to hammer metal. The fullers were used to make grooves on swords. There were bricks, saw horses, chisels, and even a blacksmith forge.

"They're building weapons," I said, picking up a hammer.

"Not just weapons," William answered.

"Fortified ones. They're welding spells into them."

"Spells?" Fish gasped. "What kind of spells?"

"Like the guards?" I cut in. "How could they possibly know spells from Magia?"

I always knew the guards in Magia put spells on their weapons. They used them when they were at war with the dragons. I'd heard horrible stories about their spells, how they tore you apart from the inside out.

"Wendell," William said, making a fist.

"You think some of the guards taught him their spells?" I asked.

William looked thoughtful. "Even I know some of their spells. It wouldn't be hard for Wendell to practice them."

"I thought Wendell had no powers?" I reminded him. "Didn't you send him here as a human?"

"Wendell may not have powers," William said, looking away. "But the warlocks do."

Fish began shaking his head.

"Why did you have to send him here?" he yelled. "Of all places, why here?"

William's face became red with fury. "He would have ended up here no matter where I sent him. He was meant to die here. Can't you understand that?"

"No, I can't," Fish shot back. "We killed Simon in Magia, why not kill Wendell there as well?"

"You fool," William hissed. "*You* killed Simon, not me. I am the king. I cannot betray the Tree of Life. *It* tells me when to kill Wendell, not *you*."

William sighed. "At first, I was convinced I couldn't kill Wendell because I was king, that's why I gave the throne to James. When I realized what the Tree of Life wanted, I knew I had to send Wendell here."

"You mean to tell me that a *tree* didn't let you kill Wendell?" Fish asked.

William corrected him. "The Tree of Life has already recorded when Wendell will die. That date cannot be changed or altered. I must be patient and wait for the right time."

"But why does he have to die here?"

"Enough questions," William yelled. "We have other matters to worry about."

William stormed out, yelling for us to follow him. Once outside, William waved his hand, sending a spell toward the guest house. The ground vibrated when his spell hit a wall. It spread quickly, wrapping itself around the entire house.

"What did you do?" Fish asked.

William looked toward the house. "I'm keeping Steven and his friends out of there."

"You know what this means, right?" Fish said.

William nodded. "Steven is helping them."

"I knew he was no good," Fish said, spinning around.

Fish stomped his way back into the mansion and up the stairs. I tried to calm him as he marched his way to Vera's room. I knew she had it coming, but I didn't want to see her fighting with her father. There was no telling what Fish was about to do.

Fish kicked her door open. "Daddy's home," he said, walking in.

Vera was sitting on her bed, listening to music. She jumped up when her door flew off its hinges. Fish took three giant steps and pushed her against the wall.

"What are you doing?" she screamed.

Fish took hold of her chin and made her look at him. "I'm only going to say this once," he said, through his teeth. "If I ever, ever, catch you around Steven again, you will know pain like no one has ever felt. And, if that scumbag comes calling on you, he will find out *why* they call me Fish."

Tears streamed down Vera's face. I was sure this was the first time Fish had spoken to her like that.

"Do you understand?" Fish said, moving his face right up against hers.

"Y…yes, Father."

"Damn right," Fish answered. "And it's about time I start acting like one."

Vera burst out in tears when Fish released her. I heard her cry Steven's name as he walked out.

William and I hurried out of the room when we heard Fish kick another door. I quickly ran, trying to stop him.

"Have you gone mad?" I heard Delia yell.

Fish was grabbing her by the arm as I reached the room.

"Listen here, Delia," Fish said, pulling her toward him. "We've spoiled and coddled that girl her whole life. It ends here, today. Understand?"

"What are you talking about?" Delia asked, pulling her arm from his grip.

Delia looked a bit shocked when Fish took hold of her arm again. "Be a mother!" he shouted. "You're not her best friend, you're her parent. I'm not standing by and allowing her to get her way because you think she may get angry with us. I'd rather see her angry than lose her."

"Lose her?" Delia asked nervously.

Delia looked at William. "What does he mean? Why would we lose her? What did you show him?" Delia asked, pulling away from Fish.

William didn't answer. When he exchanged glances with Fish, I knew what Delia was talking about.

William could see into the future. He knew when and how things would happen. The only thing was, he couldn't say a word about it. He always said it would change how the future would play out. In that moment, I knew he had shown something to Fish about Vera.

"William, please," Delia cried.

"I am truly sorry," William answered.

William turned to leave. "Am I too late?" Fish asked him.

William kept his back to him, looking straight ahead. "I'm afraid, I cannot tell you," he said, then he walked out.

I tried to follow William, but he said, "Goodnight, Ethan," over his shoulder and disappeared into his room.

I wasn't sure what to do. I could hear Delia crying from where I stood. Vera was doing the same as I past her room. I thought of comforting her, but I was still upset that she had lied to me.

I decided to retreat to my mother's garden. It had become a place to clear my head. The more time I spent there, the more I understood my mother's love for it.

I sat on a bench, trying to take in the day's events. Although I had been here a very short time, I felt a mountain of problems on my shoulders. Sadly, I knew things were only going to get worse from here. What had I gotten myself into? I chuckled as I remembered how excided I was about finally coming here. It felt like years ago, not days. I questioned if I would be as happy had I known the troubles I would be facing.

I pulled out the wooden ring my mother had given me, hoping her little gift would make me feel better. I turned it in my hand, looking at the tiny waterfall that sat inside of it. Magia's trees were very detailed. I could make out the mountains and even the river. Tiny speckles floated in whatever liquid was in the ring. It was making me a little homesick.

I held it up when I noticed a tiny figure near the waterfall. "It can't be," I said, trying to make out who it was.

I was about to put it on when I heard someone behind me. It was Steven, and he was returning with the men who had been here looking for him. They were still carrying large pieces of metal.

I hid behind some bushes, trying to get a better look. I watched as Steven made his way toward the guest house, crashing into something that couldn't be seen. I knew it was William's magic, Steven would never get past it.

I wanted to laugh when Steven and his friends put their hands up, trying to understand what was blocking them. Were they trying to feel the air? I chuckled as one of the warlocks touched William's invisible wall. He flew back about twenty feet, crashing into a tree.

"What the fuck?" Steven said.

"I'm afraid you are no longer welcomed here," I heard William say.

I didn't even see him come out.

Steven spun around, a look of shock on his face. "What did I do?" he asked.

"Let us in, Old Man," one of the warlocks spat.

William waved his hand, sending the

warlock over the gate and off the property.

"Anyone else?" William asked.

Steven swallowed hard. I knew he feared William's magic.

I readied myself when I noticed one of the warlocks trying to sneak up on William. I was about to jump out when two shiny objects flew across the yard, and into the warlock's back.

"Time to peel off the dirt," I heard Fish say.

It was then I noticed the two objects were hooks, and they were attached to a wire that was coming from Fish's arms.

The warlock screamed in agony as Fish pulled back on the hooks, skinning the man alive. When the man stopped screaming, Fish flicked his arms, causing the hooks to retract back into his sleeves.

Fish slowly looked at Steven. "Ready for a face peel?" he asked.

It was comical when Steven and the remaining warlock began to run. They ran in place before their feet carried them away. William waved his hand, sending them over the gate to join their friend.

"Why didn't you kill them?" Fish asked, running to William's side. "We could have been rid of Steven once and for all."

"Thea would never forgive me," William said, looking down at the dead warlock.

"Besides," he said, kneeling. "There is still hope for him."

He touched the skinless warlock, allowing his blood to spread across his fingers.

"I will not kill him until it is necessary," William said, holding the blood to his nose.

"Hope?" Fish said in protest. "You still think he can change?"

"Perhaps," William said, rising to his feet. "Did you not notice his neck?"

Fish squinted his eyes. "His neck?"

"No scar, no promise."

"Maybe he hasn't gotten a chance yet?" Fish suggested. "How do you know he wasn't going to make that promise tonight?"

"They had a scar," William said, looking down at the dead warlock.

When Fish tried to argue, William put his hand up. "I would much rather worry about other matters, Fish."

"Like what?"

William looked down again. "It would seem Simon's men are coming back to Salem. Perhaps looking for the new arrivals, like this man."

"How do you know this guy was a new warlock?" Fish asked.

"He didn't turn to dust," William pointed out. "Someone has shown the new ones how to mix the aging potion properly. I realized that when I cleaned up Ethan's mess at Wayne's house."

"Great, now we have to clean up bodies?" Fish said.

William chuckled. "Silly witches," he said,

waving his hand.

Within seconds, the dead warlock turned to dust, leaving behind only his clothes.

"William, I'm worried about their weapons."

William sighed, "So am I, Fish. I need to think of a weapon for Ethan. Soon, he will be too weak to use his magic. He will have to rely on his fighting capabilities to defend himself."

"You want me to make him one?" Fish offered. "There's tons of tools in the guest house."

"No, his staff will have to do for now."

"Is he a good fighter?" Fish asked.

William gave him a sideways glance.

"Have you ever fought a guard before? Ethan has," he said with pride.

I stayed behind the bush until William and Fish went back into the mansion. I couldn't understand why William thought I would weaken. Why wouldn't I be able to use my magic?

I searched my thoughts for any memory he may have given me. None of them explained why I would feel weak.

I sat back on the bench, pulling out the ring again. The thought of being back in Magia made me happy. This ring, my mother's gift, was the only thing giving me happiness right now. I imagined myself near the waterfall, mounting Attor, my favorite dragon. I could picture myself flying around as I gazed into the glass ring.

I spun the ring, moving it across my fingers.

It was light as a feather, causing me to wonder what kind of wood the bottom half was made of. I slowly slipped it onto my finger, within seconds I was gone.

Chapter Eighteen: The Whip

The ground beneath me disappeared as I spun away. Speckles of light surrounded and carried me away. I was back in a vortex, the same vortex that had taken me into the human world. This vortex was different from the last. When we left for the human world, I had the sensation of falling. This time, I felt I was being lifted.

My heart came alive when I realized what this meant. I was going home.

I took a deep breath, exhaling a loud cheer as I imagined all the amazing things I would be seeing. Magia was truly a magical garden. You could hear the draping ivy on the trees whistling from a mile away. Every color you could imagine came alive on all the flowers that grew there. Precious jewels paved the trails coming down from the mountains and straight to the river. It was an enchanted vision I never grew tired of.

The fragrance of Magia's flowers brushed my face. I closed my eyes, knowing I would soon be there. The speckles of light began to fade away. My heart raced as I waited to feel the earth under my feet.

I kept my eyes closed as the sweet roar of the waterfall filled my head. Moments later, I felt Magia's air hit my face.

"Home," I whispered.

"Ethan!"

My eyes shot open, shocked to hear my mother's voice. How could she possibly know I was coming? I thought I would have to search her out when I got here.

I spun around, almost falling back when she threw her arms around me.

"Ethan," she said, squeezing me.

"Mother."

"Are you hurt?" she asked, pulling away from me.

She began checking my face, my arms, my chest. "Where is the damage?" she asked.

"Mother, I'm not hurt."

"James," she yelled.

"Did you know I was coming?" I asked.

She ignored me, lifting my arm to see if I was hurt. "Was it a spell?" she asked.

"Mother, I'm not hurt," I repeated.

There was a loud roar over our heads. I smiled when I saw my father flying down on a dragon. He dismounted, holding a bottle in is hand.

"How bad is he?" he asked.

"I can't find anything," my mother answered.

"Father," I said, trying to give him a hug.

He almost knocked my teeth out when he pushed the bottle to my lips.

"Quick, drink," he said, trying to drown me with the liquid inside the bottle.

I pushed the bottle away.

"I'm not hurt," I said for the third time.

"How weak are you?" my father asked.

I stepped away from them.

"Will you please calm down. I'm not hurt or weak. I assure you, I feel fine."

"Not hurt?" my mother asked. "But you used the ring?"

I laughed. "Are you disappointed?"

"There was no danger?" my father asked, confused.

"I can leave if you want," I offered. "Maybe, come back when I'm bleeding?"

I laughed again.

"Are you not happy to see me?" I asked, spreading my arms.

My mother sighed. "Of course, we are."

I wrapped my arms around her as I winked at my father. "Next time I come," I said, giving her a kiss on the head, "I promise I'll have a blood trail behind me."

My father gave me a pat on the back. "It's

good to see you, Son."

I offered my hand, waiting for him to shake it. His eyes were glued to my arm. I followed his eyes, realizing what he was staring at. I still had a few leaves on it. They were dried and looked more like scabs, but it was enough for him to notice.

I pulled back my arm, hoping he wouldn't tell my mother what he'd seen.

"Is everything okay, Ethan?" he asked.

"All is well," I lied.

My father looked back down at my arm.

"Thea, his arm," he said, pointing.

My mother was quick to grab my arm. She held it out, pulling back my sleeve. There was a gasp, then a suspicious look.

"I'd know Sharron's handiwork anywhere," she said, ripping the top of my robe open.

She slapped her hands to her mouth when she saw my chest. I didn't realize how many leaves were still on me.

"I'm fine," I assured her.

"Ethan, what happened?" my father asked.

I considered their eyes, realizing I couldn't tell them about the apple. If this is how they were going to react, I would keep my problems to myself.

"I was learning how to ride a bike?" I lied again. "That hill did a number me."

"You fell off a bike?"

My father wasn't buying it.

I was about to come up with another lie

when I noticed something.

"Why are the both of you wearing human clothes?" I asked.

They quickly looked at each other, seeming nervous.

"Have you been spying on me?"

My mother looked away. She didn't realize it, but she always did that when she was about to lie.

"I didn't feel like wearing a heavy dress today," she answered.

"So, you wore that old, long skirt instead?"

I looked at her shoes. "Do those boots keep you cool?"

I looked at my father, he was wearing jeans.

"Since when does the sun in Magia make you hot?"

My father dropped his shoulders.

"Just tell him, Thea."

She looked at me. "First, tell me why you used the ring?"

I explained how I was feeling homesick.

"I pulled out the ring because I wanted to see Magia. Isn't that why you left it?"

"You mean, you don't know why I left it?" she asked surprised.

"You didn't tell him?" my father gasped.

She shook her head. "I assumed he would figure it out."

"Are you going to explain things to me, or should I wait for you to come out of a closet?"

I waited, praying they would give me answers.

"I left you that ring hoping you would never need it," my mother finally answered.

"What do you mean, hoping I would never need it?"

She didn't answer.

"Does this have something to do with William?" I asked.

"What did you just call him?" my father asked. "He's your grandfather. Have some respect."

"He demanded I call him that," I explained. "He also asked me to call my uncle and aunt, Fish and Delia."

"Wait," my mother said, stepping forward. "Why did you ask if my father had something to do with the ring? Does he know you have it?"

"No, I felt perhaps you didn't want him to know."

"You can never show him this ring," she said firmly. "I went through a lot of trouble so he wouldn't sense it."

"Is that why it's made of wood?" I asked.

She grabbed my arm, pulling back my sleeve again. "You see this," she said, running her fingers along the leaves. "You're lucky to show up here with just these leaves on your arm. I expected worse."

Still holding my arm, she looked at my father. "Give me that bottle."

My father placed it in her hand. She held it up. "Drink," she ordered.

I tried to reach for the cup. "No," she said, tightening her grip. "Use your other hand."

I took the bottle and drank the liquid inside of it. She pointed to my arm. "Watch this."

I was amazed when the leaves began falling to the ground. New skin grew back in the places where the leaves had just been. I began to feel stronger, realizing just how tired I really was.

"This is why I left you that ring," my mother said, releasing my arm. "If I know my father, you'll be needing it."

"I don't understand?"

"Ethan," my father said, putting his hand on my shoulder. "You've never been hurt before, not in Magia. You've never needed the healing powers of the River of Life. In the human world, you will grow weak as time goes by. Here, you've always had the river to keep you strong. It was in the food you ate, the water you drank. It's how wizards stay strong, stay alive."

"Even your grandfather must come here to drink it," my mother explained. "Without this water, his powers would fade away, leaving him weak and vulnerable."

I always knew about the Secret River of Life. All wizards knew its powers. It was the reason wizards had magic, the reason why we flew, why dragons could speak. It gave life to everything in Magia, including the fairies. I just didn't realize I would grow weak without it.

I remembered my mother was born in the human world. She never needed the river to survive, or to use her powers.

"Why did this not happen to you?" I asked.

"Isn't it obvious? I wasn't born here," she explained. "The river couldn't take what it never gave me. I was born with powers, the daughter of a witch and a wizard. I didn't need the river until I lost my powers to Simon. When the river gave them back to me, I had to drink from it to stay strong."

I looked at my father. "Do you need the river to stay strong?"

"Now, I do."

"Now?"

"I almost died here," he explained. "The river gives life, and so it gave it to me. I was reborn, adopted by Magia. Although I wasn't born a wizard, the river claimed me as its own. It gave me powers to survive, powers to adapt to this world. If I were to leave, I would soon lose those powers. I would return to my human form, leaving my witch half intact."

"But you," my mother said, caressing my face. "You're like your grandfather. You belong to Magia. You were conceived in the human world but born in this magical land. You're not meant for the human world. You belong here."

"Then, why allow me to leave?" I asked.

She sighed, looking uncomfortable.

"It's your destiny," she answered. "As much as we hate it, certain things must happen."

I was starting to piece together the puzzle. I wasn't going to tell her, but I had already put it all together.

"May I ask you something, Mother?"

She nodded.

"Why don't you want William knowing about the ring?"

She began to grind her teeth. "Because that stubborn man likes to do things the hard way."

"I don't understand."

I could see she was struggling to find the words.

"When we still lived in Salem," she began, "your grandfather allowed certain things to happen, things that caused me pain and suffering. He explained that sometimes we need to suffer to find ourselves. I was headstrong and stubborn, suffering was necessary, so I could change, but you're not like me," she said, brushing my cheek with the back of her hand. "You're different. You're a good boy. You found yourself many years ago. My father doesn't realize there's no need for you to suffer. He doesn't see what I see. If he knew about the ring, he would take it away from you, thinking he was helping."

"That's why it's made of wood," my father added. "William can't sense it."

"I came here often," my mother said, "when I was fighting my battle with Simon. It was a ring like this one that helped me through it. I just wanted to give you the same fighting chance."

"You're expecting me to get hurt. Aren't you, Mother?"

She bowed her head, tears flowing down her cheek. "I'm expecting you to fight back," she whispered.

My father gathered her in his arms. "We'll always be here, Ethan. Always waiting, always ready. Use that ring whenever you need it. There is no shame in asking for help."

My mother pulled away from him, reaching for my hand. "Please, tell me what's been going on in Salem. Don't miss a single detail."

I decided to be honest with them. I couldn't take the tortured look on their faces. I gave details about the troubles I had my first day in Salem and everything after that. My mother cringed when I told them about the poison apple, and how it skinned me alive. She was not surprised to hear about Steven.

"I knew he would go to the dark side," she said in a sad voice.

I wasn't sure why, but I told them about Viola. My mother seemed suspicious of her.

"Do you know why she sits there all day?" she asked. "Why there? Why the bakery?"

I told her I wasn't sure, but she seemed harmless. When I told them, William wanted me to have a weapon, my father had a confused look on his face.

"But, you already have one," he pointed out.

"I do?"

"Yes, I left it for you, the day we paid you a visit."

I pulled out the small knife he had placed on my chest, unsure why he thought this was a weapon.

"You want me to fight with this?" I asked, holding it up.

I was shocked when my father took the knife, gave it a shake, and exposed what it really was. The knife had been a handle this whole time, with a gold whip coming out of it.

"This is not an ordinary whip," he said.

He looked around, spotting a large bolder nearby. He cracked the whip, snapped it toward the bolder, exploding it into thousands of pieces. He pointed to a tree, cracked the whip again, and cut the tree in half as if it were made of paper.

When he shook the whip again, it disappeared back into the handle. My mother held out her hand.

"Where is the wand I gave you?"

I pulled it out, placing it in her hand.

"I didn't give you this to just fly around," she said, with a big smile.

Before she could show me its secrets, we heard footsteps behind us.

"When will you learn, Thea. You can hide nothing from me."

"Father," my mother gasped.

Chapter Nineteen: Broken Leg

My father bowed his head as William approached. My mother had her shoulders back, ready to fire back at him. She knew he was about to give her hell for this.

"Did you really think I wouldn't sense the ring?" William asked. "I knew about that ring the moment it left your fingers."

My mother pointed out her chin. "I don't care if you're upset, Father. He's my son, and I want to help him."

"We both do," my father confessed.

"Good," William said, crossing his arms behind his back. "Then you have done exactly what I needed you to do."

My mother was about to argue but stopped when she realized what he'd said.

"What do you mean, we did what you

needed us to do?"

William shook his head. "Thea, my plans always revolve around knowing how your mind works. I knew you would help him. He's your son, I expected nothing less. I knew I couldn't give him a ring. It had to come from you, of your own free will, just as I gave you mine."

My mother's face became flushed, her mouth agape.

"And, may I add," William continued. "I never *allowed* you to suffer. I would have taken your place in an instant if I was able. Doing things, the hard way, as you put it, is my way of making sure things don't change. You really think I wouldn't have saved you if I thought for one moment I knew you could die?"

My mother bowed her head in shame, knowing he had heard every word she said.

William continued. "If I knew that something bad was going to happen, like being certain you were going to break a leg, do you think I should stop it?"

She didn't answer.

"What if," he said, pacing, "I kept you from flying that day, thinking it would stop the future. Do you think your leg would be safe now?"

Again, she said nothing.

"What if I told you, I knew exactly how that leg was going to break. Let's say I changed it, stopped it from breaking; it would still break, but now, I would have no idea how. You see, Thea, I knew how those horrible things would happen to you, but I also knew you would come out alive. If I had changed things, protected you, I would have never known if you would survive. And that, my child, I could never live with."

William glanced at me. "Ethan's future is written," he said, looking back at my mother. "Nothing you do is going to change it."

"I can't let him suffer," my mother cried.

"That is why you must stay here," he answered. "It was agreed."

"May I say something?" I asked, stepping forward.

William gave me the floor.

I took a deep breath, hoping I could find the words to tell them how I felt.

"When I left Magia," I began, "I asked no questions. Yes, I questioned why suddenly, I could leave this land. Again, I asked no questions. I arrived in Salem only to have William give me orders. He ordered me to call him William, for one. Again, there were no questions. I was told where to work, where to sleep, even told how I should dress. All the while, I asked no questions. I have stayed silent as others around me seem to know what's going on. It's no secret to me, I figured it out. People talk in whispers, keep secrets, thinking I don't understand. I've killed men, knowing it wouldn't be the last time. The only thing I don't understand is why my parents wouldn't believe in me enough to know I can handle it?"

William nodded, a smile spread across his face. He looked at my mother.

"You know the outcome, Thea. Don't try to change it. Allow his leg to be broken."

"I'm sorry, Father," she whispered.

Brows furrowed, William took notice what my parents were wearing.

"Were you about to leave for Salem?" he asked.

My father was quick to change the subject.

"Thea was about to show Ethan what she did with her wand."

Not another word was said. I spent the rest of the day with my parents. My mother showed me a few tricks I could do with her wand. I was surprised it could change into a sword. William left to speak with the other wizards, but he didn't stay away for long.

"It's time to go, Ethan," he called.

I said my goodbyes to my parents and stood next to William. My mother ran and gave me one last hug.

"I love you, my son."

I had to stop myself from asking her about the blood promise. Who had she made the promise to and why?

"We'll have to pull off the rings together," William instructed.

I nodded and looked at my mother again. Whatever her reasons, I knew she had done it for me.

"Goodbye," I said, pulling off my ring.

We were gone in seconds.

As we travelled through the vortex, William placed his arm on my shoulder.

"Thank you, Ethan."

"Why are you thanking me?"

"Thank you for not telling your mother what I've asked you to do."

I laughed. "Well, now I understand why."

We shared a laugh.

"Yes, your mother can be quite impulsive."

"Impetuous, is more like it."

"You have no idea," he said, shaking his head.

When the speckles of light disappeared, I felt the earth under my feet. It was dark, but I could still see the lights on in the mansion. That meant everyone was still awake.

"How long have we been gone?" I asked.

"Only moments," William answered. "You will find that detail very important one day."

We made our way back to the mansion. Delia was drinking from a cup when we walked in.

"Where have the two of you been?" she asked.

"Ah, coffee," William said, reaching for a pot.

Delia started laughing. "It was Thea, wasn't it?"

"You have to ask?" William said, taking a

seat next to her.

"Oh, Ethan," Delia said, taking a sip of coffee. "Sean came looking for you. He brought you a grinder. It's on the stove."

Her words were music to my ears. I could only hope it was as delightful as the others.

"You gonna share that thing?" Fish asked, walking into the kitchen.

Delia rolled her eyes. "He's been smelling that thing since Sean dropped it off."

I laughed, reaching for the grinder. I unwrapped it and cut it in half, making sure my half was bigger.

"How are the both of you still hungry?" William asked Fish.

"These are Sean's grinders we're talking about," Fish answered.

"Do we have soda?" I asked.

"In the fridge," Fish said, taking a seat. "Get me one, too."

I gave Fish his half of the grinder and opened the refrigerator. There were so many flavors to choose from.

"What's in the orange cans?" I asked.

"Orange soda," Fish answered with a mouth full of food.

I grabbed two cans, but dropped them when I heard Delia scream.

"Someone help him!" she shouted.

Fish was foaming at the mouth. His face was quickly turning different shades of purple and blue.

He began shaking, grabbing at his neck.

"Open the door, quickly," William ordered.

William was already pouring liquid down Fish's throat. I helped him tear away his clothes as we dragged him outside.

"Fish!" Delia kept screaming.

I mounted my staff, knowing what I had to do. William quickly threw Fish over it.

"Hurry," he said in a panic.

I took to the sky, rage coursing through my veins. I knew that grinder was meant for me. It was an act of a coward. Why couldn't they face me? If they wanted a battle, I was prepared to give it to them.

"Please, help me," Fish said, gasping for air.

The liquid William had given him wasn't working. There was nothing oozing from his pores, no vomit in sight. I wasn't sure what to do.

I slowed down when Fish's neck began to split open. He gaged on his own blood as the poison tore him apart. His ears began bleeding, then his mouth. He was dying, the poison was too strong. When Fish's eyes began popping out of their sockets, I panicked.

I grabbed his arm and slipped on my ring, we were instantly pulled into the vortex.

I tried waving my hand at him as we travelled to Magia. I was hoping my magic would help. I thought of every healing spell I knew, nothing was working.

"Please, don't die," I said, trying to stop the

bleeding.

I did everything I could, but he was only getting worse. Fish was no longer fighting for his life, only convulsing from the pain. He was in shock. His face shook as foam slid down his chin. I put my hand over his heart. I could hardly feel a heartbeat. He exhaled one last breath, then went completely limp.

"No!" I shouted.

I felt a sharp ache shoot right through my heart. I felt crushed, heartbroken.

I hovered over the ground in Magia, holding my dead uncle. We arrived too late. There was nothing to be done. He was dead.

"It should have been me," I said, bowing my head.

"You came back," I heard my father say. "Did you forget something?"

I looked over my shoulder, he was coming out from the trees. His smile disappeared when he noticed the tears streaming down my face. His eyes moved down to see who was with me.

He gasped. "Fish!"

He broke into a run, a panicked look on his face. Shock shined across his face when he saw the condition Fish was in.

"He's dead, Father."

"The hell he is," he said, jumping on my staff. "Fly to the river, hurry."

I took to the sky, flying as fast as I could.

"Just fly right into it," my father instructed.

"Almost there," I said, over my shoulder.

I knew Fish was dead, but I didn't want to steal my father's hopes. If flying Fish into the Secret River of Life was going to help my father through this, I was more than willing to do it.

"Fish, dammit," my father said, shaking him. "Open your eyes. Don't you die on me."

He was gone. No amount of water from the river was going to bring him back. Perhaps if we had reached the river earlier, but now, there was no saving him.

"Fish," my father cried.

When we reached the river, I pointed the staff down and flew right into it. I knew there was no point, but I had to do it for my father.

The moment we were under the water, my father shook Fish, hoping the river would revive him. Fish's dead body only moved with the flow of the river. My father shook him again, desperately trying to save him. After a few moments, he finally gave up. He slowly pulled Fish toward him, wrapping his arms around his dead friend. I could hear his sobs under the water. It was one of the saddest moments I had ever lived through.

I reached out and tapped my father on the shoulder, motioning towards the shore.

My father held Fish tight as we made our way out. I helped him drag Fish, leaving him on the river's edge. My father collapsed to his knees, breaking down in loud, choking sobs.

"Fish," he cried, over his dead friend.

My heart ached as my father dragged Fish's dead body closer to him, sobbing like I'd never heard him before.

"I love you, kid," he said, as he choked on his sobs of pain.

"I'm sorry, Father."

I stepped back and gave him a moment. I knew they had been great friends. Fish was like a brother to him. I understood my father's pain. For many years, my father had done nothing but speak of Fish in the highest regard. He talked about the many funny moments they spent together. He spoke of him with love, with great respect. Fish had been the one person my father missed the most when he left Salem.

I thought of the pain I was about to impose on Delia. How could I tell her Fish was dead? What words could I possibly say to her? This would crush her, devastate her life. My mother always said that Delia was nothing without her Fish. He had changed her for the better, loved her despite Delia pushing him away so much.

I looked down at my father, thinking perhaps he should be the one to tell her. I knew he would never want Delia to see Fish like this. We would have to clean him up first, make him look as normal as possible.

"We have to get him out of here," my father said through tears. "Before your mother sees him like this."

"I think it's best," I agreed.

My father placed Fish on the ground and prepared to get up. Suddenly, he kicked Fish away.

"What the hell?"

He jumped to his feet, kicking Fish over. I gasped, realizing there was a strange man lying on the ground. The man was much larger than Fish with black hair and a beard.

"A spell," my father gasped.

His face began to light up. "That's not Fish. That's not Fish," he cheered. "The river broke the spell. It wasn't Fish."

Suddenly, he froze. "It wasn't Fish," he repeated. "That means?"

He looked at my hand. "Quick, pull off the ring. I don't care if William gets mad."

He grabbed my arm as I pulled off the ring, instantly pulling us both into the vortex.

Chapter Twenty: Just Like Old Times

My father asked for his whip as we traveled back to Salem. There was a fierce look on his face, one I'd never seen before.

"Can't we get there faster?" he said, anxiously.

His whip was at the ready. If someone had Fish, I knew they would die tonight.

"Where should I command the ring to take us?" I asked.

"You can't command the ring," he answered, glaring into space. "It takes you back to where you last used it."

Everyone was outside when we arrived. Cory and Sean were pacing the yard. Delia was in tears, enveloped in William's arms. I quickly noticed William was surprised to see my father.

"James?" he said, pulling Delia away.

Delia spun around, her eyes swollen from where she'd been crying.

"W...where is Fish?" she asked nervously.

My father ignored her, storming his way to William. "Where is he, William? It's not like before when you were weak. This time, I know you have the power to find him."

William looked at me. "I thought he was with you?"

"That wasn't him," my father growled. "That man is dead. The river broke the spell and revealed a dead warlock."

I'd never seen such a surprised look on William's face before. He truly didn't know that man hadn't been Fish.

"Where is he?" my father shouted.

"What the hell is going on?" Cory asked.

My father kept his eyes on William. "They have him, Cory. They have Fish."

"No," Delia cried.

It took William several moments to get over the shock. When he finally snapped out of it, he began giving instructions.

"You," he said, pointing to Sean, "Go cut down some branches. We're going to need them."

Delia was next. "Go get something of his person."

"What?" Delia asked.

"Something that he wears, something that belongs to him, quickly."

Delia ran into the house. William locked eyes with my father. "This is going to take a lot out of me, James. I won't be able to help you."

My father smiled. "Don't worry, we won't be needing your help."

Sean was back with the branches.

"What do we need these for?" he asked.

"Hurry, place them between your legs."

Cory quickly snatched one of them up. Sean seemed confused about the branch. My father was already waiting, branch at the ready.

William waved his hand, causing the branches to hover. Sean grabbed on tightly.

"I don't know how to fly," he pointed out.

"You'll catch on," my father said through his teeth.

We all looked towards the house, waiting for Delia to come back. She finally appeared, holding one of Fish's shirts.

"Here," she said, giving it to William.

He took the shirt, closed his eyes, and began to hum. I could literally see sound waves coming from his body. For every hum that came out of his mouth, the sound waves would move farther and farther away. His hums began to get louder. I knew the sound waves were searching for Fish.

"Hummmm," William hummed again as he spread his arms.

I mounted my staff, eager to look for Fish.

"Come on," my father said, impatiently.

Suddenly, the sound waves came shooting

back at him. William's eyes shot open, the humming stopped. He dropped to his knees, sounding out of breath.

"Quickly, he's at the Burying Point Cemetery. They're burying him alive."

In an instant, my father was gone. I pushed off and followed behind him. I was having a hard time keeping up.

As we neared the cemetery, I saw no less than twenty warlocks, throwing dirt over a fresh grave. Some were sitting near a small wall, laughing and talking to each other.

"Ethan," my father yelled. "You get Fish out of there. Make sure he's alive."

I nodded, pointing my staff in that direction. I hovered just over the warlocks, waving my hand at the grave. The warlocks jumped back when my magic hit the ground. There was an explosion of dirt and wood, exposing Fish lying in a coffin. The warlocks were sent crashing into the wall.

My father jumped off the branch, shaking his knife and exposing the whip.

"I'm not going to lie, gentlemen, but this is going to hurt," he said to them.

You could hear weapons being drawn as the warlocks jumped to their feet. My father moved closer as they made a circle around him.

"Save some for us, James," Cory said, tossing the branch aside.

He flicked his arms, exposing two blades from each of his sleeve. Sean was already in a stance, his razor swords gripped tightly in his hands.

There was a moment of silence.

Then…chaos. Two warlocks came at my father. He cracked the whip at their feet, causing them to stumble to the ground. My father cracked the whip again, cutting the men in two.

I jumped off my staff as Cory sent a head flying right by me. The sound of weapons clanging together filled the air. Sean was holding his own, slicing and cutting body parts away.

I joined the melee, waving my hand at some headstones. They were ripped from the ground and floated in the air, awaiting my command. I clapped my hands together, causing the stones to crash into each other, flattening one man's head between them.

"Ethan, behind you!" my father shouted.

When I spun around, there was a man behind me, standing perfectly still. At first, I was confused. Then he began to moan. His moans soon turned into screams of agony. I began to hear something tearing, almost like cloth. When the man's skin began to peel away, I knew it was Fish.

The skinless man collapsed at my feet. Fish was standing behind him, gasping for air.

"Sup," Fish said, trying to catch his breath.

An arrow flew just over Fish's head and right through a warlock's heart.

"Hey Ginger," Fish said, falling to the ground. "It's like old times now."

After the last head rolled to a stop, there was silence. Weapons were scattered all over the ground. Some of the weapons were cut in half where my father's whip had touched them.

"Fish," my father said, running to him.

Fish was still trying to catch his breath.

"Hey, James. Did they invite you, too?"

My father laughed. "I invited myself, buddy."

"They let anyone into this place," Fish answered.

My father was half laughing and half crying. His eyes filled with tears as he wrapped his arms around Fish.

"It's good to see you, Fish."

"I think I'm a little happier to see you, James."

My father laughed again and helped Fish to his feet. Cory rushed over, asking Fish if he was okay. Joshua and Sean were right behind him.

"I'm fine," Fish answered. "I just have dirty thoughts going through my head. Get it, dirty thoughts? I was buried alive, the dirt?"

Only my father laughed.

"Geez, Fish," Joshua wined. "You're cracking jokes, now?"

"Ginger, when did you get back?" Fish asked.

Joshua was another one of my mother's dear friends. He was as tall as Sean with red hair and very light skin. My mother always said that Cory,

Fish, and Joshua were like brothers, living together for most of their lives.

"Just now," Joshua answered. "William told me where you were."

"What are we going to do about that?" Sean asked, pointing towards the dead warlocks.

We all looked, there was blood and body parts everywhere. Just as Sean said that, puffs of dust began drifting into the air. The sound was everywhere. Puff, puff, puff was all you could hear as the warlocks turned to dust.

We all looked up. William was hovering over us. "Can you *please* hurry? I can't hold this shield forever," he yelled down.

Although no one was around this time of night, William made sure we wouldn't be seen. His shield covered over two blocks.

"Always thinking, William," my father yelled up.

With Fish sitting behind my father, we took to the sky. We explained to Fish about the imposter. He couldn't believe the man had dared to enter his house.

"Did he fool Delia?" Fish asked.

My father squinted his eyes. "Why does that matter? He fooled all of us."

"Yes, but did he fool my wife?" he asked again.

"Well, yes," my father answered.

"Delia has some explaining to do," Fish hissed.

I couldn't understand why Fish would blame her. How could she possibly know that would happen?

When we landed near the back door to the kitchen, Fish jumped off and headed inside.

"Lucy, you have some *splainin* to do," he said, walking in.

I heard Delia scream his name the moment he was inside. We followed him in, packing ourselves into the kitchen.

Delia was about to throw her arms around her husband. "No," Fish said, pushing her back by the forehead. "You're not touching me."

"What?" Delia said, stepping back.

"How could you *not* know that wasn't me?" Fish asked. "What if he stayed the night? What if, he wanted to play fireman with you?"

I suppressed a giggle. My father's shoulders were already bouncing up and down from a quiet laugh.

"I know how much you like that game," Fish continued. "Were you going to ask him to pull out his hose?"

"Fish," Delia said, eyeing us. "You're embarrassing me."

That was it, I couldn't hold it in any longer. The room engulfed in laughter. My father couldn't catch his breath. Everyone laughed, everyone but Delia and William, that is.

Cory thanked Sean for his help.

"Hey, can I keep the branch?" Sean asked.

William snatched it from him. "No," he said, returning his attention to Delia and Fish.

Sean quietly left out the back door.

"How could you not recognize that it wasn't me, Dells?" Fish was saying.

"Are we quite finished?" William asked.

"You idiot," Delia said, wrapping her arms around Fish. "I would have known the moment he kissed me."

I couldn't help but notice how worried William looked. He didn't crack a smile once. I think my father noticed.

"William, are you alright?" he asked.

William hung his head, something that was very unusual for him to do. "I'm troubled, James. Very, very troubled."

"I'm fine," Fish assured him. "Nothing a good bath can't handle."

"Please," William said, in a perturbed tone. "Sit down, I need to speak with all of you."

"I'll make some tea," Delia said, heading to the stove.

We all sat at the table, eyeing William the whole time.

I was shocked when he said, "I'm going back to Magia, and I *will not* be returning."

"What?" my father gasped. "You can't. Ethan needs you. You promised you would watch over him."

William sighed. "Just as I asked you to watch over my kingdom, I ask you now to stay with your son."

"William, I don't understand," My father said. "What brought this on?"

William was clearly uneasy, I just couldn't understand why. I noticed his hands shaking. It was subtle, but I noticed.

"You can't just tell me you're leaving and not say why," my father said. "Thea will ask questions."

"I will speak with Thea when I return to Magia," William answered.

"You'll have to speak with me now, Father."

Chapter Twenty-One: Good Bye

I looked over my shoulder, my mother was standing at the back door. There was an angry look on her face. She was giving my father the evil eye.

"Don't leave dead bodies behind if you don't want me to follow you," she said, making her way in.

She tossed a piece of paper on the table.

"I found this in his pocket. It's a layout of the mansion. Every nook and cranny is described in it. Someone who knows this house has betrayed us."

Frustrated, William pounded his fist on the table. "Why didn't I see that?"

"Okay, that's it, Father," my mother said, taking a seat next to him "You're going to explain what the hell is going on. I want to know everything. So, spit it out."

We spent the next hour bringing my mother up to speed. "I don't understand," she said, shaking her head. "Why would the imposter eat the grinder? I mean, if he knew it was poisoned, why would he willingly eat it?"

"I don't think he knew," my father answered. "They seem to be very disorganized. I don't even think they tell each other their plans. It's as if someone is giving them individual orders. I see no communication between them."

"You think it's someone who is new at this?" Cory suggested.

"I believe so," William answered.

"That can't be why you're going back to Magia," my father said. "There has to be another reason."

William's hands were shaking more and more. He had to put one on top of the other when it wouldn't stop.

He took a deep breath. "I think I've been poisoned," he confessed.

"Father," my mother gasped. "Are you alright? Let me heal you."

He motioned for her to stay seated.

"Someone has been poisoning me, slowly," he continued. "I haven't been feeling well. I just assumed it was my old age finally getting the best of me. When James said it had been an imposter tonight, I knew something was wrong with me. I sat next to the man, we even spoke a few words."

"Now it makes sense," my father said. "You would have normally caught that."

"Now you see my problem," William answered.

"I still don't understand, Father. Why go back to Magia?"

"The poison is slowly affecting my nervous system. I will have to stay in Magia until I heal."

"Will you be able to come back once you heal?" my father asked.

William shook his head. "Don't you understand, James? Someone is trying to get rid of me. They know I'm here. I pose a lot of problems for them. That's why they've been finding ways to kill me. With me out of the way, they can get to Ethan."

My mother didn't look surprised.

"You can't leave him alone, not now. You promised me, Father."

"They've been trying to poison me, too," I reminded them. "You don't see me leaving."

"Foolish boy," William answered. "The Black Witch wants you alive. She's been sending her men to poison a wizard. She told them to look for a man with unusual powers. They've been searching for said wizard for months. That's why I didn't want anyone to know who you were. I wanted them to come after me, but your little fight at the lake with Netiri confused them. One of them saw you using your magic, the one that got away, remember?"

Frustrated, I closed my eyes. "The one I sent flying into the water."

"Yes, the very one."

"So, the warlocks assumed Ethan was the wizard the Black Witch wanted dead?" Cory asked.

William nodded.

"Wait, that means they know Netiri is helping us," Cory pointed out.

"Shockingly, the man never got a good look at Netiri. His eyes were glued to Ethan," William said, looking back at me.

I leaned back in my chair, feeling like a fool.

"I'm sorry, William," I said, hanging my head in shame.

"Father, but now they'll keep coming after Ethan. They won't stop until he's dead."

"Not if the Black Witch has a body," he answered. "And, since I must leave to heal myself, why not give her mine?"

"I don't understand," my mother asked confused.

"I need the poisoning to stop," William answered. "We all saw what it did to the imposter. If she believes I'm dead and out of the way, she'll order the poisoning to stop. She can't take a chance on hurting Ethan."

My mother glanced at me, not really seeming surprised when he said that.

"What's the plan?" Cory asked. "How will we make the Black Witch think you're dead?"

"We need a body," William answered.

"There's one outside," my mother said, pointing toward her garden. "I brought him with me, but he's in pretty bad shape."

"Perfect," William murmured.

"Does she even know what you look like?" Fish asked.

"If she's been watching, she'll know who I am. It's the warlocks who didn't know, not her."

"When are you leaving?" my father asked.

"Straight away. I'll leave you instructions before Thea and I depart."

"No, I'm staying here, Father. I need to watch over my son."

William held up his hand. "James can watch over him just fine. You're leaving with me."

"The hell I…"

William reached over, tapping her on the head. She instantly closed her eyes, resting her head on the kitchen table. She was out.

"May I speak to you in your study, James?" William said, pushing his chair back.

My father got to his feet. "Wait here," he said to us.

When they left, Delia got up to make more coffee and tea. "It's going to be a long night," she said, putting a pot of water on the stove.

Cory ran his fingers through his hair. He sat back, looking up at the ceiling. Fish was staring at Delia while she made the tea.

"Vera in bed?" he asked her.

"Hours ago," Delia answered.

Fish looked at Joshua, who was almost sleeping.

"What about you, Ginger? Where's the wife?"

Joshua looked up with one eye half closed.

"I sent her to her mother's. You think I want her here?"

Fish looked at Delia again.

"Don't even think of it," she said, with one hand up. "I'm staying with you."

Their words only made me feel guilty. It was obvious Joshua didn't want his wife in danger, even Fish was thinking the same.

I couldn't get William's words out of my head. "*She can't take a chance on hurting Ethan.*"

Why this Black Witch wanted me alive was a mystery to me. Who was she? And, why did she want me, of all people? How did she even know about me? I had never been here before, how was it possible that I was the reason she was willing to kill William?

I sorted through my thoughts, trying to find something that would explain things. I recalled a memory my mother had shown me. The Black Witch was there when Simon tried cutting me out of my mother's womb. Even then, the Black Witch wanted me, but why?

"Fish, what are you doing?" I heard Delia ask.

I was pulled from my thoughts only to find

Fish poking my mother with a straw.

"Creepella is snoring," he laughed.

I reached over and pulled the straw from his hand. "Leave her," I said, tossing the straw over my shoulder.

Delia slammed a cup of tea on the table, almost burning Fish in the process.

"How can you joke at a time like this? You almost died tonight," she said, breaking into a sob.

Fish quickly gathered her in his arms.

"It's okay, baby."

"I can't do this again, Fish. I just can't," she said, burying her face in his chest.

Joshua pushed his chair back with force. He punched a wall before walking out of the kitchen.

Cory sat, his arms crossed in front of him, staring at me. How I wished I had the ability to read minds like William. I'd give anything to know what Cory was thinking.

"Going to the party?" Cory asked out of the blue.

"Party?" I asked confused.

"Yeah, the party to kick off the season. They even have a parade."

How could he think of a party at a time like this? I looked at Delia, who was still crying in Fish's arms.

"I don't think so," I answered.

"Why not?" Cory asked.

I wasn't sure if I liked his tone. It was a little aggressive.

"Everyone likes a party," he continued. "They'll be lots of people there."

"I'm not really in the mood for parties."

"You mean, you can't think of a single reason you should attend this party?"

"What are you doing?" Fish asked him.

Cory ignored him. "You can get all dressed up, do a little dancing."

"I don't dance," I said firmly.

"I can teach you," he shot back.

"I never said I didn't know how to dance."

"Then you should go."

"Cory, leave him alone," Fish said, pulling away from Delia.

"Stay out of it, Fish," Cory hissed.

"He doesn't want to go," Fish answered.

Cory kicked his chair back and got in Fish's face. "Ethan can answer for himself. I need you to stay out of it."

"What's up with you?" Fish asked.

"Don't you understand?" Cory yelled. "William is going back to Magia and leaving us with him," he said, pointing to me. "He needs to learn how to think like William, be as smart as him. We can't afford for him to miss anything."

Cory looked at me, leaned over the table, and got inches from my face. "Can you think of any reason why you shouldn't go to that party?"

He asked the question slowly, hugging every word. "Can you?" he shouted.

Fish tried to pull him away, but Cory

slapped his hand away.

"He has to think for himself, Fish. We can't hand him all the answers."

"Maybe he doesn't have the answers," Fish shot back.

"He has to!" Cory shouted. "Our lives depend on it."

The moment Cory said that, I understood.

"I'm the bait," I said, realizing what he was thinking. "I'm the one she's looking for."

Cory leaned over again. "Yes. Can you think of a better way to find her?"

I looked him in the eye. "I'm going to that party."

Cory smiled. "And, we'll be waiting, I swear it."

Just then, my father and William walked back in. "Was someone shouting?" my father asked.

"We were laughing at Thea," Cory lied. "She's snoring."

"I see, a joke at my wife's expense."

Cory and I eyed each other. I gave him a nod, assuring him I wouldn't say a word. We could speak later, away from the over protection of my father.

"Now for the body," William said, making his way towards the garden.

Once outside, we all looked at the mangled body, wondering how this was going to work.

"William," my father said, shaking his head.

"This man was poisoned. What would make them think it was you?"

"And, who was that poison meant for?" William asked.

I instantly knew his plan. William really was a genius. "I'll go get the grinder," I said, heading back inside.

When I got back, William had already turned the dead warlock into a perfect carbon copy of himself.

"Place the imposter not too far from the mansion," William instructed. "Make sure the sandwich is under him. We don't want a human trying to eat it."

"You really think this will work?" my father asked.

William nodded. "Even if they check him, they'll find the poisoned food in is stomach, believing I ate it."

"That makes perfect sense," Cory said in awe of him.

Cory took the grinder from me. "Come on, Fish, let's get him out there."

"I'll help you," Delia said, leaning over.

"Wait," William said, stopping them. "There's one more thing. Under no circumstances are you to tell anyone that I am alive, not even your family. Only those who are here must know the truth."

"What about Vera?" Delia said. "She'll be brokenhearted."

"Would you rather she be dead?" William shot back.

"What about Sharron?" Cory asked.

William looked around. "Is she here?"

"Well, no."

"There's your answer."

There was silence.

"What are we supposed to do, about a funeral, I mean?" Delia asked.

"William already instructed me to build a fire," my father informed them. "We'll recreate the same kind of fire we burned Samuel in. They'll be searching for that."

My father looked at us all. "We'll have to act as if William is *actually* dead. They'll be looking for any signs of deception."

Once everyone agreed, Cory and Fish dragged the imposter away. We followed William back into the kitchen. I heard my mother's snores before I even walked in.

My father sat her up, kissing her gently on the mouth. "I'll miss you, my love."

He gave her a kiss on the head, and leaned her against William. "Good luck keeping her away from here," my father said.

"I'll worry about that when the time comes," he answered.

He looked at me. "Don't forget what I've asked of you, Ethan."

"You have my word, William."

He reached for my mother's hand, taking

hold of her ring. When he pulled both rings off, they were gone.

Chapter Twenty-two: Denim

Loud screams awoke me from a sound sleep. It was Vera, and she was in hysterics. I felt as if I hardly slept a wink. I looked towards the window, it was still dark. Red flashes of light, coming from outside, confused me.

I hopped out of bed and headed for the window. There were red trucks and police everywhere. "The body," I said, remembering what we'd done.

I quickly changed into my robe, slipped on my shoes, and headed for the door. When I heard voices coming from downstairs, I headed in that direction. I saw my father talking to some officers as I made my way down.

"I don't know why someone would do that," my father was saying. "I assure you, everyone in this house is accounted for."

The officer lowered the volume on his radio as he wrote down everything my father was saying.

"And, you're sure you didn't see a body near your property?" the officer asked.

"I've been in bed for hours," my father answered. "I didn't see anything."

The officer looked at my father with suspicious eyes. "The neighbors said it looked like someone who lives here. Are you sure no one is missing?"

"I've doubled checked, officer."

The officer looked towards the stairs. "Why do I hear someone crying?" he asked.

"I'm afraid my daughter has been grounded, officer. Broke curfew, you know how those things go."

"Yeah, I got one of those," the officer answered. "Well, sorry to bother you. Must have been a prank call."

"Have a good evening," my father said, closing the door behind him.

"Did they find the body?" I asked.

"No, thank goodness," my father answered.

"I thought we wanted them to find it?"

"Not them, Ethan. That would cause too many problems. Lucky for us, the warlocks found him before the police did. They took the body before the police arrived. The neighbors must have seen the body and called the police."

"So, why is Vera crying?"

He sighed. "She tried sneaking out of the house. Fish caught her. I believe what you heard was a temper tantrum."

I followed my father into the kitchen.

"I'm having some coffee, you want some?" he asked, reaching for a pot.

"No thank you, Father."

"Ethan, what did William tell you? Just to be safe, don't call me Father."

That was going to be hard. I didn't know if his name could escape my lips. "James," I said, awkwardly. Well, that wasn't so bad. "You really think the warlocks took the body?"

"I know they did. Cory and I were watching out for them."

"Now what? Do we start grieving?"

My fath…I mean, James, poured himself some coffee and took a seat. I took a seat next to him.

"We're not supposed to know he's dead yet, Ethan. If that were really William, we would have all been sleeping. Considering that it's not unusual for William to disappear, we wouldn't go out looking for him. Normally, I would have thought that a prank call as well. I'm sure the warlocks will make it a point to inform us that they've killed him when they're done with the body."

"How long do you think it will take?"

He took a sip of coffee. "I'm not sure, a couple of weeks maybe? If I know them, it won't be too long."

"May I ask you something, James?"

He nodded.

"It's just that, well, I couldn't help but notice how the others fight and kill like it's normal. I mean, they go right back to their lives as if nothing has happened. How can they do that?"

He thought it over. "Well, considering what we all went through with Simon, it became natural for us to fight like that. I know we've kept that part of our lives from you, Ethan. Your mother and I went through many struggles to get to where we are today. The others, well, they lived through that journey with us. There's a world you don't understand here. We live among humans. We've made it our job to stay invisible to them. We live as they do. Work hard as they do. We try not to intrude in their lives. Although we've always been here, the humans have no idea witches are real, much less the battles being fought around them. Imagine if they knew what kind of dangers existed."

"What would happen if they discovered us?"

He huffed. "Madness," he said, taking a sip of coffee.

Although this conversation was interesting, I was beginning to feel tired.

"What do you think of Salem?" James asked.

I had to think that over.

"I'm beginning to understand why you both

loved it so much. I didn't think much of it when I first arrived, but now, I see the magic."

"It even smells different here," James said, with a faraway look. "Something about this town captures you, makes you fall in love with it."

"I suppose."

He put his coffee down.

"You fight just like your mother."

"I'm sorry?"

He smiled. "She used whatever she could get her hands on and turned it into weapons when she fought. I noticed how you used the headstones, reminded me of your mother."

I rubbed my eyes.

"Why don't you go back to bed," James suggested. "It's only four in the morning."

"Yeah, I think I will."

"Do you have work later?"

"Yes."

"I'll come wake you. Get some rest."

I hurried back up the stairs and into my bed. I was out as soon as my head hit the pillow.

I had so many dreams that morning. Scattered images running through my head didn't let me sleep much. I knew I had a huge task ahead, and I was prepared for it. If ever there was a time to prove I was a man, this was it.

By morning, I felt like a different person. I stood in front of my closet, staring at my robes. Somehow, I didn't feel the need to wear them today. It was time. Time to take off the robe.

I picked out a pair of jeans, grabbed a green t-shirt and got dressed. These clothes felt odd on me. They hugged every inch of my body, I wasn't used to that. Although my robe was more fitted than William's, it never fit me quite as tight as these jeans. I tucked in the t-shirt, unsure if I was doing it correctly.

When I grabbed the wand, I realized I had no place to put it. I looked down at myself, searching for a place to hide it. I tried putting it in my back pocket, but only half of it fit, making it clearly visible. I settled for hiding it in my sock, that would have to do for now.

I grabbed the ring, which fit perfectly into my front pocket, and set off for the bathroom. I checked my hair in the mirror, Vera was right, it did look like a cow had licked it to one side. I ran my fingers through it, settling for leaving it messy. It was a day for change, why not change everything.

I stepped into the hallway, feeling as if I was wrapped in leaves again. I wasn't used to feeling denim on my skin. It felt odd but rather comfortable. It was certainly cooler than my robe, but I was never going to admit to that. I took a few steps, trying to get use to the shell-like texture on my legs. The shirt felt as if I had painted it on. It was a snug feeling I wasn't quite sure I liked.

I could hear James' laughter in the kitchen as I made my way down the stairs. I knew it had to be Fish making him laugh. I made my way in.

"So, he takes the branch," Fish was saying, "puts it und…"

Fish froze, looked at what I was wearing, and lit up. "Well, it's about time."

Delia did a double take when she looked up from the stove. Her eyes traveled the length of my body, almost undressing me, at least, it seemed that way.

"Is that what you were hiding under that robe?" she asked, a bit flushed.

"Hey, Delia," Fish said, giving her a dirty look. "Wipe your mouth, you have some drool coming out."

"You idiot," Delia said, looking back down.

James laughed. "Good morning, Ethan. Come join us for breakfast."

"I don't think I can sit," I said, looking down at the jeans.

James laughed. "You'll get use to them. It took me a while to get use to the robes all the wizards wear in Magia. I felt a draft for the first year I wore it. Don't even notice it anymore."

I took a seat, bending my legs very slowly. It felt like the jeans would tear at any moment.

"Do you miss wearing jeans?" I asked.

"Of course, I do. Just as you will miss wearing your robe. It's what you're accustomed to."

Delia served me up some of her horrible, salty eggs. "Enjoy," she said, with a big smile.

"They look wonderful, Delia," James said,

kicking me under the table.

When I looked at him, he motioned for me to look under the table. He shook something, and motioned again. I took a peek. He was holding a paper bag.

"Hurry, before she turns around," James said, in a whisper.

Fish quickly went to distract Delia.

"Have you noticed all the spider webs?" Fish said, pointing up.

The moment Delia looked up, I threw the eggs into the bag. I quickly set the plate back on the table. I began making scraping sounds on the plate with the fork.

"Webs, again?" I heard Delia say. "We get a lot of those, don't we?"

Fish checked to make sure the deed was done. "Yeah," he said, stepping away from her. "I'll have to spray for spiders again."

"It's no wonder the house doesn't smell like chemicals," she said, returning to the stove.

She noticed my empty plate. "How were the eggs?" she asked.

I smiled. "Mmmm," was all I could say.

James made his way out the back door, tossing the bag in a barrel just outside the door.

"I'll go empty the trash," he said, picking up the barrel.

Fish winked and handed me a glass of orange juice. It only made me wonder just how often he did that. Delia's cooking was truly horrible.

"Thanks for breakfast, babe," Fish said. "I'm gonna head out with the guys."

When James returned, we thanked Delia and made our way into town.

"Salem hasn't changed much, has it?" James said on the way to the deli.

"This place will never change," Fish answered. "I think that's why I like here so much. I can always count on Salem to feel like home."

"I think it will always be home to Thea and me," James said, looking around. "I sure do miss this place."

"Why don't you come back?" Fish asked.

"Perhaps, one day."

I was enjoying my walk. It was nice not to hear remarks about my robe, or rude comments about it being a dress. There was, however, a lot of people staring at me, mostly women. One even said hello, in a very funny tone, as she passed me.

When we reached Essex Street, I became a bit uneasy. Why were people still staring at me? Again, mostly women.

Had I put my clothes on wrong? Was there something sticking to me? Maybe the t-shirt was backwards? I even asked James. He only smiled and said, "Trust me, you look fine."

"There's Sharron," Fish said, pointing.

She was coming out of a market, holding a bag of herbs. "I want to say hello to her," James said, heading her way.

Sharron gave James a hug, kissing him on the cheek. "So nice to see you, James. How is Thea?"

"She sends her love."

Sharron looked at me, nodded, and returned her attention to James. "Will she be join…"

Sharron cut off in mid-sentence. She slowly turned her head, and began looking up and down my body. "Oh my," she said, turning a rosy color.

"We're headed to the deli," James said. "I just wanted to say hello."

"What's that, dear?" Sharron said, peeling her eyes away from me.

James tried not to laugh. "We're late. Ethan needs to get to the deli."

"Yes, of course," she said, returning her eyes to me. "You'll have to bring him along when you come visit." Again, her eyes traveled the length of my body.

"Dirty, old lady," Fish said, when we walked away.

James laughed. "I don't think Ethan realizes what's going on."

What were they talking about? Did I look stupid? I knew I shouldn't have worn these clothes.

"I think he almost gave Sharron a heart attack," Fish answered.

"Okay, what's going on?" I asked, stopping.

"Morning," a woman said, passing us by.

I thought her head would spin as she looked

over her shoulder at me.

"What was that all about?" I asked the two.

"Get used to it," Fish said. "It's not such a bad problem to have."

"I have a problem?"

Fish laughed. "Yeah, and it's a problem a million other guys would kill to have."

"Leave him alone, Fish," James said, playfully. "He'll find out soon enough."

We continued walking. The whole way to the deli, I got stares from different women, all gawking at me. One woman gave me a piece of paper with some numbers written on it. I wasn't sure what to do with it.

"Put it in your pocket," Fish said to me.

"Why?" I asked.

"So, you can call her."

"Call her what?"

"Come on," James said, with his arm on my shoulder. "I'll explain later."

Chapter Twenty-Three: Donut

I found myself searching for Viola the moment we neared the deli. The bench was empty. Where was she? A feeling of disappointment washed over me. I was really looking forward to seeing her today.

"I dropped Vera off early," Fish said to James. "Cory said he would take her home. I grounded her last night."

"Yes, I heard," James answered.

James and Fish headed to the bakery to speak with Cory. I paused at the empty bench, wondering where Viola could be. I looked up and down the street, but she was nowhere to be found. It was unlike her not to be here.

Sean startled me when he tapped on the glass, motioning me to come inside.

"You're late," he said, waving me in.

I took one last glance down the street before going inside.

Susan was filling the display case with sliced meats. "We have a lot of work to do," she said, not bothering to look up.

I grabbed an apron. "I'll get right to work," I said, heading to the back.

"Hey, you lost the dress," Sean said, the moment I walked in.

"It's not a dress," I said, reaching for today's orders.

"There's some pepperoni in the walk-in," Sean said, cutting some vegetables. "Cut the whole case, then get started on the salami."

"Okay."

I came out of the walk-in with my hands full of pepperoni. Susan walked in, paused to look at me, and continued walking. "You're not wearing a hairnet," she hissed.

She walked out the back door, slamming it behind her. Sean shook his head. "She'll come around, you'll see."

I had grown use to her foul mood. I hardly took notice of it anymore.

I spent the next hour slicing all the meat in the walk-in. Sean left two cases of iceberg lettuce for me to chop. He and Wayne left to service the van.

"Some help out here, please," Susan called. She was trying to reach some boxes when I came out. "Sean usually gets those for me," she said, stepping aside.

I easily reached up and grabbed them. They weren't even that high. Why couldn't she get them?

"Where do you want them?" I asked, turning around.

She quickly looked up. "Um, just put them on the counter."

Had she been staring at me?

When I turned to place the boxes on the counter, I saw Viola sitting outside. She seemed to be looking for something. She wouldn't stop looking up and down the street.

"May I take a short break?" I asked Susan.

"Y…yes, but don't be long."

I took off my hairnet and apron, and headed for the door. Viola looked up when she heard the bell ding. She seemed surprised to see me walking out. She immediately looked at what I was wearing, pausing at my jeans.

"I didn't think you were coming today," I said, taking a seat next to her.

She looked at me from the corner of her eye.

"I overslept," she said, shyly.

She wore yellow today. I do believe it was my favorite color now. Again, the dress was two sizes too big for her. Why would she hide her figure under all that fabric? It brought back memories of the clothes my mother used to wear. She also hid her figure under oversized clothes.

"No book today?" I asked, when I noticed she hadn't brought it.

She shook her head, seeming nervous.

"Is something wrong?" I asked.

She glanced at my jeans. "No."

"Hey, you in the mood for a donut? I'll go get us one," I said, heading next door.

I hurried to the bakery, pondering over what kind of donuts to get us. Vera was standing behind the counter when I walked in.

"Hey, Vera. Can I have two donuts? I'll pay as soon as I get my first check."

Vera was like a statue, staring at me with a strange look on her face.

"Are there anymore chocolate ones?" I asked.

"Um, yeah," she said, staring at what I was wearing.

"Well, can I have them?"

"Y...yeah," she said, opening the display case.

I headed for the door the moment she gave them to me. "Thanks," I said, over my shoulder.

I was almost skipping my way back to Viola. I was truly happy to see her today. With all the horrible things going on in my life, she was a breath of fresh air.

"I think I took the last two chocolate ones," I said, handing one to Viola.

I sat next to her again, taking a bite of my donut. "Aren't you going to eat yours?" I asked, with a mouthful of donut.

Something was different about her. Why was she so nervous today?

"You changed your clothes," she said, glancing at the jeans again.

"It's just clothes. I'm the same person."

"Hardly," she said, looking away.

What did she mean by that?

"Didn't you like the robe?" she asked.

"Of course, I did. I just thought it was time for a change. Why, do I look stupid?"

She half smiled. "Quite the opposite, actually. I still think the robe looked much better on you."

"Why? Because it made me look special?"

She finally took a small bite of her donut. "You don't need clothes to make you look special. You stand out no matter what you wear."

I smiled. How could I tell her I thought the same of her? She brightened up my day by just showing up.

"Listen," I said, leaning back. "I was thinking, they're having this party next week. Maybe you and I could go together?"

"I don't go to parties."

"That would make two of us."

She squinted her eyes. "Why do you want to go with me?"

"Why wouldn't I? We're friends, aren't we?"

"We are?"

"You don't consider me a friend?"

"I suppose."

She kept fidgeting and biting her bottom lip.

"So, is that a yes?" I asked hopeful.

Just then, Vera approached us.

"Ethan, may I speak with you?"

"I have to go back inside," I answered. "I really don't have time."

"It's about the dance."

What now?

"I'll be right back, Viola."

"Yes," Viola said, the moment I got up.

I looked down at her.

"Yes, what?"

She looked at the ground. "Yes, I'll go with you to the dance."

I smiled. "Then, it's a date."

I went to go see what Vera wanted. I was still a little upset with her. I hadn't forgotten the lies she spat about Viola.

"How may I help you?" I asked her.

"It's about the dance, I changed my mind."

"Changed your mind?"

"Yes, about going with you."

"I don't recall asking. Besides, I already have a date."

"What? With her?" she said, pointing to Viola. "But she's wicked ugly."

Her tone was so arrogant.

"And, I'm a dork," I answered. "We make a perfect couple, don't you think?"

I left her standing there, her mouth agape. I knew Vera wasn't used to rejection. I had always given into her. There hadn't been a wish I hadn't tried to grant.

"So, you going to eat that donut," I asked, taking a seat next to Viola again.

"What did *she* want?" Viola asked.

"You're not jealous, are you?" I teased.

Viola looked in Vera's direction. "Maybe not of her personality."

Did I just hurt her feelings? I think she misunderstood my teasing.

"She has nothing for you to be jealous of," I assured her. "Vera wishes she was like you."

A bright, golden smile spread across Viola's face. "You really think that?"

I moved a bit closer. "I'll tell you a secret. I would notice you walking into a room, before I ever noticed her."

I looked down at the donut in her shaky hand. "Now, eat that donut before I eat them both."

She smiled, taking a big bite of her donut.

After my break, I hurried through the day, anxious to speak with James. I had so many questions. Like, what did people wear to parties? Do I pick Viola up, or walk there? Salem wasn't very big, you could easily walk to where you were going.

I was cleaning the walk-in floor when I heard the bell ding. "Anyone here?" I heard someone say.

I leaned the mop against the wall and went to see who it was. I looked around for Susan as I made my way out. Where was she?

"How may I help you?" I asked the customer

"I have a package for Sean Gurry," a man in a uniform said.

"He's not here right now, but you can leave it with me."

"I'll need a signature," the man said, holding out a pen.

"I can sign for that," Susan said, entering the room.

"I didn't see you come in," I said to her.

"I was out back, throwing out the trash," she said, reaching for the pen.

The moment she clicked the pen, a strange blue dust blew in her face. She slapped her hands to her face, screaming as the man ran for the door. I jumped over the counter, waving my hand at the man. He flew back, crashing into one of the display cases.

Susan dropped to the floor, her face melting as if it were butter. I heard a spell spinning as I tried to get the wand from my sock. The spell hit my back, launching me across the room.

I waved my hand before the warlock could spit out another spell. Within seconds, every knife that had been hanging in the back, was now floating and awaiting my command.

The man gasped, then tried to make a run for

the door. I waved my hand again, sending the knives right to him. It sounded like Sean was cutting meat when the knives speared him to the wall.

"Ethan!" James said, storming in.

I staggered to my feet, stunned but not hurt. I ran to Susan. Her hair was already lying on the floor. She was literally melting.

James pulled out some petals from his pocket. He reached down and placed them on whatever was left of Susan's face. I recognized those petals, they were from the flowers in Magia.

"Let's hope they work here," James said, holding Susan's head up. "I don't think there's much magic left in them."

Suddenly, the front door flew off its hinges. Sean came storming in. "Susan!" he said, running to her.

"Stand back," James said, holding up his hand. "She can't be moved yet."

Sean gasped. "Who did this to her?" he asked.

I pointed to the wall.

Sean spun around, walked over to the dead man, and tore his head off with his bare hands.

"It's working," James announced.

Sean ran back to his wife. Her hair was already growing back.

"Suze," he said, kneeling beside her.

"Is she going to be okay?" I heard from the door.

I was shocked to see Viola standing by the door. How much had she seen? She didn't seem bothered by the severed head near her feet. Why wasn't she scared? Better yet, why wasn't she screaming?

"She's going to be fine, Viola," James answered. "She just needs a minute."

James knew her name? How could that be? He'd never met her, that I knew of. He answered her as if they were good friends. Did my mother know her? I remembered mentioning Viola to both my parents. Why didn't James tell me he knew her? Maybe I never mentioned her name to them?

"You know her?' I asked surprised.

"Yes, that's Justin's daughter.

Chapter Twenty-Four: Justin

I looked at Viola, shocked to learn who she was. I knew her father, Justin, from a few visits he paid my mother. Justin had tagged along with Fish and Delia when they came to Magia. I learned his story from my mother.

Justin had loved a human girl but left her when he learned Simon wanted to kill her. It was his way of protecting her. He knew if Simon found out he had fallen in love with a human and impregnated her, he would have sent his men to dispose of them both.

My mother said Justin always watched his daughter from afar, keeping a watchful eye. When Simon was killed, Justin sought her out. By then, it was too late. Viola's mother had been killed by warlocks, dismembered, and thrown into the woods. Justin lost his mind, blamed himself for her death.

He left Salem, thinking himself unworthy of Viola's love. The guilt of not being here to protect them sent him to a dark place. My mother never saw or heard from him again.

"Ethan," James said, pulling me from my thoughts. "Go next door and get Cory."

I looked down at Susan, she was almost back to normal. Sean was holding her hand, telling her how much he loved her.

"Ethan, go," James ordered.

I paused at the door, locking eyes with Viola. I could see the resemblance now. She looked so much like her father.

"Are you okay?" Viola asked.

I tried to smile. "I'm fine," I said, brushing my fingers across her face.

I walked out, knowing I would do everything I could to protect her.

"Cory," I called, walking into the bakery.

"Back here."

I walked to the back of the bakery. Cory and Fish were standing in the far back, talking in whispers.

"How is Susan doing?" Cory asked.

"Better, the petals worked."

"Is James ready?" Cory asked.

"He asked me to come get you."

"Tell him I'll be right there."

I nodded and looked at Fish. He had a worried look on his face.

"What's going on?" I asked.

"Tell James, I'll be right there," Cory said again.

I left the bakery feeling uneasy. What were they up to? I had a bad feeling about this.

When I gave James the message, he and Sean exchanged glances. They still had Susan on the floor. Viola was already gone.

"Sharron is on her way," James said. "She can take her home. They'll be safe there."

Sean kept his eyes on Susan. There was a fierce look spreading across his face. It almost seemed that he would explode with anger.

"She's fine, Sean," James assured him. "We won't let this happen again."

"We're ready," Cory said from the door. Fish was standing right behind him.

When they asked me to stay with Susan, I knew what they were up to. James and Fish had been at the bakery all morning. It was obvious they were planning something.

Sean placed some aprons behind Susan's head. "Leave her here until Sharron arrives," he said to me.

"Take me with you," I said, facing them.

"We won't be gone long," James said, heading for the door.

"This isn't your fight," I yelled.

"Stay out of it," James answered.

"Don't take another step," I warned.

When they ignored me, I waved my hand,

sending them flying back into the deli. I waved my hand towards the door, repairing it and sealing it shut. I leaned down, pulling the wand from my sock. I had to wave my hand again when James tried stopping me.

"Wall," I shouted.

They flew up, and slammed hard against the wall, where they stood.

"I learned that from my mother," I said, unshrinking the wand.

"Dammit, Ethan, put us down," James yelled.

"I'm sorry, Father. You'll have to forgive my rudeness, but you're not going anywhere."

They kept yelling for me to put them down. I ignored their pleas and readied myself to leave. Sean was trying with all his might to pull himself away from the wall, but my magic was stronger than his.

"I'll put you down when I return," I said, heading for the door.

"Ethan, where are you going?" James asked.

I smiled. "I won't be long," I said, then walked out.

I made sure to hang closed signs on both shops. I locked the doors and closed the blinds. I was in the air moments later.

There was something I needed to find, something that would calm all the fighting. I knew the others were worried about their families, wondering who would be next. What they didn't know was, I had just figured something out.

I had been watching the warlocks, studying their every move. I tried to find reasoning behind their actions, questioning how killing us would benefit them. I found no answers, no reasons behind all the attempts on our lives. So, I watched them, trying to find a reason why they suddenly hated witches again. I found none.

Weeks before I got here, the warlocks had been living in harmony with the witches. There were no fights, no deaths. Life in Salem was good, peaceful. I was surprised the others didn't notice what I had. Why was it, every time they attacked, the humans were conveniently not around. Even today, not one human walked into the deli. We were usually very busy. Humans would have been sitting at all the tables, enjoying their grinders. Why would today be any different?

The day they tried burying Fish alive, I didn't see a human once. The warlocks were throwing dirt on Fish's grave with no worries, never looking over their shoulders for humans. I knew warlocks didn't want to be discovered in this world. It would pose too many dangers for them as well. Bullets were more than capable of killing us. Human weapons did damage, and the humans had many of them.

No, it was convenient for warlocks and witches alike to stay undiscovered. William said the warlocks were disorganized and not very bright. He was wrong. The warlocks were very intelligent, their attacks well planned. They stuck together in bans, rarely traveling alone. Where there was one, you could certainly find another. Why would one come alone today?

My family and friends were blind to what was going on. All they thought of was killing warlocks, even hunting them when possible. They didn't know there was no need to kill them, no need to fight.

The warlocks weren't trying to gain control of Salem, someone was controlling them. I realized that today when the warlock came alone with no real purpose for his attack. Sean posed no threat to them. Why kill him? Sean was one of them, stronger and more skilled than any of the other warlocks could ever be. That's why the Black Witch wanted him. Susan had only been hurt because the wrong person was hit with the spell. If it had been Sean, the outcome would have been different. It was the same when Fish's imposter ate the grinder. It had been meant for me, a potion to control my mind. William was confused when he said it had been meant for him.

I also noticed something else, a scar on the warlock's neck today, and it wasn't from a blood promise. William had been wrong about that, too. The warlocks hadn't made a blood promise. Someone had given them a potion, one that would make them easy to control. I saw what that potion did on Fish's imposter. It was the signature of the black witch. Her spells and potions left a mark, showing her who she had control of.

The only thing I couldn't figure out was, who was controlling the humans? Why were they conveniently not around every time something happened? Someone was protecting them, making sure they wouldn't be hurt. I knew it couldn't be The Black Witch. Why would she care if humans were hurt? A spell, perhaps? But who would know such a spell? Especially a spell to cast on all the humans. William could certainly be responsible, but I knew that wasn't possible. He would never risk changing the future.

I flew away from Salem, desperate to find Netiri. I already knew what William was having him do, so it would be easy to find him. I had to warn Netiri about William being wrong. We didn't need to spy on the warlocks, we needed to help them. They were as much a victim as we were. I wasn't buying the whole witch and warlock battle. This world was big enough for us all. We had enough enemies, why make enemies with each other?

I flew until I reached a camp, one I had seen in my mother's memories. She had been tortured in this camp, set on fire and burned alive. I could almost hear her screams of agony drifting in the air. I pictured the chains Simon had used to restrain her. I imagined her bloodied face, her tortured body. She had been so brave, so defiant.

I shrunk the staff, placed it in my pocket, and began making my way into the grounds.

The place was quiet with not a soul in sight. I knew Netiri had to be here, I could almost feel him. I slowly walked past a few empty cabins, taking note of a fire still burning nearby. Someone had been cooking. By the looks of the overgrown grass and shrubbery, it was clear why they chose this location. It had not been used in years by humans.

"Netiri," I called.

"Ethan?"

I spun around, Netiri was coming out from behind a cabin.

"What are you doing here?" he asked, quickly making his way to me. "I thought it was the police again."

He looked in all directions. "You can't be seen here," he said in a whisper. "The police have noticed trespassers. The warlocks will return the moment they realize it wasn't them."

"Are there warlocks here?" I asked.

"Yes, Ethan. Get out of here, before they see you."

"Where are they?"

"Down by the lake. The police were here moments ago. That's why we left."

"And they didn't see the fire?" I asked motioning to it.

"I just built that fire," Netiri explained.

He looked nervously around the camp. "You need to get out of here, before you're seen. I won't be able to explain why I know you."

"Where is the lake?" I asked.

Netiri's eyes began to change color. "Ethan, you're going to destroy all my hard work. Why did you come here, anyway?"

"To stop you," I said flatly.

I began to tell him my suspicions about the warlocks. I explained how I didn't believe they wanted to start a war with us again. I wasn't sure if Netiri believed me.

"You think the Black Witch has a spell on them?" he asked.

"She isn't using a spell," I explained. "She's using a potion to control their minds."

"So, that's why William told me not to eat or drink anything they gave me," Netiri said, looking away.

This surprised me. "William knew?"

"Why else would he tell me to only eat what I prepared, to only drink from a closed container."

I thought back to the day Wayne had been poisoned. Susan was asking William how to tell the good warlocks, from the bad.

"What's going to happen?" Suzie Lou asked. "How can we possibly know which warlocks are friend or foe? We can't go around killing all of them."

"She's marked them," William answered. "It's not hard to spot the scars on their necks."

William slipped. He really did know.

Netiri was staring into space. "A potion," he murmured. "That makes sense."

"Are there any warlocks here without scars on their necks?" I asked.

"No."

"How do I get to the lake?"

Netiri had a look of shock. "Are you crazy, Ethan? All the warlocks here have scars. They'll attack the moment they see you."

"Shall I find the lake myself?"

Netiri shook his head. "You're as crazy as your mother," he said, leading the way.

We made our way through the trees until the lake was in view. I stopped Netiri before making our way out of the trees.

"What is it?" he asked.

"I'm not sure if my plan is going to work," I explained. "If it doesn't, I want you to leave."

"Are you out of your mind? You can't fight that many men alone."

I smiled. "You don't know me very well, do you?"

I walked around him and out of the trees. I could hear weapons being drawn the moment they spotted me. I ignored everything around me and pulled out my ring.

My mother was too predictable, I knew what else she had placed in the ring. It was water from the secret River of Life. She'd meant for me to break it open and use it if I became too weak. Her little gift was going to come in very handy.

I knew the magic in the ring wouldn't last very long on the warlocks, my father had given me that peace of the puzzle.

"If I were to leave, I would soon lose those powers. I would return to my human form, leaving my witch half intact."

I made my way into the water, spears flying over my head. I tapped the ring and broke it open, and slowly allowed the magic water to mix into the lake. I waved my hand again, sending all the warlocks diving into the lake.

All you could hear were splashes as the warlocks hit the water. The vomiting came fast, emptying their stomachs of the potion. Green, bright mist drifted into the air. I smiled, knowing it had worked.

I faced Netiri. "Explain it to them, tell them I'll be back. I need a moment of their time."

"Where are you going?" Netri asked.

"I need another ring," I said, holding the broken one out.

I was hoping the broken ring would still take me to Magia. I was truly counting on it. When I slipped it on, I was pulled hard into the vortex.

Chapter Twenty-Five: Attor

I opened my eyes when I heard the roar of the waterfall. I was back in Magia and grateful the ring had worked. I jumped back when a flame of fire went right over my head.

"My favorite dragon," I said, turning around.

A roar of fire filled the sky as Attor spread his massive wings. William was standing right next to him, and looking healthier than ever.

"Poisoned, huh?" I teased.

William smiled. "Was I believable?"

"You even fooled me, Grandfather."

"I was afraid of overacting a bit," he laughed.

"Don't think they noticed."

"I see you've taken off the robe. Human clothes look quite well on you."

I looked down at myself. "It seems to be a big deal for some reason."

I smiled at Attor. "Hello, old friend."

"Greetings, Ethan."

Attor was leader of the dragons and my grandfather's main guard. He was black as the night. His eyes were bright yellow with red circles around the irises. I played with him as a child, flying all over Magia. My Grandfather loved him and considered him a true friend.

"I see you figured things out," my grandfather said. "You were faster than expected."

"Your puzzles are not easy, Grandfather."

"Your mother is *still* trying to figure them out."

We shared a laugh.

I held up my hand, showing him the ring. "Was this of your doing, Grandfather?"

He held up another ring, a carbon copy to the broken one on my hand.

"I made three of them, in fact. I destroyed the one your mother gave you, replaced it with my own. I knew you would be needing more than one."

"Of course, you did," I said, under my breath.

He held it out as he approached. "Ask your questions quickly, Ethan. You need to get back."

I took the ring from him, placing it into my pocket. "Why did you really leave?" was my first question.

He sighed. "It was necessary. I didn't lie when I said the Black Witch wanted me out of the way. I knew I had to find a way to distract her, take her attention away from me. I'm almost certain she's been listening to every word we say."

"What? How is that possible?"

"She's in the mansion, Ethan. At least, her eyes are."

"What are you talking about?"

"Do you remember what I said about the Black Witch taking things from right under our noses, and replacing it with one of her own?"

"Yes."

"I'm afraid, she's taken Vera."

My heart sunk. "But, she was there today, at the bakery."

"That isn't Vera, it hasn't been Vera for a very long time."

"Is it the Black Witch?"

William looked thoughtful for a moment.

"I'm not sure. That's why I haven't acted yet. I must first find out where Vera is being kept. I'm positive she's still alive."

"Does Fish know?"

He shook his head. "He knew there was danger coming. He just didn't know what kind. When I warned him to take good care of her, he coddled and spoiled her instead."

"They were going to replace Fish, weren't they? That's why that imposter was there? Another set of eyes?"

My grandfather raised one eyebrow. "They're trying to replace all of them. I would stop it if I wasn't certain it's going to flush them out. I need to know who's helping her. Besides Wendell, that is."

"Why didn't you warn the others? Why wouldn't you at least tell me? Why wouldn't you tell Fish about Vera?"

"And, what do you suppose Fish would do if he knew his daughter had been taken? She would be dead before Fish even got to her. Her life depends on us finding the Black Witch first."

"We have to find Vera, Grandfather."

"What do you think I've been doing?"

"Is there anything I can do to help?"

He looked toward the waterfall. "Just do as I have instructed you. Don't let the imposter suspect you know anything. Nothing can change, the future must stay the same. We can trust no one, not even our friends. The Black Witch knows dark spells, and she knows how to use them. I have no doubt the darkness is helping her. Making her believe I'm dead will reveal her plan to me. I can't act until I know it."

"Can you tell me why you never told Cory about all of this?"

"I told no one. The Black Witch is becoming good at what she does. It took me days to figure out that wasn't Vera. Besides, they would react differently if they knew the truth. The Black Witch is watching for changes."

I told him what I had done with the warlocks. "I'm going back to speak with them when I leave here."

"Good thinking, Ethan. Now we can flush her out. Make her do her own dirty work."

"She won't have a choice," I said, proudly. "She must face me, or no one."

My grandfather's eyes beamed with pride.

"How did you know it was safe to call me Grandfather?" he asked.

I smiled. "Because, we're in Magia."

He shook his head. "Why couldn't your mother have been as observant as you."

"Your skin," Attor said, leaning toward me. "What is that odd smell?"

"Oh," I said, looking at my arm. "That's Sharron's leaves. They left my skin feeling funny. I think that's why that warlock's spell bounced right off me today."

Attor leaned in again, placing his cold nose right up against my skin. "You've been near Wendell," he said, pulling away.

"What?" I gasped.

I tried to think back, remember all the people I spoke to this morning. No one stood out.

"Can you think of anyone?" My grandfather asked.

"So many people," I said, shaking my head.

My grandfather looked at Attor. "Are you certain it's him?"

Attor blew fire into the air. "I'd know his scent anywhere," he hissed.

My thoughts were racing, trying to picture every face I'd encountered throughout the day.

"I can't see it," I said, frustrated.

"Perhaps your encounter with him was brief," my grandfather suggested.

"I had a lot of those today," I said, remembering all the women that approached me.

As I tried to retrace my steps, I thought of something. If Wendell had dared to come near me, that meant he would do it again.

"He's testing me," I said, figuring it out. "He wants to see if I can sense him, doesn't he?"

My grandfather smiled. "Your mother should be ashamed of herself. She was never this intuitive."

"Thank you for having faith in me, Grandfather."

He gave me a nod. "By the way, I asked James to send for some friends of mine. They know Salem's woods like the back of their hands. If anyone can help you find Vera, they can."

"Who are they?"

He looked towards the sky. "Old friends," he said, almost mesmerized.

"I have to get back," I said, reaching for the ring.

"One more thing," my grandfather said. "It's the warlocks, you realize some of them are helping her willingly, don't you?"

"For what reason?"

He sighed, seeming disappointed. "I thought you had figured it out."

"I suppose asking would do me no good?"

He nodded knowingly. "Netiri is waiting."

I pulled off the broken ring. I was gone in seconds. When I arrived back at the lake, Netiri was still talking to the warlocks. Their earlier aggression was gone. I hoped that meant they believed him.

Netiri joined me the minute he realized I was back. "They're confused," he informed me. "Some of them don't even remember coming here. The last thing they remember is eating or drinking something. As soon as the effect from the potion was broken, their tones were different. Their attitudes and even their voices were different too. Ethan, these are good men."

"I suspected as much," I said, heading to the group.

I jumped on a rock that was at the edge of the lake. I looked around, grateful my plan had worked. These men looked tired. I was sure some of them hadn't eaten in days. I knew their actions were due to the potion. The Black Witch had them thinking of nothing but following her orders.

"I have no quarrel with you," I began. "Netiri has explained the situation we are faced with, has he not?"

They all nodded knowingly. I continued.

"Eat only what you cook. Drink only what is

sealed. The Black Witch will use any methods possible to control your minds. She doesn't care about you or us. You've lost friends because of her. Gained enemies because we didn't know she was behind it. The killings must stop," I said, looking around. "Don't allow your minds to be poisoned by her lies. She belongs to the darkness; her intentions serve only herself. Some of the spells she's using are from a dark spell book. There's only one place she could have acquired it. I think we all know where that place is."

A very tall warlock stepped forward. He was black skinned with braided hair.

"I never agreed to help anyone. I don't even know what I'm doing here. I have a family, children. I've been trying to live an honest life."

"And you still can," I answered. "It's of no fault of your own that you are here. The Black Witch needs bodies, robots to do her bidding. She knows dark spells, some we've never heard of. I'm afraid she used some of those spells to make a potion, one you obviously took."

I looked at the other men. "Witches and warlocks have lived in peace for years. There is no need to start another war. We're friends, comrades. We bleed the same color, share the same pain. We have no reason to hate you, we're brothers."

I pulled out the ring William had given me.

"In this ring," I said, holding it up. "Lies the only thing capable of breaking the potions effect. I challenge you to bring your brothers here, meet me so that I may help them. Don't allow them to live their lives as robots, not for her, not for anyone."

There were rumbles among them. I lowered the ring, hoping they understood.

I spun around to face Netiri. "Answer any questions they may have. Come find me when they bring more warlocks. Lie to them if you must. Promise them power and glory, just get them here. I have to break the potion's effect before it's too late."

Netiri's eyes kept changing. "You've really grown up, kid. You sound just li…"

"Yes, like my mother. I know."

He laughed. "I was going to say, like your father."

"I have to get back," I said, pulling out the wand.

"Where are the others? he asked.

I chuckled. "They're hanging around."

I was in the sky moments later.

I could see people standing outside the deli when I got back to Salem. They seemed confused to see a closed sign hanging on the door. I quickly found a safe place to land and tucked the wand back into my sock. I used the back door to enter the deli only to find angry faces awaiting me. They were still glued to the wall. I waved my hand, allowing their bodies to slowly slide down.

James was glaring at me. "Sorry I took so long," I said.

Cory held Sean back when he tried coming

at me. "Hear him out, first," Cory said, pushing him back.

"What the hell was that all about?" James growled at me.

I stood my ground. "I told you, it's not your battle to fight."

"Where did you go?" he shouted.

I had no choice, I had to tell them. I began to explain what I had figured out. No one was surprised the Black Witch wanted Sean on her team.

James spun around. "I wonder if she knows who you really are?" he asked Sean.

Sean quickly disagreed. "I've told no one, not even my wife. The only reason you know is because William gave me away."

"What is he talking about?" Cory asked him.

James and Sean exchanged glances. The subject was quickly changed.

"What else did you find out?" James asked me.

I held up the broken ring. "I can break the potion's effect with the ring. I used the water from the ring you and mother gave me."

I didn't want to tell him that William had replaced the one they had given me. For reasons I couldn't yet say, I had to keep it from them.

"The water from the secret river," James said, realizing what I was talking about.

"It worked?" he said, taking it from me.

"Just long enough to break the effects," I

explained. "Several of them didn't even remember how they got there."

As my father looked down at the ring, my eyes moved over to Sean. My father's question had me intrigued. Who was he? Better yet, what was he? Sean's strength was unhuman. I didn't miss how easily he tore that warlock in half. It was without effort, without the slightest trouble. Even when he shook my hand for the first time, I had noticed his unbelievable strength.

I gazed around the room, trying to find clues as to who he was. I thought of his unusual swords, the odd way he had chosen to conceal them. I searched my head for anything I had missed. The only thing that stood out to me was the amount of bread Sean consumed.

My father handed the ring back to me.

"Clean things up," he instructed. "We'll have to help Netiri gather up the warlocks. I don't want anyone else getting poisoned. We'll meet at the mansion once the deli is closed for the day."

I was about to respond when, "At once, my liege," Sean answered.

My jaw dropped as Sean obeyed James' orders. For a moment, I had thought James was talking to me. He was speaking to Sean; giving him orders, commands.

"Porteus?" I asked, in a very low voice.

Chapter Twenty-Six: In Love

James was quick to pull me into the back of the deli, he was almost dragging me.

"What is he doing here?" I asked, pulling away from him.

James waved his hand around, motioning me to stay silent. "The others will hear," he said, making sure no one was behind us.

I always knew the guards could disguise themselves like that. It was a mind trick they were gifted with. Porteus really didn't look like Sean, but he was making us believe he did. Porteus had used his mind to trick me many times before, making me believe he was my grandfather. It was one of his favorite games to play with me.

"Kneel before me," he would say. Once I kneeled, Porteus would laugh and lift his mind trick, pointing and laughing at me.

Although everyone thought Porteus looked like Sean, his real appearance would have scared half the town away. Porteus was seven feet tall with alligator-like skin and blood-red eyes. His head resembled that of an owl. His human-like hands stood out in direct contrast to his long, leathery tail. His talons, capable of cutting a man in two, were twice the size of both my hands. He was a king's guard. Loyal and obedient. Obeying orders was in their blood, that's why my grandfather left Porteus guarding James. I should have known he would follow him here.

"Where is the real Sean?" I asked.

James realized he would have no choice but to tell me the truth.

"When we discovered someone was teaching the Black Witch spells that only the guards knew, I realized I would need Porteus."

"When did he arrive?" I asked.

James checked again, making sure no one was listening. "The night they tried burying Fish alive," he said, nervously looking toward the front. "The real Sean is nearby. We sent word about what happened to his wife. He's probably there now."

"You're lying," I said, taking a step back. "Porteus has been here longer, hasn't he?"

James seemed a little shocked by what I was saying. That cemented it, he *was* lying.

"I saw the bread, James. I know how much the guards like it."

Frustrated, James closed his eyes.

"Where is the real Sean?" I asked again.

He didn't answer. I could tell by his silence that he was worried.

"She already has him, doesn't she?" I asked, figuring it out.

"That's the least of our problems," James said, shaking his head.

"What do you mean?"

He looked towards the front. "That damn lizard has fallen in love with Sean's wife."

It took me a moment to absorb what he just said. When it sunk in, I erupted into laughter.

"It's not funny," James hissed. "He *actually* thinks he can stay here, make her happy."

I laughed some more.

"Don't tell him you know it's him," James warned.

"He's in love," I said, shaking my head.

It only took the love bird a few minutes to get the deli back to normal. I tried to contain my laughter as I turned the closed sign over. Porteus, I mean Sean, couldn't understand why I was laughing so much. I knew I would have to refer to him as Sean, even in my thoughts.

"So, Sean," I said, as humans began lining up to place their orders. "Should I work in the back, or out here?"

Just then, Wayne walked in. "What's good, boss? Any deliveries ready yet?"

"Work the counter today," Sean answered.

"We fell behind."

I had to admit, Porteus made a pretty good Sean. He seemed to know exactly what to do.

By the end of the day, I caught myself looking out the window, hoping to see Viola. I mopped the floor, glancing over my shoulder every time someone walked by. Why hasn't she come back yet? Had she really been scared? Was she in shock? Why had she not told me she was a witch? Did she know who *I* was?

I was wiping down the counters when I heard a soft tap on the window. I looked up, smiling when I realized it was Viola. She was wearing a blue cotton dress with sunflowers along the collar. There was no book in her hand, no bag. I took note of her long, brown hair. It was messier and more tangled than I'd ever seen it.

I quickly made my way around the counter, eager to speak with her. The bell dinged as she opened it.

"You fixed that pretty fast," she said, looking at the door. "What kind of spell did you use?"

When I didn't answer, she looked my way.

"Why didn't you tell me?" was the first thing I said.

She bowed her head. "I wasn't sure if you were *like them*," she answered.

"You mean, a witch?"

She nodded.

I wanted to tell her I wasn't a witch, but I

had to keep my word to William and not tell anyone what I was.

"Why didn't you tell me you could fly?" she asked, looking up at me.

I was stunned, not knowing what to answer. "You saw me?"

She nodded. "I've seen you twice."

She looked down again. "Don't worry, I won't tell anyone."

I believed her. Something about this girl told me she would never betray me.

"I'm not a witch," I confessed.

Her honey-brown eyes sparkled as she looked up at me. "What are you?"

I sighed. "I can't tell you."

She began fidgeting, pulling on her fingers.

"I just wanted to make sure you were okay. I was worried."

She was about to turn away and leave.

"About me?" I asked, moving closer to her.

She bit her lip. "I went next door the moment that man tossed you across the deli."

"*You* warned them?"

She half looked at me. "I knew they would help you, like they helped me. I understand what I am because of them. I sort of discovered my magic by accident. One of them was close by the first time I realized what I was. They helped me understand who I am. Cory has been very nice to me."

I would make it a point to find out more

about her. I had a lot of questions, but my talk with her would have to wait. Right now, I just wanted to be near her.

I smiled as she nervously played with her fingers. She was so sweet, so beautiful. Her tangled hair fell across her shoulders, covering half her face. I could see her thick, brown eyebrows furrowing as she swallowed thickly.

"Okay," she said, turning for the door. "I'll be going along now."

"No, wait," I said, gently grabbing her arm. "Are you in a hurry?"

"Um, not really," she said, looking at my fingers around her arm.

I released her. "I'm not going to hurt you," I said, moving closer. "I just want to spend more time with you?"

She slowly gazed into my eyes. "Why?"

"All cleaned up?" Sean asked, coming out of the back.

I turned. "Yeah, mind if I get out of here now?"

"Didn't James say to meet him at the mansion?" he asked.

"No," I said, taking off my apron. "He said for *you*, to meet him there."

I pulled off the hairnet, waved goodbye, and walked out with Viola.

"Where are we going?" she asked, as we made our way down the street.

"I want to show you something," I said,

looking up and down the street.

I knelt, pulled up my pant leg, and took the wand from my sock. "Come on," I said, grabbing Viola's hand.

I had nothing left to hide. She knew so much about me. She knew I could fly, so why not have some fun with it?

I found a safe place to grow the wand and placed it between my legs. I held my hand out to her. "Want to come for a ride?" I asked.

She looked around.

"We won't be seen," I assured her. "It's dark now, we'll only be a flash to people."

She bit her lip, then swung one leg over the staff, taking her place behind me.

"Wrap your arms around my waist," I instructed.

I slowly felt the warmness of her body as she placed her shaky hands on my hips.

"I'm ready," she said.

"You call that holding on?"

I reached for her wrist, pulling her hand forward, and around my waist. "Like this," I said, reaching for the other hand.

I could feel her breath on my neck. I looked over my shoulder. "I won't drop you, I swear it."

I waved my hand, causing the staff to hover. Viola drew breath, digging her fingers into my skin. I realized she would be too frightened sitting behind me.

I jumped off, moved her forward, and took

my place behind her. I felt my heart beat faster when her hair brushed across my face. She smelled like sunshine, bright and fresh.

"Put your hands over mine," I said, grabbing the staff tightly.

I could feel her heart pounding as she slowly placed her hands over mine.

"Hold on tight," I whispered into her ear.

I took to the sky, leaning my body forward. I wanted to feel her close to me, take in the fragrance of her hair. I flew high above the clouds, hoping to reach the stars. Viola pointed at the moon. It was shimmering over the ocean. I guided the staff in that direction, flying us just over the water.

"We're flying," she said amazed.

I expected to hear screaming, like Vera had done the first time she flew with me. Viola was treasuring the moment, even spreading her arms as the air hit her face.

"You're not scared?" I asked.

She leaned to one side, gazing into my eyes.

"Not when I'm with you."

I leaned forward, pressing my lips to hers. Her lips were sweet. I kissed her slowly, trembling when my tongue found hers. I let go of the staff, wrapping my arms around her. She leaned back as I pulled her to me. I could feel our hearts beat as one.

"Viola," I said, gently running my tongue along her lips.

"Kiss me again." she whispered, pulling me closer.

I found her lips again. It made me feel happy when Viola would shake from my touch. She was happy to be here; happy to be with me. I flew miles across the ocean, our lips never parting once. It would be a moment in my life that I would never forget.

I was convinced I was so in love with Vera, years of being next to her proved that to me. I never imagined how wrong I really was. I was a drooling fool around Vera, never knowing what to say to her. With Viola, I knew exactly what words to say. I felt like myself, unlike the babbling idiot I used to be around Vera. Viola made me feel alive, made me appreciate every moment.

I was finding true love, real and pure. I had feelings I never knew I was capable of. There were butterflies in my stomach, fluttering and moving about. I wanted to shout from the highest mountain, tell the world how wonderful she was. Nothing compared to this moment. I was happy, utterly and completely happy.

When I pointed the staff back to Salem, I held Viola all the way back. It gave me pleasure to feel her quiver from my touch. Every time I spoke, her face would light up. I took note of the tangled mass upon her head, knowing the reason why.

My mother had told me about witches, how their hair became a knotted mess when they were in love. It was a sign to show others she was taken and very, very much in love.

"Your eyes," Viola said, gazing at me. "They're turning blue."

I already knew what she was talking about. It meant I was in love. I had inherited that from my witch father. When he fell in love with my mother, his eyes had also turned blue. A mark of love, as he put it. I knew only Viola would see them blue, my eyes would look normal to everyone else.

As we neared Salem, I asked Viola where she lived. I didn't want her walking the streets alone at this hour.

"Can you head to the deli?" she requested. "I can walk home from there."

"Nonsense," I answered. "I'll take you right to your door."

She became nervous. "Please, just leave me at the deli."

"It's very late, Viola. You shouldn't be out alone."

"I'll be fine," she insisted. "I prefer to walk alone."

She was becoming uneasy. I decided to grant her wish. I just wasn't sure if I would be able to stop myself from following her. I just wanted to make sure she arrived home safely.

The streets were empty when we arrived at the deli. I asked again if I could walk her home.

"Will you grant me just this one thing?" she said, brushing my face with her fingers. "Don't follow me home. I'll be just fine, I promise."

I couldn't say no to that. I gave her a long kiss goodnight and watched her walk away from me.

She waved over her head before disappearing around the corner. I put the wand back into my sock and almost skipped my way home.

When I reached the mansion, the others were still awake. "Ethan, is that you?" James called, as I closed the front door.

I walked into the kitchen only to find everyone having a late supper.

"You're still up?" I asked, pulling out a chair.

"Where have you been," James asked.

I leaned over, making sure no one would hear me. "I was on a date," I whispered to him.

He leaned back, brow lifted.

"I see," he said, with a big smile.

"Are you alright?" Delia asked.

"Never been better," I said, reaching for some of her horrible food.

Chapter Twenty-Seven: Liar

I talked to James for a few minutes before heading to my room. He said Netiri never called him. He assumed they hadn't found many warlocks yet. We agreed to look for him in the morning. Besides, I didn't have to work in the morning. The deli was usually closed on Tuesdays, something that made me very happy.

I inquired about Susan. James said she was doing fine. Of course, Porteus was with her, something James wasn't happy about.

"He's giving himself hope," James said. "She belongs to another."

As I made my way up the stairs, Vera appeared at the top. She had her arms crossed in front of her, tapping her foot on the floor. I had to remind myself that wasn't her.

"Where have you been?" she hissed.

"If you must know," I said, reaching the top. "I went for a walk."

A confused look washed over her. "Why are your eyes different?" she asked.

"My eyes?"

"Yes, they're brown. Why are they brown?"

I realized my eyes had always been blue for Vera. I had loved her since childhood. This imposter had obviously been able to see what Vera could.

"Who were you with?" she said, grinding her teeth.

I smiled. "I'm afraid that's none of your business."

I headed down the hall and into my room. I lay in my bed, not bothering to undress, and looked up at the ceiling. Thoughts of Viola danced in my head. I couldn't help but wonder why she didn't want me to walk her home. In fact, where did she live and with whom?

I thought of her fidgeting, the way she bit her lips. There wasn't anything about her that I didn't like. I knew she was self-conscious about her weight, but I thought she looked beautiful. It didn't bother me that she hid her body behind lose clothing. I found it refreshing that she didn't feel the need to wear tight clothes like Vera and some of the other girls around Salem. I found her modesty attractive, alluring even.

I thought of her for hours, allowing myself to drift away with her in my thoughts.

By morning, I couldn't wait to see her. I knew I had to go with James first; we had to find Netiri. Not wanting to waste a moment, I sprang out of bed and into the shower.

As I showered, I thought of the many places I could take Viola. Perhaps a picnic would be nice. I was pretty sure I could make one of those grinders for us. I would pack a basket and spend the day with her.

I was rinsing off when I felt someone's hand on my shoulder. I spun around, Vera was standing behind me, stark naked. I quickly shut the water off.

"What are you doing in here?" I said, reaching for a towel.

"Ethan, please. I was wrong," she said, trying to pull the towel away. "We belong together, we always have."

I yanked the towel back, wrapping it around my waste. "You need to get out of here, Vera. Go back to Steven."

I turned to leave, but she wrapped her arms around me, holding me back. "I made a mistake," she said, leaning her head on my back. "I didn't realize how much I truly loved you. Let's start over, just you and me. Fly me to the lake again, take me and make me yours. I know you want me, just as much as I want you."

I grabbed her hands with force, pushing them away from me. "Don't waste your breath," I said, walking out.

"You'll regret this," she yelled.

"I'll take my chances," I said, over my shoulder.

She began screaming at the top of her lungs, calling for her father. Moments later, Fish and James stormed into the room, with Delia right behind them. I was still in the towel, Vera was still naked.

I couldn't imagine what they were thinking. Here we were, me with only a towel, Vera was dripping water all over.

"What the hell?" Fish gasped.

"It's not what it looks like," I tried to explain.

Vera ran into her mother's arms. Fish quickly threw a blanket around her.

"He had his way with me," Vera cried.

"What?" James yelled. "Ethan would never do that. I raised him better than that."

Fish spun around, facing James. "Yeah, then why was she in the shower with him," he said, pointing to me. "Huh, James? Why is my daughter naked and crying?"

I had to stop myself from telling Fish that wasn't his daughter.

"I didn't touch her," I assured him. "She came into the shower, uninvited."

Fish's face became red. "Are you telling me my daughter threw herself at you? Be careful how you answer," he warned.

"He's always loved me," Vera cried. "He even tried to force himself on me the other day. He became angry when I told him I was in love with Steven."

"She's lying," I said, defending myself.

"Tell them, Ethan," Vera said, pulling away from her mother. "Tell them how you flew me to the lake and tried to almost undress me."

I bowed my head. I couldn't bring myself to tell them she was right. Not about today, but about the lake. I did want her, but that was before I realized I didn't truly love her anymore.

"He just used me," Vera cried into her hands.

"I didn't touch her," I tried to explain.

Fish took Vera into his arms, glaring at James. "What are you going to do about this, James? Are you going to let him dishonor my daughter?"

James exhaled one long sigh. "If what she's saying is true, Ethan will do the right thing."

"Of course, it's true," Fish said offended. "Vera has no reason to lie about this."

"And Ethan does?" James shot back.

Delia spoke up. "Ethan has always loved Vera, we all know that. He's loved her ever since I can remember. I can understand how he would lose control of himself."

"Because she's so irresistible?" James said with sarcasm.

"You listen here," Fish said, passing Vera

over to Delia.

He got in James' face. "You better make this right. I'd hate to see years of friendship go down the drain just because your son couldn't keep his hands off my daughter."

James moved closer, almost touching his nose against Fish's. "And I'd hate to see our friendship destroyed because you have a spoiled daughter that doesn't like to lose."

For a moment, I thought they were going to fight. James' fist was at the ready.

I was relieved when Fish stormed out of the room with Delia and Vera right behind him.

"I didn't touch her, Father. I swear it."

He held his hand up. "I believed you the first time."

I breathed in a sigh of relief. I thought I would have to spend hours explaining myself to him. I was thankful he had faith in my word.

"What happened?" he asked.

I told him everything. He couldn't believe Vera would offer herself up like that.

"I know she's spoiled," he said. "I never thought she would be that kind of woman."

I had to tell him the truth. I couldn't stand by and let him think the worst of the real Vera.

"I have to tell you something," I said, nervously. "I was told to keep this to myself, but I feel it necessary to clear things up. I don't think I have a choice."

"Wait," James said, looking toward the

door.

He made sure the door was locked. "Get dressed," he ordered. "We can't talk here."

I quickly changed into my robe. It was faster than trying to get my jeans on.

James was waiting when I returned.

"Give me your hand," he said, holding his out.

The minute I placed my hand in his, we were gone. As we travelled through the vortex, my father asked me to explain things to him.

"That's not Vera," I said flatly. "Grandfather said it hasn't been her for a very long time."

"They have her?"

"Yes."

"Why would they need her?"

"Grandfather doesn't know. He told me to not say a word to anyone, especially Fish."

"Yes, I can see why," my father said, looking away.

"What are we going to do?" I asked. "Fish believes her. I don't want him thinking I'm capable of doing something like that."

He sighed. "We'll think of something. I'll talk to William, explain what happened."

I bowed my head, trying to find the words to thank him with.

"Thank you, Father."

"Why are you thanking me?"

"You believed me, without a doubt in your mind."

My father lifted my chin with his fingers, making me look at him. "You're my son, Ethan. I know the man I raised. I would never doubt your character or your word. I raised a man of honor, a man with dignity. Nothing could make me doubt you. Don't ever forget that."

My eyes spilled over. I threw my arms around him. "Thank you, Father."

When we arrived in Magia, we both took to the sky, searching for my grandfather.

"Of all days for him to hide," my father said when we couldn't find him.

"Why don't we try the castle," I suggested.

My father nodded, and we headed that way.

Chapter Twenty-Eight: The Castle

You could see the castle's turrets from miles away. Its glass towers send rays of light all over Magia. Guards stood just outside the gatehouse, gold and silver spears in their hands. My father pointed to the flag, signaling that the king was in.

We flew over the tower and into the massive courtyard. I never grew tired of seeing just how beautiful the castle was. Its glass walls were imbedded with precious jewels. A garden-like courtyard beckoned you to smell its flowers.

"There he is," my father said, pointing to one of the ramparts. "William," he called.

He was on the far side of the castle, looking out towards his kingdom. He quickly made his way down when he saw us.

"Is something wrong?" he asked, approaching us.

"I had to tell him, Grandfather. He knows about Vera."

"Did you tell him in Salem?" he quickly asked.

"No, in the vortex," my father answered.

Grandfather seemed relieved by that.

"Please, continue."

My father began to explain what happened. When he was done, my grandfather kept shaking his head.

"What purpose would that serve her?" he wondered.

"Should I bring Fish here?" my father asked. "We can tell him the truth."

"No, James. It's too dangerous for Vera. There must be a reason why they picked her, of all people. They replaced her for a reason."

"The imposter's intensions seem clear," my father said. "She wants our loved ones to hate Ethan."

"No, it's something else," my grandfather said, looking away. "Something we're not seeing."

"Are you certain the real Vera is still alive?" my father asked.

"Yes, I can still feel her."

"Grandfather, why can't you find her like you found Fish?"

"You think I haven't tried that?" he answered. "She must be behind heavy walls, protected by spells."

"Fish is very upset," my father said. "He believes every word the imposter said to him."

My grandfather's eyes lit up. It was like he was piecing a puzzle together. "You say she screamed for him?" he asked me.

"Yes."

"I see," he said, staring into space. "She's expecting him to react how a father would."

"That's exactly what Fish did," my father said. "He feels his daughter's honor is at stake."

William was thoughtful for several long moments. "I see," he said again.

"What are you thinking?" my father asked.

My grandfather smiled, and I wasn't sure I liked it. "I'm thinking, we have a wedding to plan."

"What?" I gasped. "I'm not marrying that witch."

"Calm down, Ethan," my father said. "No one is asking you to marry her."

My grandfather raised his eyebrows, looking straight at my father.

"You can't be serious, William."

"It's what she's expecting, James. We must find out her reasons. We can delay the wedding, make up lies and keep pushing it back. That will give us time to figure things out."

"I can't believe my ears," I said, shaking my head. "You really expect me to marry that woman? We don't even know who she really is."

"That's not what I said," my grandfather

answered. "I'm only asking that you make her *think* you're going to marry her. Just until we find out what her plans are. Why would marrying you help the Black Witch?"

"And if we find Vera first?' I asked.

"I'll kill the imposter myself," my father answered.

I thought of Viola, what would she think of me? I couldn't do this to her.

"Don't tell her," my grandfather said, reading my thoughts. "There's no reason she has to know."

I thought it over. I wasn't sure if I was willing to risk losing her.

"You love her?" my grandfather asked, seeming surprised.

"Of course, he doesn't," my father answered. "He just met the girl."

My grandfather shook his head. "And, how long did it take *you* to realize you loved Thea?"

My father looked at me, realizing how I felt.

"Do you love her, Son?"

I thought of her nervous ways, her constant fidgeting, our first kiss. "Yes, Father. I love her."

I wasn't sure if he was happy to hear that. He didn't seem very pleased with my announcement.

"Where is Thea?" he asked my grandfather.

"In the village," he answered. "She's still very angry with me."

As they spoke, I began to think of the places

I would search first. If finding the Black Witch was going to avoid this marriage, I would make it a point to find her.

I was no longer paying attention. I was too wrapped up in my own thoughts. I couldn't help but wonder, why would this imposter risk so much? Why would she take a chance on being discovered? Did she not think I would question her lies? I knew the real Vera would never do something like this.

I looked at my loved ones, confused as to why they didn't question the same thing. And, why wouldn't we tell Fish the truth, explain that searching for Vera would put her in danger? I knew Fish. He would never act reckless when it came to his daughter. He would have never thought it possible that I would take advantage of her like that. Why did he believe her so easily? Why didn't he question her about using the shower in my room? He knew there were at least six other showers in the house. Didn't he wonder why she chose mine?

Even Delia didn't ask a single question, never even bothered to hear me out. That wasn't like her. Delia questioned anything that didn't make sense to her.

My grandfather gave me a subtle nod, checking to see if my father had noticed. At that moment, I knew I had figured it out.

"We have to go," I said, interrupting their conversation.

"Yes," William said, stepping back. "Keep me informed of any changes."

I knew he meant that last comment for me. I returned the nod, knowing he would understand.

"Good," he said, looking at my father. "I'm sure Fish and Delia are waiting."

"I'll delay the wedding as much as I can," my father assured him. "I don't think Fish would want to rush into things anyway."

"Yes, of course," my grandfather agreed.

We locked eyes before my father pulled off his ring. "I'm proud of you," he said, before we disappeared into the vortex.

Someone was pounding on the door when we got back. "James, we need to talk."

It was Fish, and he didn't sound happy.

"Why aren't you opening the door?"

My father swung the door open. "I needed a moment with Ethan," he explained.

"Is he still calling Vera a liar?" Fish asked.

How could my father not see it? It was clear as day now. That wasn't Fish.

"Calm down, Fish," James said. "I had to hear his side of things. You have to give me that."

"What's to hear?" Fish answered. "She was naked, he was in a towel. Isn't it obvious what happened between them?"

James sighed. "Very well, Fish. I won't risk our friendship over this. Ethan will do the right thing."

"Damn right he will," Fish hissed. "I expect

him to ask her properly, too. Vera deserves that."

"Ask her properly?" James asked.

Fish pointed his chin out. "He needs to ask her to marry him."

I wanted to kick him across the face, I almost couldn't stop myself.

"I'll marry your daughter," I growled. "But I'll be dammed if I ask her for anything."

"Enough, Ethan," James said, holding his hand up. "There's no reason to get upset. Fish knows you'll be true to your word."

Fish stood his ground. "You're not taking that away from Vera. You've already taken her virtue. The least you can do is ask her to marry you, swear that you will stay by her side."

I was about to answer, but James put his hand on my chest, stopping me from saying another word.

"Ethan will promise no such thing," James said, moving closer to him. "You have his word, that will have to be enough."

Fish made a fist. "We'll see about that," he said, storming off."

James kept his eyes on him as he stomped his way down the hall. Even after Fish was gone from view, James kept his eyes in that direction. I could almost see him solving the puzzle.

"Those bastards," he murmured.

I almost fell to my knees, thankful he'd figured it out.

"Don't say a word," James warned, as he

slammed the door close. "Do you know?" he quickly asked.

I nodded.

"What the hell is going on?" he said, looking away. "When? How?"

"What do we do now?" I asked.

He ran his fingers through his hair.

"I hate William's puzzles," he said, shaking his head.

"What about the others?" I asked. "What if…?"

"Don't talk Ethan," James said, leaning against the door. "I'm sure they're listening."

He stepped away from the door, pulling out a phone.

"What are you doing?" I asked.

He dialed some numbers. "Calling some friends," he said, holding the phone to his ear.

After a few moments, a loud, shattering noise came from downstairs.

"Now what?" James said, heading for the door.

We descended the stairs, shocked to see broken glass everywhere. Fish appeared at the top of the stairs, Delia was right behind him.

"No!" Delia screamed.

"William," Fish said, taking the stairs two at a time.

I hadn't noticed William's fake head on top of the broken glass. How Fish and Delia saw it from where they stood was laughable. It was clear they were about to give us the performance of their lives.

It made sense now, why these imposters were here. They thought William was dead and gone, allowing them the freedom to take our friends. William was right, making them think he was gone would flush them out.

"Why?" Delia was weeping.

James gave me a nudge, prompting me to react. I felt foolish, but I knew it was necessary.

"Grandfather," I yelled.

It was obvious they knew who I was. There was no point in calling him William now.

My father followed suit, crying and shouting William's name.

"Who would do this?" Fish cried.

"We're sitting ducks now," Delia said, throwing herself into Fish's arms.

My father pretended to console me, gathering me in his arms. He glared at Fish.

"I don't want my son seeing this. He's been through enough already."

"I understand, James," Fish answered. "Take him upstairs, I'll take care of things."

We were in my room moments later.

"Stay in this room," my father instructed. "I won't be long."

"Where are you going?" I asked.

"I need your mother," he said, removing the ring.

Chapter Twenty-Nine: Fire

I sat near the window, looking out into the night. My father hadn't returned yet. I wondered what was talking him so long. The day had turned into night, causing me to worry a bit. I knew we still had to build a fire to burn William's fake head. I still didn't know the purpose of that. William was a wizard, not a witch. We didn't do things that way.

I was finding it hard to keep my eyes open. I had drifted off a few times, bumping my head on the window. I couldn't get Viola out of my head. She was the only reason I was keeping my sanity. I longed to hold her, tell her how I felt about her. I could picture her golden-brown hair, her honey-brown eyes, she wasn't like other girls I'd met. She was sweet, kind hearted, and although I didn't know her very well, I knew she was thoughtful.

I drifted off again, Viola running through my every thought. When I opened my eyes, it was daylight. I stretched my arms, still feeling a bit tired.

I had fallen asleep leaning against the wall, but I sat up when I heard someone hammering just outside my window. I looked out, my father and Fish were building the platform we would be setting on fire. Cory was there, looking visibly upset. I searched for my mother, she was nowhere in sight. Had my father not found her?

I rose to my feet when I heard the doorbell. There were voices coming from downstairs. I heard a woman weeping, asking how William had died. I recognized that voice. It was Sharron. I quickly changed out of my robe, putting the jeans back on.

I made my way towards the stairs, pausing at the top. Sharron's eyes were swollen from crying. Joshua was consoling her, assuring her that things were going to be alright. She choked on her sobs when she saw me looking down at her.

I searched her eyes, making sure it was really her. Her pain was real, her heart shattered.

"Ethan," she cried, running up the stairs.

I met her half way.

"Xander loved you," she said, throwing her arms around me. "I just can't believe he's gone."

I knew Sharron truly loved my grandfather. My mother said she'd been in love with him for many years. I felt bad we were lying to her.

I was trying to make myself cry. I felt silly trying to fake my sorrow. Not wanting to cause any suspicions, I waved my hand at myself, bringing a flood of tears.

"He loved you, too," I said, squeezing her. "He always called you a friend."

"He will be missed," she sobbed.

The doorbell was constantly ringing, every witch in Salem wanted to pay their respects. Donna was here with her sister Kym, too. One after the other, the witches of Salem made their way in. I didn't know half of them, some even came from far away. They wore corsets and draping skirts; some wore witch hats.

Van after van pulled up the driveway, quickly filling the house with flowers. Hundreds of people stood outside, waiting to come in. I was surprised to see how many people knew my grandfather. He was loved, respected. I even spotted a few humans paying their respects.

The doorbell rang again. Fish let go of Delia to go answer it. I quickly made my way to the door when I realized it was Viola. She was holding a small bouquet of flowers in her hand. She wore a long, black dress, her hair pinned up in a bun.

Fish stood aside as she made her way in. Her face lit up the moment she saw me. She couldn't hide the happiness she felt. I felt the same way.

"Hello, Viola," I said, softly.

"I heard what happened," she said, looking

down at the bouquet. "I'm very sorry for your loss. I know how it feels to lose a loved one. I share in your sadness."

Before I could say another word, Fish's imposter put his arm on my shoulder. "In the midst of all the sadness," he said, with a wicked smile, "We have one good thing to be happy about."

He swung his other arm over, patting me on the chest. "This guy is going to be my son-in-law. He and Vera are engaged and very much in love."

My heart sank, I wanted to kick the imposter across the room and tear him to pieces with my bare hands.

Viola slowly looked up at me, her eyes filling with tears. She began to tremble as she waited for me to deny it.

"Ethan?" she said, in a shaky voice.

I bowed my head, unable to tell her the truth. I could almost hear her heart breaking as she dropped the flowers and ran out the door.

"Viola!" I said, pushing Fish away.

Fish grabbed the back of my shirt, pulling me back. "What is Vera going to think?" he said, closing the door.

I made a fist, trying to control myself.

"Why don't you go comfort her," he said, crossing his arms in front of him. "Isn't that what a fiancé should do?"

I shook with rage, feeling a desperate need to kill him. I couldn't take his presence or the sound of his voice.

"Besides," Fish continued. "How can you compare a good steak to ground beef?"

In a flash, I had the wand in my hand. I grabbed the imposter by the neck, opened the door, and took to the sky with him hanging off the staff.

"Ethan!" I heard my father shout.

I flew over Salem, unafraid if human eyes saw me. I couldn't get ahold of myself, my anger had taken over. I never imagined I could feel this way. The hate coursing through my veins was leaving a bitter taste in my mouth.

The imposter was fighting to free himself, kicking and trying to unglue his hands from my staff.

"It's pointless," I shouted.

"Let's talk about this," he said, trying to convince me to stop. "I'm your uncle, remember?"

"You're no uncle of mine," I said, flying faster.

I wasn't sure where I was going, but I needed to get there fast. This man was going to talk, I would make sure of that. I'd had enough of all these rules. If this was going to change the future, I was prepared to suffer the consequences. How many more loved ones did my grandfather think I could take losing? I had been patient—obedient. Now things were going to be done my way.

I flew, unsure where to take him. Then I remembered a fort from my mother's memories, I quickly pointed the staff in that direction.

I flew to a town named New Bedford. Fort Rodman sat near the ocean, just a few miles from where I was. It was a vivid memory my mother had shown me. It's where Simon had tried to cut me out of her womb, the same place my mother discovered the Black Witch was helping him.

The fort came into view. I hovered a mile back, making sure no one was around. I could only see a couple of joggers, running on a trail behind the fort. The fort itself was intimidating, standing three stories high and made of cement. There was greenery growing on the top of the wall that surrounded the fort. Streams of rust stains ran down the back of its walls.

I remembered seeing a courtyard in my mother's memories, so I knew I could fly over the top to get in. I noticed the cannon holes had been blocked up with bricks and cement. Some of the bricks seemed out of place, as if someone had moved them at one time.

When the joggers were a good distance away, I made my way in. I quickly flew over the top and into the courtyard. The moment my feet touched the ground, I felt something odd. There were vibrations on the grass where I stood, like sound waves traveling through the ground.

I threw the imposter to the ground, waving my hand to put him to sleep. I couldn't shake the feeling washing over me. Why was the ground vibrating?

I looked all around me. There were corridors

surrounding the courtyard I was in. The place looked abandoned with debris lying everywhere. I spied two massive wooden doors that made the entrance. Just in front of it, I saw pieces of scrap wood lying on the ground.

I waved my hand at the imposter, making him float high above my head. I began to gather the wood, placing it right under him. When I had a good size pile, I woke him up.

I stepped back, staff in hand, as the imposter opened his eyes. He began to kick and wave his arms. "What witchery is this?" he yelled.

He gasped when he noticed the pile of wood under him. "What are you going to do to me?" he asked.

I smiled. "I'm going to burn you alive," I said, flatly.

The man began to shake. "Ethan, what's gotten into you, boy?"

I waved my hand, sending my magic towards his feet. His foot exploded on impact, sending his toes flying across the courtyard.

The man cried out in pain. It only made my smile grow wider. "If you say my name again," I growled, "I'll aim for your face next."

"P…please, help me. I'm going to bleed to death."

I slowly shook my head. "That's not how you're dying, scum. I have other plans."

I waved my hand, igniting the wood under him. The man quickly bent his legs, pulling them away from the fire.

"I figure you have three chances," I began. "For every question you don't answer, I move you closer to the fire."

The man closed his eyes, a squeaking sob escaping his lips.

"Where is my real uncle?" I asked.

He tried to catch his breath. "I…I am your real uncle," he lied.

"Wrong answer," I said, waving my hand.

He begged me to stop when he was jerked closer to the flames.

"Where is he?" I asked again.

A look of anger washed over him. He finally gave up on the charade and glared down at me.

"Go ahead. Kill me, pretty boy. I'd rather burn alive than feel her wrath. Nothing you do to me will compare to what she's capable of."

"You don't know me very well, do you?" I said, waving my hand again.

I lowered him enough to burn what was left of his feet. The man only closed his eyes, trying to hide his pain.

"Pain is a funny thing," I said, moving closer. "We can take it at first, until it travels through our nerves," I said, waving my hand again.

I watched as the fire reached his knees. He finally broke, sending his cries of pain throughout the courtyard.

"Where is my family?" I shouted.

"Go fuck yourself," he hissed frantically

through his teeth.

I raised my hand, prepared to wave it again. I stopped when the vibrations on the ground became stronger. I knelt, placing my hand over the grass. I could clearly feel it now, but what was causing it?

I quickly rose when I heard voices behind the wooden doors. I moved closer when I couldn't hear what they were saying.

"We can roll a joint in here," a voice said. "Nobody comes here. We can kick it for a while."

It was the humans.

I noticed the vibrations got even stronger when the humans tried pushing the doors open.

"There's a lock on it, dumbass," I heard another voice say.

I put my ear against the door. I could hear their steps. They were leaving. I looked down when I noticed the vibrations slowing down. Then it hit me, it was a spell. The Black Witch must have cast a spell around the fort; I assume to keep out the humans.

I realized I was wrong when I spotted tools and sheers, along with footsteps next to the debris. Someone had been here, and it was humans. If she wasn't trying to keep the humans out, what purpose did the spell serve?

I tapped my staff on the ground, breaking the spell's effect. Steam came rising from the ground. I heard a crackling sound as the spell was lifted and revealed what the fort really looked like.

What my eyes beheld truly shocked me.

"The fort in my dreams," I gasped.

Chapter Thirty: Fort Rodman

My jaw dropped when the steam cleared, revealing an enormous flat-screen TV hanging on one of the walls. On the other end was a platform with three nooses mounted to it. There were weapons scattered everywhere as if someone had suddenly dropped them.

I was about to demand the imposter explain, but he was already dead. I looked in every direction, trying to piece things together. I couldn't get over how many weapons were left behind. "A battle," I mumbled.

I had seen my mother fighting in her memories, she clearly fought here as well.

I began making my way through one of the corridors only to find strange looking masks lying on the ground. I reached for one, dropping it back down when I saw Sharron's face looking back at me.

I kicked over the other masks, gasping when I recognized the faces. I reached for the one that looked like Joshua, touching the skin-like surface. It looked so lifelike. I would have thought them real heads if I didn't know any better.

Donna's face was there along with Sean and his wife. Almost everyone I knew. I was intrigued, questioning how these masks worked. Fish's imposter was even built like him. Same voice, same posture. How did they manage that?

I looked down at Joshua's mask and slowly placed it over my face. I jumped back when the mask sucked itself to my skin. It covered my ears, my neck, every part of my face. I froze when images began running through my head. I could see the bakery, Joshua was putting some pies into the oven. Hundreds of moments from his life were being fed to me.

At first, I thought they were memories. I soon realized they were details given to me by the mask. Every secret Joshua had was being revealed by the mask. I kept it on as I looked down at myself. It was no surprise that I had on Joshua's clothes. I was even built like him. So, this is how the imposters had fooled us so easily.

I pulled off the mask when I spotted something odd. Near the masks, was a stack of black witch hats. Some of them had been tossed to one side, burn marks all over them. Why would they be burned?

I made my way farther into the corridor, the staff gripped tightly in my hand. I stepped over blankets and opened food cans, making my way into another corridor.

I found a small fire burning, a cast-iron cauldron hanging over it. I moved closer, leaning over to see what was in it. A strange substance was boiling, beige in color. Lying on a table next to it, were molds shaped as faces. I realized this is where the masks were being made.

On the table were pictures of my loved ones with red circles around their faces. I picked up a picture that was facedown, gasping when I flipped it over. It was a picture of Viola, sitting just outside the bakery.

"No," I said, as it slipped from my hands.

I spun around, running toward the exit of the corridor. I knew they were going after her next. I had to get there before they did. I ran faster, desperate to get out of here. I had to fly back to Salem and find out where she lived so I could save her.

I was in the first corridor I had entered; daylight was just ahead. The moment I neared the courtyard, I was struck with something hard right in the jaw. There was a crackling laugh as darkness filled my head.

My eyes shot open when I felt a stinging sensation on my feet. The stinging soon became unbearable as I tried to get up. I was unable to move, realizing I was strapped to a table. I was soaking wet, sopping in something I wasn't quite sure of.

I slammed my head back down, unable to take the terrible pain I was feeling.

"Like that?" a raspy voice asked. "I hear your kind enjoys it."

It was a woman's voice.

I was having trouble breathing as I searched the room for the voice. I tried to free myself from my restraints.

"Why isn't it working?" the raspy voice asked.

"Give it time," a man's voice answered. "He'll calm down in a moment. The needles finally stopped breaking. There must have been a protection spell on his skin."

I couldn't see who it was, who *they* were.

"Give him another needle," the raspy voice ordered.

I heard footsteps, then…pain. I gripped the ropes that bound my wrist, never giving them the satisfaction of knowing my pain.

"He's just like his mother," the man's voice said. "I warned you it wouldn't be that easy."

"Use a longer one!" the raspy voice shouted.

I braced myself for the pain I was about to feel. Unfortunately, I wasn't disappointed. The searing pain took my breath away. I knew I wouldn't be able to take much more of this.

I exhaled when water was poured over my face. Soon after, my breathing became labored.

"So, you're the prodigy son?" the raspy voice asked. "I've been waiting a very long time for you."

I was in and out of consciousness, trying with all my might to free myself. I was becoming weaker by the moment. I almost couldn't keep my eyes open.

"Wake him up!" the raspy voice shouted. "Keep inserting the needles so he learns to stay awake."

I felt fingers running along my forehead. A horrible, rancid stench made me turn away. The fingers moved down to my chin, forcing my head back. I gasped when I saw who was standing beside me.

"Not having fun, are we?" the Black Witch asked.

Her glossy looking eyes were dark as the night. I could see no pupil, iris, or sclera. They were lifeless, solid black and deadly. Thin strands of grey hair covered her nearly bald scalp. The cloak she wore covered most of her, but I could see wrinkled, sagging skin on her arms.

She ran her dirty, long nails across my lips.

"Not in the mood to answer questions?" she asked, poking my nose. "It's a good thing we have a way of making you talk."

She gave the order for the torture to continue. My body bounced up and down as another needle was inserted into my foot. The pain was unbearable. I had to force myself not to scream from the pain.

I felt her nails again, this time on my neck.

"I'm afraid we're not making you feel at home," she said, almost kissing me. "Would it make you feel better if we used knives instead? I came prepared, in case you're wondering."

"What do you want, witch?" I said through labored breathing.

She laughed, tightening her grip on my neck. "Isn't it obvious? I want you, but not before you make me a little promise," she said, breathing her putrid breath into my mouth.

She climbed onto the table and straddled me. I looked away as she ran her fingers along my chest.

"What are we hiding under here?" she asked, ripping my shirt open.

Her crackling laugh echoed throughout the corridors.

"You'll love me soon enough," she said, leaning over me. "I'm going to be your new wife, loving and caring. Nothing in this world will ever separate us. We'll have children, two of them, and live happily ever after."

I was struggling to keep my eyes open. I knew I would feel the wrath of another needle if I didn't stay awake.

"Feeling tired?" she asked, stroking my hair. "You have your mother to blame for that. She left something very important behind, something I found when she left with Simon."

She leaned back, pulling something from her cloak. A wicked smile spread across her face as she held up a leaf. I instantly recognized it was from Magia.

I'd heard all the stories about the leaves, how they weakened wizards and took their powers. A wizard's energy is too strong, causing the leaves to feel pain whenever they are near. The leaves had developed a defense against the pain the wizard's energy caused them. It was the one thing wizards feared.

"I despise your mother," the Black Witch continued. "She never offered to show me how she broke her blood promise. She dared to seek me out, almost begged me to help her, only to take the secret with her. I still go over that day in my head," she said, looking away. "How did she do it? How could she possibly push away the darkness?"

She looked down at me again, her dark eyes full of evil.

"If I can't have my life back, she doesn't get to live happily ever after. She made a deal with the devil, and I'm here to collect her debt."

I looked through blurry eyes, finding it almost impossible to stay awake. The water the leaves had soaked in was making me weaker.

"I think we need another needle," she said, over her shoulder.

When I began to shake my head, she leaned over me again. "Did you know you were promised to me?" she asked. "I don't like it when people break their promises."

I shouted cries of pain when I felt another needle being inserted into my other foot.

She wrapped both hands around my neck. "I can make it stop," she whispered as her rancid breath brushed across my face. "One little promise will end your pain. I'll settle for a question—for now."

She released my neck, holding out her hand.

"Give it me," she ordered.

I still couldn't see who else was here. I only saw one of the masks being placed in her hand. When she placed the mask over her face, my heart sunk.

It was the spitting image of Vera. She had her hair, her body, even her scent.

"I believe you have a question to ask me?" she said, leaning over me. "I promise to say yes."

I didn't answer.

"This should be easy for you," she said, touching my lips. "You've always loved her, had dreams about her. Well, now she can be yours."

The mystery as to why she had chosen Vera was clear. She thought I loved her, would do anything for her. It had been true at one time, but now my heart belonged to another.

"Go to hell, witch," I said, almost spitting at her.

Her loud, crackling laughter echoed off the walls. She rolled off the table, ripping the mask from her face. "Drag him into the other room," she said, turning on her heels.

She laughed again, shaking her head wildly.

"Melanie," she shouted down the corridor. "Where is my precious sister?"

Chapter Thirty-One: The Smiling Witch

A cloth was placed over my face just before the ropes were cut away. Someone pulled my ankles, dragging me off the table. They pulled me to the floor, my head hit the ground with a thump. My arms were lifted up, pushing my wrist together. I felt a rope being wrapped tightly around them. They gave one last yank before letting my arms drop.

Whoever was dragging me was having a hard time. I could hear them huffing, trying to catch their breath. They dragged me for several long moments, stopping when we reached some stairs. I knew this because my head was bouncing, hitting each of the steps.

I began to smell the strong odor of mildew, it got stronger the more we moved. I closed my eyes, trying to command the ropes to rip away. The leaves had done their damage, leaving me too weak to defend myself.

Suddenly we stopped. The cloth was swiftly pulled away.

"Ethan!" I heard someone scream.

All I could do was allow my head to fall sideways, I had little strength for anything else.

"You're gonna die, fuckin' witch."

I recognized that voice. It was Fish.

"Fish," I whispered.

"She's not alone," Fish warned.

"Silence," the Black Witch yelled at him.

"Fish," I said again. This would be the second time I thought he was dead.

I was falling into darkness. I could feel a numbness traveling throughout my body.

"Leave him alone!"

With my eyes half open, I could see the real Vera. She was alive. Someone took hold of my ankles. I could only gasp as the needles were pulled from my feet.

"Father," I managed to say.

"If you don't pick him up, I'll cut her head off," I heard the Black Witch say.

There was silence, then two massive hands grabbed me by the shoulders. It took me a moment to realize it was the real Sean. As he carried me across the room, I saw Susan. The Black Witch had a large dagger to her throat.

"You swore to me," a woman cried.

~ 321 ~

"Shut up, Melanie," the Black Witch answered. "You've done nothing but give me trouble. Giving us those flying branches is the only good thing you've done."

"You said you would use them to fly away from here," she cried. "You swore you would never return."

The dungeon was filled with crackling laughter. "You're as stupid as these half breeds," the Black Witch answered. "So easily distracted. I kept them busy with the warlocks, making them believe another war was coming."

"I'm going to kill you," Fish shouted.

I couldn't see where his voice was coming from. How many people were in here? I could hear Vera's cries as Sean leaned me on a pole.

"Tie him to it," the Black Witch ordered.

I could see the agony in Sean's eyes as he reached for a rope. When he leaned over to grab it, I saw just how many people the Black Witch had captured.

This was a dungeon used to keep prisoners. There were jail cells lining all the walls. Steel bars kept my loved ones at bay. Delia was unconscious, draped over a cement bed in a cell. Vera was next to her, holding Delia's hand tightly. Fish was in the same cell with them, ropes tied around his wrists and feet.

I was shocked to see Joshua in one of the cells. He was badly beaten, leaning his head on the steel bars. That meant there was another imposter in the house.

"Did I miss anyone?" the Black Witch asked.

I searched for her voice. It was getting harder to see clearly. She seemed proud of herself, claiming victory with her smile.

When Sean had secured me to the pole, the Black Witch ordered him back into his cell.

"If you try using your magic," she warned. "I'll make sure you get your wife back in pieces."

When had they taken her? I knew Susan had been hurt with a spell. Last thing I remembered, Sharron had taken her to her house.

"Don't you love distractions," the Black Witch said, when she noticed I was looking at Susan.

She pushed Susan into an empty cell.

"While they were trying to save their precious Susan, I was kidnapping the real one. No one noticed when she walked out the back door."

I was beginning to realize what she'd done. She didn't need the warlocks to fight her battles. They were just distractions, puppets to lead us away from what she was really doing. She had been taking our loved ones right from under our noses.

I tried to ignore my pain as the Black Witch picked up a glass of water, throwing it in my face.

"There," she said, placing the glass on a table. "You should be nice and weak by now."

My head felt like it weighed a hundred punds. I was finding it hard to hold it up. "Do your best, Witch," I said, trying to keep my eyes open.

She ordered Melanie to gather wood. When Melanie didn't move, the Black Witch slapped her across the face.

"You're useless," she said, as Melanie fell to the ground. "The Smiling Witch indeed. I still haven't forgiven you for befriending that half-breed."

Melanie held her cheek. "I should have listened to her," she cried. "I should have walked away and forgotten all about you. She was right, you belong to the darkness now."

The Black Witch laughed. "You think I didn't know you were helping them? I knew you were trying to get rid of me. Why do you think I used you, huh? You were willing to do anything so that I would leave. Asking you for those flying branches was all I wanted from you. I made you believe I would disappear and stay in the darkness forever."

The Black Witch glared at her sister.

"He was promised to me," she said, pointing at me. "Simon made a deal with me, and I kept my end of the bargain. I want what was promised to me. He has to marry me. How else will I get my children back?" she said, glaring my way.

"You killed your children," Melanie shouted. "You cut them into pieces, you heartless witch. Nothing is going to bring them back, nothing!"

The Black Witch smiled. "Says you," she said, in the evilest voice.

Melanie staggered to her feet. "I won't let you do this," she said, making for her sister.

The Black Witch blew powder in her face, laughing her crackling laugh as Melanie hit the floor. "That should take care of you," she said, looking towards the corridor. "Wendell, bring some wood," she ordered.

There was no answer. She yelled again.

"Wendell, get in here."

Again, no answer.

Fish quickly turned his head and stared down the corridor. I knew what he was looking for. He thought perhaps the others had arrived. I knew this wasn't so. I would have felt my father by now.

Suddenly, Wendell came out of the darkness, needles still in his hand. He was just as my mother described him. Thin, pointy nose and beady looking eyes. He didn't seem to like the way the Black Witch was talking to him.

"Let's get one thing straight," he hissed at her. "I am not your slave. Never speak to me as such. We have a deal. I teach you wizard spells and in return you give me the dark spell to take his powers," he said, motioning to me.

I could see her crackling laughter was annoying him.

"Do as I say," the Black Witch answered.

"Before I return you to the mud I found you in."

Wendell stormed off, but returned moments later carrying an armful of wood. He threw the pile at her feet.

"Get on with it, witch. I'm getting impatient."

I struggled to free myself as the Black Witch approached. She leaned forward, breathing her rancid breath straight into my mouth. The stench moved slowly through my nose and into my lungs. I felt I would vomit. I wanted to thrust a dagger straight through her heart, but I was far too weak to move. This would be the end of me. I had failed in every way possible. I thought of my mother as the Black Witch began moving piles of wood closer to my feet. She smiled, revealing a fire spell spinning in her hand. She slowly held it up, showed her yellow teeth, and threw it under me.

I could hear my loved ones screaming my name. I wanted to beg for their forgiveness, tell them it had been a mistake to believe in me. I thought of Cory, he knew I was never capable of saving them.

It felt like torture as I waited for the wood to catch fire. It was only prolonging my horrible death. I hung my head, looking at my hands that were bound in front of me. I drew breath, realizing how close they were to my pocket.

The Black Witch became impatient, spitting down at the wood. There was a puff as the wood ignited, sending flames close to my feet.

"I'll stop the fire," the Black Witch said. "I only need to hear one simple question."

She reached for the mask she had thrown on the ground. "Can't forget this," she said, placing it over her face.

In an instant, Vera was standing before me. I knew what the Black Witch wanted, and I was never going to speak those words.

"Ask me!" she shouted. "Before I let you burn to death."

"W...will you," I struggled to say.

"Go on," she said, moving closer.

"G...go straight to hell?"

She slapped me hard across the face, giving me the perfect chance. I slipped my fingers into my pocket, desperately trying to get the ring to slip on. Sean jumped to his feet, grabbing the steel bars in front of him. He spat out a spell when he realized I was reaching for something. Wendell tried to warn the Black Witch when Sean threw the spell across the room.

The spell hit my front pocket, ripping the material away. The ring came out and fell directly into the fire.

"No!" Sean shouted.

Crackling laughter filled the room.

"I think I'll kill you first," the Black Witch said, heading towards Sean.

Suddenly, she spun around when an explosion came from the fire. The fire began to burn a bright green, sending speckles of light straight through me. They entered my body like daggers, sending a thunder-like blast throughout the room.

Waves of energy came from my body, causing the ground to shake. My feet began to heal themselves, a thrust of energy shot through me. The pain I was feeling drifted away. The fire no longer burned me.

I looked down at my feet, commanding the ropes to rip themselves away. My clothes were as if fire had never touched them, the tear in my shirt, gone. I held out my hand, commanding the staff to find me. I wanted to laugh when the staff flew into the dungeon, hitting Wendell in the back of the head.

"Kill him!" the Black Witch shouted.

I was shocked when about a hundred warlocks came running from every corridor, weapons held tightly in their hands. Their eyes were black and glossy. They had a scar running across their necks. These warlocks wanted to help her and for that, they would die.

I looked at the Black Witch. "I knew you wouldn't fight alone."

I could smell her putrid breath as a smile slowly spread across her face. "You'd be surprised what kind of friends I have."

She pulled something from her cloak, slamming it to the ground. A cloud of dust filled the room, blinding me to where she was.

"Ethan, behind you," Fish shouted.

Chapter Thirty-One: The Cloak

I slammed the staff on the ground, propelling myself across the room. I waited for the dust to settle, spinning the staff in my hand. I slapped it on my palm, wrapping my fingers around its tip. When I felt it sharp as a blade, I held it over my shoulder.

"Ethan, let us out," Fish shouted.

I ignored him. This was my war, my fight. They were here because the Black Witch wanted *me,* and it would be *me* who would kill our enemies.

I was filled with fury, thirsty for their blood. Their deaths would be quick, the Black Witch would quickly follow. I planned on returning the favor. She would know the pain from the needles.

I tightened my grip on the staff as the dust finally settled. The moment I could see angry faces staring back at me, I threw the staff across the room. I waved my hand, sending my magic right behind it. "Find," I chanted.

There was a flash of green as my magic reached the staff. The staff began to curl and move like a snake, seeking out its victims. I smiled as body after body fell, a gaping hole through their hearts. When the last body was down, my staff floated, awaiting my command.

I turned and faced Wendell, who was hiding like a coward behind a table. I looked at my staff, motioning toward the coward. It went right through the table, and straight into Wendell's head. It flew him back, nailing his head to the cement wall.

I waved my hand again, commanding the needles into the room. I could hear them clanging together as they made their way in. No less than twenty of them floated all around me. It was then I realized why they had been so painful. They looked more like daggers, thick and long, with razor edges.

They floated around my head as I searched the dungeon for the Black Witch. I had an uncontrollable need to kill her. It was all I could think of. I wanted her to feel every needle. I would start with her head first. I planned on making her eat them. I would force them down her throat. Her eyes would be last. I would wear them around my neck like a badge of honor. Her death would be the ultimate reward.

"Ethan! Where are you?" someone shouted behind me.

I made the needles spin around, pointing them in the direction of the voice. I remained motionless, searching the dungeon for the Black Witch.

"Ethan!" I heard again.

It was my father, and he wasn't alone. Cory ran into the room, stopping when he noticed the floating needles around my head. My father almost slammed into him. He already had his whip in hand. They both looked at the carnage on the ground, returning their eyes to me.

My father slowly walked toward me. He kept eying the needles floating around me. With every step he took, the needles followed him. They were ready to strike, kill the moment I commanded it.

"Ethan. Look at me, son," my father said, nervously. "It's over."

I had my back to him, my eyes still dancing around the dungeon searching for the Black Witch.

"Ethan," my father said softy. "It's me, son. I came to take you home."

He slowly began to walk around me. He suddenly froze when the needles readied themselves to strike.

"James," Cory whispered. "It's Fish and Delia. They're alive."

My father kept his eyes on me. "Go get them out, but walk very slowly."

The needles slowly turned in the direction Cory was walking, assuring he wasn't coming toward me.

"He's just going to help them," my father said, holding up his hands. "Don't attack him. Put the needles down, son."

I could hear Vera's cries as Cory tried to open the cell doors.

"On the wall," Fish said. "I see a set of keys hanging."

I could hear Cory's footsteps. He was walking slowly, cautiously. The needles clanged together as they followed his every move.

My father pulled out a phone, he was speaking to someone moments later.

"Porteus, capture Delia and Susan. They're imposters. Find Joshua, too."

He snapped the phone shut, his eyes on me the whole time. "Ethan, the needles, you have to put them down. You're going to hurt our friends."

How could he think I would ever hurt them? I had no intentions of sending the needles their way. The magic I had hit them with was strong, filled with fury, like I was. I would save that fury for the Black Witch.

"What's wrong with him, James?" Cory asked. "I don't think he can hear you."

He was wrong. I could hear all sound around me. I heard the cell doors open, Sean taking his wife into his arms. I heard the moment Delia came to, asking where she was.

"He killed them all in one shot," I heard Fish say. "I've never seen anything like it."

"What?" Cory gasped.

"His staff, it came to life. It took them all down—at the same time."

"Be quiet," my father warned them. "The needles are pointed your way."

"What is he staring at?" Fish asked.

"It's just a dead warlock," Cory answered, "with Ethan's staff through his head."

"But that was Wendell," Fish gasped.

Cory was right, it was just a dead warlock. The magic from the mask had worn off, revealing who had been wearing it. It was never Wendell, *he* was never actually here.

I looked towards the back of the dungeon, noticing a black cloak on the ground. The bricks I had noticed earlier were gone, leaving a whole in the wall. She had flown away, grabbed Melanie's flying branch and escaped.

Cory followed my eyes, pointing when he spotted the cloak. "There's something under it," he said, heading that way.

The needles prepared themselves, ready to kill if she was there.

"Ethan," my father said, moving a bit closer.

He froze when two of the needles spun around, taking aim at him.

I kept my eyes on Cory as he reached for the cloak. When he picked it up, there were bones lying under it.

"How did she do that?" I murmured.

How was it possible that she was never here? Who had flown away? I knew her touch had been real, her rancid breath, her crackling laugh. Had my mind been playing tricks on me? That couldn't be. I saw her, she was here.

"It was only her bones," I murmured.

"Stay back" I heard my father say. "He's not himself yet. Don't get close to him."

Soon after, I felt a soft hand caressing my face. "Come back to me, Ethan."

It was my mother. Her touch sent a cooling pulse, traveling throughout my body. I heard the needles fall to the ground as I collapsed in her arms.

I felt trapped in a bad dream, with the Black Witch laughing next to me. She was holding a bouquet of flowers in her hand, a strange man, wearing a cloak, waited at the end of an altar. He was looking down at a book in his bone-like hands. Was it a bible? I couldn't see it very well from where I stood.

The Black Witch slowly threaded her arm around mine, pulling me gently towards the altar. She laughed her wicked laugh as we neared, causing my skin to crawl. She was savoring this moment, almost devouring me with her dark, glossy eyes.

When we reached the altar, I noticed the book wasn't a bible at all. It was the strangest book I'd ever seen. I could make out two skull-like faces on the cover, with a black cloth covering them. Two skeleton hands were next to them, as if trying to pull themselves out of the book. A bronze latch sat at the top right of the book, keeping its secrets safe inside.

I gasped when the faces on the book began to slowly move back and forth. The hands were reaching out, as if pleading for someone to help them. I could see cloud-like figures, souls, being absorbed into the pages. Every time a new soul was absorbed, the demon would smile as his book became thicker and thicker.

It didn't take me long to understand what he was holding. It was a powerful spell book. One that held the black spells my grandfather had told me about. The more souls the book collected, the more spells it would reveal to the demon. However, the book needed people's sorrows and pain to stay strong. Without it, it would lose all its power.

When he tapped the latch, I heard the agony in the moans of lost souls coming from inside. The man flipped the pages, stopping when one of the pages came to life. The words drifted out of the book and floated near my mouth.

"Open your mouth," the demon instructed.

His raspy voice echoed through my ears, whispering to obey him. I couldn't make out what the words said, they were spinning too fast for me to read. I tried with all my might to look away, but my head wouldn't budge. I slowly opened my mouth, causing the words to slow down. Just as they were about to enter my mouth, I realized what the words read. *Will you marry me?*

"No!" I shouted, as I was pulled from my nightmare.

I sat up. I was on a bed of flowers, my clothes drenched in sweat. I felt warm rays of light brushing across my face. I knew instantly where I was.

"Ethan."

I felt my mother's touch again.

"I'm here, son."

It took me a moment to realize it had been a dream. It had seemed so real, so vivid.

"Give him a moment," my grandfather said.

I grabbed at my chest, realizing how fast my heart was pounding. Racing thoughts began going through my head, recalling the events from the dungeon.

"She wasn't there," I murmured.

"She would never make it that easy," my grandfather said. "The darkness is guiding her."

"The darkness," I said, remembering the man in my dreams. I visualized his red eyes, his bone-like hands. "A demon," I said, looking away.

"That is her *real* army," my grandfather said. "The warlocks served only as a distraction, even fooling me."

I recalled her words, the evil smile she had when she said them. *"You'd be surprised what kind of friends I have."*

I rose to my feet, feeling I had already lost the battle. How could I possibly fight against demons? I didn't have enough knowledge to fight them. Could they even be killed?

I looked at my grandfather, making sense of the instructions he had given me. He slowly nodded, assuring I was on the right track. But, what track was that? I still wasn't sure how he expected me to do it.

"The leaves," I said, remembering. "She has leaves from Magia."

"That can't be," my mother said. "I brought them all back home."

"Not all of them, Mother. You left some at the fort when you left with Simon."

I could see the color draining from her face. She was remembering. "No," she gasped.

"What about Wendell?" my grandfather asked. "Was he with her?"

"It wasn't Wendell," I informed him.

I explained about the imposter.

"It was his soul," my grandfather answered.

"His soul?" I asked confused.

He nodded. "The darkness has given the Black Witch many spells, some of which we've never heard of. I'm afraid she's going to make this very difficult for us."

"Is that why you ask me to…" I froze, remembering my mother was there. I knew William didn't want her to know the journey that lay ahead.

"I don't think she knows about Cory," I said, remembering what the Black Witch had said.

"What do you mean?" my mother asked.

"When I saw the others," I explained. "She asked if she had missed anyone."

"I see," William said, looking away.

"What does that mean, Father?" my mother asked.

He looked thoughtful for a moment.

"It has to be someone Cory doesn't know," he said, mostly to himself. "Someone only the others have met."

"What are you saying?" my mother asked. "You think someone is telling her all the people we know?"

"Yes. Someone who hasn't encountered Cory, never saw him near the others. Why else would they not take him?"

I told him all about the masks. He didn't like hearing that. He agreed we should help the warlocks, take them to the lake as planned.

"They are innocent mules," he said, somberly.

When I got to the part about the needles, my mother slapped her hands over her mouth. She knew all too well about those needles. It had been Simon's favorite choice of torture.

"I'm so sorry, Son," she cried. "I never wanted you to suffer the things I had."

I looked at her tear-filled eyes, knowing I would never tell her about my suffering again. She wasn't strong enough to know what still lay ahead. William was right. She would do the impossible to help me.

I knew it wasn't going to be easy, but I would have to face the unknown without her help. I would reject her gifts or any kind of magic she was so willing to give me. There was a reason William was making her stay here, and I had just solved that mystery.

When I placed a mask over my face, I was able to absorb any knowledge of that person's life. Any secret they kept was quickly revealed and given to me. I knew there was one secret the Black Witch desperately wanted, and only my mother's memories could give it to her.

It all made sense. William was protecting my mother. He feared she would be captured and drained of her memories. Her memories would be fed into the mask, giving the Black Witch what she wanted. It was the one secret my mother had, and the one the Black Witch desperately wanted. *How had my mother broken the promise?*

It all made sense now. The Black Witch wanted out of the darkness. My mother had shown her it was possible. She wanted kids, a husband, a happy life. She hated that my mother made it seem so easy. They had both made a blood promise, but only my mother had pulled herself out of that dark place. And if the Black Witch couldn't figure out how my mother had done it, she was determined to take anything my mother loved.

That was William's real reason for wanting to leave Salem. He was the only one capable of stopping my mother. He knew she was forming a plan, and he needed to keep her here, in Magia.

William nodded knowingly.

"Do you understand?" he asked.

I looked at my mother. "Perfectly," I answered.

I knew William was blocking our thoughts from her. My mother had no idea we were having a conversation in our heads. William knew her all too well.

I told my mother about her friend, Melanie.

"The Black Witch doesn't seem to like that you call her sister the Smiling Witch."

Brows furrowed, my mother looked at me confused. "What are you talking about? No one knows I call her that."

"I heard it with my own ears," I assured her.

"You told no one?" William asked.

"No, Father. I call her that silently, in my head. She has dimples, they're more obvious when she smiles."

He looked away, not liking what he was hearing.

"I didn't see anything wrong with her when we took her home," my mother continued. "The powder only put her to sleep."

William was still looking away.

"Well, we should go now," my mother said, taking hold of my hand. "Your father is waiting.

He must be very worried."

I kissed her hand, saying goodbye in my head. I wanted to tell her how much I loved her, how much I respected her. She had truly gone through hell; the needles were just a dent in her suffering. It wasn't hard to guess how she'd broken that blood promise. What the Black Witch wanted couldn't be found in my mother's head. She was born with it. She had determination, bravery, and most of all, love for others. She loved those around her more than she loved herself. I was certain the Black Witch wasn't capable of that.

I looked at William. "Are you ready?"

"I'm ready," my mother replied, thinking I was talking to her.

When William nodded, I waved my hand, sending my mother right to him. I was gone in seconds.

"Ethan!" I heard my mother shout.

Chapter Thirty-Two: Magical

Two weeks had passed. Salem's trees were vibrant with color. It made it easy to understand why it was my mother's favorite time of year. There was a certain smell in the air, a freshness I couldn't explain. The smell of caramel and cinnamon came from every coffee shop. The tourists had tripled once October came, bringing business to all the shop owners.

The spooky hay rides and haunted happenings enjoyed their share of tourists. There were witch hats and costumes as far as the eye could see. Cory's bakery was busier than ever. He had to make three times the bread to keep up with the demand of grinders we sold at the deli.

Sean and Susan were doing better than I thought they would. It was as if nothing bad had happened. There was no trauma, no shock after they were rescued. It was business as usual for them.

I couldn't say the same for Joshua. He had packed up and left Salem that very night. He told my father he couldn't go through that nightmare again, and my father understood why. I knew he and Joshua were together the night they were tortured. Joshua had been very different after that. I felt his fears when I put on that mask. Joshua was still living with torment.

Porteus was upset when William called him back to Magia. He begged and pleaded to stay, but William said he was too emotionally involved. I still laughed at the fact that he was in love with Susan. In fact, my father had instructed him to capture Susan's imposter. Porteus settled for killing her instead. We found her in pieces when we arrived at Sharron's house. Joshua and Delia's imposters had fled by the time Porteus went looking for them.

Netiri had been busy finding warlocks. We had already taken hundreds of them to the lake. Salem was safe for now, at least the humans were.

When I returned from Magia, the others were burning the imposter's head. They had built a platform following every detail of William's orders to the end. We all cried our fake tears and shook hands with all the mourners. It took us weeks to get rid of all the flowers in the house. Even now, you could still smell their fragrance.

Vera was heartbroken, believing William was truly dead. We knew we couldn't tell her the truth.

I stayed behind when the mourners left, watching my father. Before the fire could burn out, he took a small blanket and placed it over the fire. He pulled the blanket away, repeating the process. Was he sending smoke signals?

"What are you doing?" I had asked.

He looked up at the smoke. "Following Williams instructions," he answered.

I spent my time looking for Viola. No one seemed to know where she lived. Every day, I stood outside the deli, waiting for her to take her place on the bench. I even stayed for hours after the deli was closed. I thought I would see her when Salem threw a parade, I was sadly disappointed.

I took a chance and went to the dance, hoping to find her there. She never came. I only stayed a short time, frustrated with the number of women who kept asking me to dance.

I had to find her, explain that it had been a lie. I planned on being honest about Vera. I would confess how I had once loved her. I would show Viola that my feelings have changed.

Throughout all this madness, I couldn't help but notice how Steven had disappeared. He didn't come to the funeral and wasn't at the fort. I found it odd that there was no sign of him anywhere. In fact, Vera hadn't asked for him even once. In Magia, she did nothing but talk about him. Now, it was as if he was never born. I also found it strange that Vera showed no signs of shock. She acted as if nothing had ever happened to her.

I never told William how the Black Witch kept putting the Vera mask on. For some reason, she wanted to look just like her before I asked my question.

I couldn't get the recent events out of my head. I was walking the streets of Salem, trying to sort through every detail.

"Ethan," I heard from behind me.

I was pulled from my thoughts, turning to see who it was. Vera was waving a piece of paper in the air.

"I found her," she yelled.

She came running down the sidewalk, her black hair bouncing off her shoulders. She was out of breath as she held out the paper.

"I found her," she said again.

"Found who?" I said, taking the paper from her.

"That girl, the one you've been looking for."

My heart began to race. "Viola?"

I looked down at the paper. There was an address written on it.

"Where did you get it?" I quickly asked.

"Well, she spends a lot of time at the library. I have a friend who works there. He gave me the address."

I looked down at the paper again.

"I know the two witches she lives with," Vera continued. "They're very protective of her. I guess they took her in when her mother died."

"She lives with witches?" I asked surprised.

"Don't we all?" Vera said, then headed on her way.

I was overcome with happiness. I became anxious to speak with her. I looked at the address again, recognizing the name of the street she lived on. It was going to be easy to find her. She lived on one of the streets with the red and blue lines on it. It was near a pirate ship docked at the pier.

I squeezed my way through the crowds. My day had just gotten a lot better. I had a smile from ear to ear. I began walking faster. I could see the pink house from where I was. I finally made it to her front door, straightening out my shirt. I knocked on the door and stepped back as I messed with my hair. I knocked again when there was no answer.

A tall, short-haired woman answered the door. Vera was right, she was a witch.

"How can I help you?" the woman asked.

"Afternoon," I answered politely. "Is Viola home?"

The woman eyed me. "Who wants to know?"

"My name is Ethan Wade. I'm a friend of hers. May I speak to her?"

"Who is it, Renee?" I heard from inside the house.

"It's the kid from the deli. He wants to see Viola," the woman named Renee answered.

Another woman was quickly at the door, a fierce look on her face. She also had short hair, but was much shorter than Renee.

"She doesn't want to see you," she hissed. "You broke her heart. Haven't you done enough?"

Clearly, this wasn't going to be easy. "If I could only speak with her I can clear things up," I said, trying to convince them to let me see her. "I won't take up much of her time, I swear."

"Shouldn't you be with your fiancé?" Renee spat at me. "Leave Viola alone. She's been hurt enough. She doesn't have time for games, or for people that want to hurt her."

She tried to slam the door in my face, but I put my foot out, blocking the door. "Please," I said, backing my foot away. "There was a misunderstanding, a lie in fact. I'm not engaged."

They both eyed me. My news seemed to surprise them both.

Renee looked at the other woman. "What do you think, Cheryl?"

The one named Cheryl gave me a dirty look.

"I'll go talk to her," she said, stepping away from the door.

Renee glared at me as we waited for Viola. I couldn't imagine what they thought of me.

"She's been locked in her room," Renee said. "You gave her hope, made her think someone loved her."

"Someone *does* love her," I corrected quietly.

"You're lucky we didn't turn you into a toad or something."

I smiled. "For that, I thank you."

Cheryl was back moments later. "She doesn't want to see him."

Renee grabbed the door. "There's your answer, buddy," she said, slamming the door in my face.

Frustrated, I took a few steps back. "Viola," I shouted. "Give me a chance to explain. It was a lie. I'm not engaged."

I waited, hoping she would come out. I didn't care that people were staring. I wasn't going to give up.

"Viola," I yelled again. "I never meant to hurt you. You fell victim to a lie. I couldn't explain it then because I wasn't able to, but if you want, you can come ask Fish yourself. I swear, he can clear things up."

There was silence.

"Viola, please. Just give me a chance to explain. I meant every word I said to you. I wasn't playing games. My feelings for you are real. Didn't you see it in my eyes?"

More Silence.

I hung my head, feeling more pain than any needle could give me. There was nothing I could do, not if she wasn't willing to hear me out.

I turned to leave, pausing when I heard the front door open. There she was, standing by the door, wearing a beautiful yellow dress. Despite the tangled hair, she was utterly breathtaking. She was looking down at her hands, fidgeting as usual.

The closer I got to her, the more I wanted to pull her into my arms. She kept her head down, nervously looking at her hands. Her guardians were standing right behind her, giving me the evil eye.

"Thank you for seeing me," I said, softly.

She only nodded.

"Viola, I'm not engaged. It was a lie. I couldn't ex..." I glanced at her guardians. I really didn't want to do this in front of them.

"Viola, will you take a walk with me?" I asked, holding out my hand.

She finally looked up, her honey-brown eyes staring into my soul. I felt horrible when I noticed how swollen they were.

"You still like leaving my hand out, don't you," I said, jokingly.

It felt like dark clouds drifting away when she smiled at me. She slowly reached for my hand.

"Stick to the lines, Viola," Renee said, closing the door.

"I know the rules," Viola answered.

I squeezed her hand, pulling her away with me. The moment we were behind some trees, I pulled out the wand.

"There's too many people around," Viola warned.

I unshrunk the wand, and placed it between my legs. "Why don't you let me worry about that,"

I said, reaching for her.

She took her place in front of me, holding my wrists tightly. "Hold on," I whispered in her ear.

I took to the sky like a flash, a blur to human eyes. I flew us to the lake, where I knew we would be alone. The moment we arrived, I prepared myself to beg. I was surprised when Viola threw herself into my arms.

"I thought you were a dream," she said, sobbing. "I kept telling myself you were too good to be true. I convinced myself I had imagined you. I felt so stupid."

"Did you imagine this?" I said, pulling her to my lips.

Her lips were as sweet as ever. I thought my heart would explode with happiness. Nothing in this world mattered more to me than being by her side. She was my other half, my true love. With her, I felt complete.

I pulled my head back when she sobbed into my mouth. "Why are you crying?" I said, wiping her tears. "I'm not engaged. I swear it."

"It's not that," she said, bowing her head. "It's just that, well, I don't understand why you like me."

What did she mean by that?

"I don't like you, Viola."

She looked up, tears flowing down her cheeks. "You don't?"

I smiled. "No. I love you."

I crushed my lips to hers, this time, she didn't cry. She ran her fingers through my hair, pulling me ever so close.

My life made sense now. I knew exactly what I wanted. If I was going to live through hell, I needed to know that she would be waiting. She made me stronger, made me a better man. I knew from this moment on, I couldn't live without her. She was my life now, my air, my hopes. I would fight the battle ahead, knowing she was the prize awaiting me. I would spend the rest of my life earning her love and making her happy.

"You know," I said, kissing her neck. "There's something you haven't said yet."

"There is?" she answered breathless.

"Yes. You never said you loved *me*."

She pulled back, holding my face in her shaky hands.

"You're so beautiful," she whispered. "I fell in love with you from the moment I laid eyes on you. I didn't need to see you in these clothes to know that. You stole my heart from the very beginning, robe and all. You didn't treat me like the others. You were kind and thoughtful. How could I not love you?"

"You talk as if you're the lucky one," I answered.

I stepped back, got down on one knee, and took her hand in mine. She slapped her hand to her mouth, gasping as she looked down at me.

"Viola, I don't need months or even years to

know I want to spend the rest of my life with you. A man should be so lucky to have a woman like you. I know I don't have a ring, but I have my heart. I promise it will always love you, always be faithful. Would you do me the great honor of becoming my wife? Will you marry me?"

Viola choked on her sobs. "Yes," she said, throwing her arms around me.

I felt like the happiest man alive. I saw the world through new eyes. The murky lake was now a beautiful place to me. The trees were alive with color, lighting up the night for us. Salem held a special place in my heart now. I had found happiness, found a new life. It was a magical night I would remember for the rest of my life.

Epilogue: Into the Darkness

I lay in bed, thinking about Viola, my fiancé. I was a changed man, ready to face what destiny had prepared for me. My reasons for fighting had changed. I was in love and happier than I'd ever been. I hadn't said a word to anyone about my engagement. I knew it wasn't time yet. I had explained the dangers to Viola. She agreed at once to keep it between us. I confided many things in her, knowing I could trust her with my life.

I would have to find ways to secretly see her, be careful to not put her in danger. She was safe for now. Turns out, those two witches she lived with were very crafty. I learned why they had Viola stick to the red and blue lines. They had placed protection spells on them, assuring Viola would be safe. I thanked them for that.

Renee and Cheryl had no idea we were engaged, but they seemed to be fine with my visits.

It took several days, but they finally stopped giving me dirty looks. On some days, they seemed happy to see me. Viola explained how they were married. She feared I would have a problem with two women being together. "Love knows no boundaries," I had said.

I had dinner there often. Renee was a pretty good cook. It beat eating Delia's horrible concoctions. Cheryl was actually a very nice witch. She had many talents, casting spells was one of them. Her protection spell was very clever. Anyone who touched Viola while standing on the red and blue lines would instantly lose the ability to walk, giving Viola time to get away. The only reason those warlocks had been able to take Viola that day was because she had strayed away from the lines. Now, even I was telling her to stick to the lines.

Netiri and I had been training for weeks. He would be coming with me on this journey. I was determined to end this nightmare as soon as possible. I only prayed that I would survive.

The Black Witch had outsmarted us. I was having trouble dealing with that. I couldn't understand these dark spells she used or comprehend how to fight against them. I had to think like her, go to a dark place, and figure it out. I would risk my soul to find her, defeat the demons who protected her.

No one knew I had gone back to the fort days later. When I realized what the masks could do, I took the cauldron that contained the liquid used to make them. The Black Witch's face was cemented in my head, giving me a perfect picture of her.

If I was going to find her, I had to learn all her secrets. I would descend into darkness, deep into the pits of hell. I had to learn about these demons and the mask was my only way.

I had already tried making one several times, tossing it aside when it didn't work. I knew the mask had to be a carbon copy of her. I knew it wouldn't work otherwise. I had to get it right. I didn't have much of the mixture left.

I had stopped trying for now, choosing to draw her face instead. I couldn't miss a single detail. Every crack on her face was vital. This frustrated me, I was certain of her features in my memory. What was I missing? Where was I going wrong?

I decided to go for a walk, clear my head before I drew her again. Perhaps the fresh air would help me think. I made my way into town and straight to Delia's alley. There was someone I wanted to see, maybe ask her a few questions. Melanie, the Smiling Witch, knew her sister better than anyone. Who better to ask?

I didn't hold anything against her. She had only wanted to help. She apologized many times already, though I told her it wasn't necessary. This told me she would be more than willing to help.

The alley was more crowded than ever.

Melanie's stand was just past the wooden witch tourists took pictures with. She also had a store, but this alley was very busy. I could see why she chose to put a stand here.

She was handing a customer a t-shirt when I arrived. Her dimpled smile disappeared the moment she spotted me. "Come again," she said to the customer.

"Afternoon," I greeted her.

"Afternoon," she said, bowing her head.

"Busy day, I see," I said, making small talk.

I knew she wanted to cry, something she did every time she saw me.

"I'm truly sorry for what happened," she said for the hundredth time.

"Please, Melanie. You don't have to apologize every time you see me."

"She wasn't always like that, you know," she said, shaking her head. "She used to be a beautiful woman, sweet and caring. That's the sister I remember, not this horrible person she's turned into. You would never believe it, but she used to be the most beautiful woman in Salem."

Her words shot through me like a bolt of lightning. I instantly knew what I was doing wrong. The Black Witch didn't always look like that, she had been a regular person at one time. I had been drawing the wrong face all along.

I took hold of Melanie's arm. "Where do you live?" I asked.

"W…what?"

"I need a picture of your sister," I said, pulling her behind me.

Made in the USA
Middletown, DE
30 June 2020